NECROPOLIS

A NEW DELHI CRIME NOVEL BY

AVTAR SINGH

This is a work of fiction. All names, characters, places, and incidents are the product of the author's imagination. Any resemblance to real events or persons, living or dead, is entirely coincidental.

Akashic Books
Twitter: @AkashicBooks
Facebook: AkashicBooks
E-mail: info@akashicbooks.com
Website: www.akashicbooks.com

For my World

Put off that mask of burning gold . . .
—W.B. Yeats

SUMMER GAMES

The papers of that time were full of the somewhat anticlimactic resolution to the story that had consumed them through the summer. A young man's dead body was recovered from a wooded area next to an old village of Delhi, the main road not so very far away. He was no older than twenty, reportedly well dressed, affluent enough to afford both extraordinarily detailed tattoos and a vast amount of metallic piercings. While the mainstream press stayed away from describing either, there were murmurs in the parties and bazaars of Delhi of fetishistic inserts in his genital area and some apparently self-inflicted injuries, including bits of metal embedded under his skin. His face was clear, according to sources in the police. There was a mark around his neck, presumably from a rope or similar restraint: it was unclear whether it had been placed there with or without his consent. He was declared to have died of a heart attack.

Around his throat was a necklace of fingers.

These fingers had been collected from a number of unwilling donors. The perpetrator of this digital crime wave had followed a simple and startlingly effective method. He followed his victims late at night. They were drawn from the ranks of the peripherally urban— rickshaw-walas, casual laborers, and the like—whose coming home late would have passed unremarked. They were incapacitated with a blow to the head, delivered from behind. An injection was administered to make sure the mark didn't awake. The absence of the digit would be noted, along with a deft bandage to minimize the blood loss, when the drug wore off. Not one man had died, though the absence of mortality, if anything, added to the morbidity of the crimes in the city's eyes.

As the collector grew in confidence, he took to even chasing his targets. Only one, famous in his village for being fleet of foot, eluded him. The rest were run down through a city that stopped its ears to their screams and were divested of the tax the collector felt they owed.

He took only one finger from each mark, and never took a thumb. There seemed to be no pattern to his culling either: his collection had just as many pinkies as ring or index fingers.

He had started in high summer, had persisted and indeed sped up through the monsoon, and by the time a hysterical city was nearing spontaneous combustion, had collected almost twenty fingers. There had been some speculation whether he would stop then, or whether the good weather would see him make the big jump across the class divide and actually start defingering the middle classes. There was a palpable feeling of relief around the city that neither hypothesis was put to the test.

The news outlets had noted that the policeman on the spot was Deputy Commissioner of Police Dayal of the Crime Branch, noted for his perspicacity in matters criminal. As the head of the task force set up to deal with the matter, he had become, over the summer and the rains, the most visible investigator into these particular outrages. His phlegmatic encounters with the press had achieved almost cult status and were relayed from citizen to like-minded voyeur via mobile phones and social networking sites.

"We had established who he was," said the DCP to the cameras and the digital data recorders in the early-morning light. "I was pursuing him. He was running away when he collapsed. Obviously, he wasn't very well." With which understatement, the policeman turned away from the press and retreated behind the sanctity of the yellow tape, and no amount of media coercion could tempt him out again. People watching at home over their cornflakes and breakfast parathas remarked, as the inevitable frenzy played out over the course of the next few days, at the resignation on the DCP's face as he said his piece. Triumph and closure were conspicuous by their absence. Various commentators would impute tiredness as a reason for this lack of emotion, as well as the deflation that would naturally ensue from the conclusion of a long and harrowing case. The thing to remember, it was pointed out, was that the abomination itself was over.

A cursory glance at the city pages of the newspapers would have served to acquaint the reader with the other irritant to Delhi's solid citizenry that interminable summer. The battles, sometimes pitched and at other times running, between gangs of self-styled vampires and werewolves, had captivated the youth and horrified the elderly and left everyone in between completely bemused. What was to be made of young adults of both sexes wearing makeup and hurling objects and insults at each other, in bus stations and on trains, in markets and parking lots? Who were their role models and what were they trying to prove and where were their parents?

The lighter pages in the city supplements of those same papers also noted the disappearance of the Colonel. She was so called because of the vaguely military outfits she wore when out on the town, which was every night. Her tight leggings and fitted epauletted jackets defined both her anatomy and her style and were further distinguished by being copied by nobody else. The fashion victims of the city had long since concluded that only the Colonel herself could carry off such ensembles. She disappeared, it would seem, on the very night marked by the discovery of the body of Delhi's own Angulimala.

A gaggle of her feminine hangers-on, bereft of her leadership, were interrogated inside their nocturnal habitats by a few reporters on the nightlife beat and a TV channel or two. How long had she been around? "Forever," declared one twenty-something. "Since before this bar was opened," affirmed another. "And that was at least two years ago." She had no family that anybody could remember. Nobody could state that they had ever been invited to her home. She came to a different bar every night and her court moved with her, and her smile and her conversation and her benevolent hold on their lives would be missed forever.

In a few days, she too disappeared from the papers and the minds and hearts of her erstwhile acolytes.

A few months earlier:
    Two a.m. in Lajpat Nagar. A bastion of the Punjabi middle class

in reasonably central Delhi. Its posher parts house the minor officials of the more déclassé embassies, while the seedier bits are populated by Afghans and Kashmiris and other outliers of Delhi's refugee cartography. There are streets here that are by no means dark, hedged about by houses that are far from empty.

One such street: a row of stores selling automotive accessories at one end, a dingy park at the other. The modest flats here brood over both store and garden. What windows there are, are barred. Smaller alleys lead off this thoroughfare. The rickshaws come here to roost at night, after the last rude boys in their dark-tinted hatchbacks are gone, stereos blaring. The rickshaws line up one next to the other and the men who ride them curl up either in the meager comfort of the bench seat, or on the open road. There is a small shack by the side of the road which is open late and dispenses tea and biscuits. If you give the man who runs it some eggs, he will make them up for you. The cold glow of sodium vapor lamps is everywhere, rendering the citizens of the night and their environs in an unhealthy yellow.

The smell of confined exhaust is still on the hot air of the Delhi night. There is no or very little breeze and the few clothes the men wear on their thin bodies are glossy with perspiration. A man turns and then turns again and calls out feverishly in his sleep, an intimacy nobody else sharing his open bedroom wants, so the others ignore him and let his ravings crawl up and down the walls and across the street.

One of them wakes then, grumbling, and shambles over to the mean park, a bitterly contested site which is sought by the middle-class denizens of the street to be secured during the day for their children and at night against just such men as he. There is a padlock on the gate, so he does his business against the outside wall. He isn't the first and a sharp male stench hangs over the whole park. An enormous old neem casts its erratic shadow over him. There are patches of darkness here, more so than out on the street itself, and perhaps he thinks, Why not? Before taking out his kit. Then he hears something, *and he turns, and he sees something that goes with what he's heard, and the combination scares him enough that the old glass syringe in his hand falls from his hand and the dirty needle in it breaks and the precious cargo on its little bit of foil falls upon the heedless ground, scattered into the dirt.*

Probably, he screams. Clearly, he runs a few steps.

Then there is a blow and he drops to his knees. There is a second one. An injection is quickly administered, one in which he has no say and from which he derives no pleasure. A finger is removed, a bandage applied, the collector disappears.

The lights are still on, the men still asleep or pretending to be, on their common pavement and on their individual cycle rickshaws, a scant few yards away. Somewhat farther and higher, the middle-class denizens of Lajpat Nagar slumber on, their fans and air conditioners perhaps more of an alibi.

But surely he screams.

———⚬———

He must have screamed, insisted Dayal, as he squatted where the man was found—newly nine-fingered and blubbering—and then squinted up into the rising sun. Daybreak was long past and the cool of that hour, such as it was, was a memory more ephemeral than the dawn itself. But Dayal wasn't fazed by the heat. He made a fetish out of reconstructing the sequence of events in crimes that he was investigating. This wasn't just in the interest of fighting crime, either: the DCP enjoyed the physical intimacy of almost being there that a faithful reiteration granted. So he'd walk and think and let his mind wander, and in time, would come to see, almost as if cinematically, what he thought had happened. The broken syringe, the urine stain, the few short steps back in the direction of his comrades: these were an open book to his colleagues too. But Dayal took it further. He caressed, as if with love, the syringe, almost bent to sniff at the ground. He was practically polite to the rickshaw-walas.

His immediate subordinate, a slow-moving Punjabi named Kapoor, heavy of manner and midriff, knew and indulged this, but the rest of the task force from Crime Branch were inclined to treat it as being borderline creepy. But even they had to admit they had precious little else to go on.

They'd all been there since before dawn and now, as the sun approached its zenith, were all slowly wilting. The sullen rickshaw men were desperate to be allowed to ride away, as much to escape the interminable questioning as to earn their daily bread. Their colleague, missing a digit as of the night before, was in the hospital and no use at all to the investigation. The heat, the lack of a lead, the surly faces of the rickshaw-walas: it was all getting a bit much for the more impatient officers, and the possibility of a broken leg or two was being freely aired as an antidote to the torpor and the mulishness of the rickshaw-walas and even, it must be admitted, to the tedium of a dying investigation. It was all talk, of course, because Dayal didn't work like that. But he was in the zone and they weren't.

"He must have screamed," he murmured again. "Did nobody hear *anything*?"

Kapoor shook his head glumly. Dayal raised his eyebrows, then his eyes to the naked sky. "It was ever thus," he muttered. "Mir noted it when Nadir Shah sacked Delhi. The refugees were harassed by their own countrymen. Nobody listens, nobody cares." Presently he asked, "Who is the local dealer?"

Kapoor indicated with a nod the hapless tea-stall owner, perhaps the longest-faced of the entire hangdog crew.

"Anything?" inquired Dayal.

Nothing, admitted the other man. Didn't hear anything, didn't know anything. Didn't seem to be lying. "Do you want me to have the local cops take care of him?"

Dayal thought about it for a moment, then shook his head. Obviously they already knew. "Tell him to confine himself to these rickshaw-walas. If he ever sells his poison to one of the kids from around here, his body will be in the Yamuna before the sun sets."

Kapoor nodded and ambled over, and then the thin music of a slap judiciously applied to a part-time drug dealer's face was lambent upon the air of Lajpat Nagar. The heavy tread of his subordinate approached again. "I have family here," said Kapoor virtuously.

Dayal nodded at him, then frowned again. "Where does he come from?" he wondered aloud. "From the trees? What is he, a vampire?"

"Like those kids?" asked Kapoor. "The ones fighting in the metro?"

Dayal looked at him and smiled. Just like them, he nodded.

Then, finally, he got to his feet. One of the rickshaw-walas approached him. "Can we go now, sir? We have to make at least our daily rents for our rickshaws. Otherwise it comes out of our pockets."

"Do you have their mobile numbers?" asked Dayal.

"Where'll they go?"

Dayal turned away. "Set them loose."

———————✦——✦——✦———————

In an over air-conditioned room in police HQ sits the cyber-crime unit. When the DCP and Kapoor walked in that afternoon, a few young police officers were on duty, sitting at the big screens of their powerful new machines. A young female officer met them at the door and escorted them in.

She knew who the DCP was and was glad of the opportunity to meet him and was flattered when he smiled in turn. The DCP was a good-looking man and he knew it. The darkly handsome cast of his features was led by an aquiline nose, which also rescued his somewhat beetling brow. Inquisitive eyes, by turns gentle and probing, gave the final touch to a visage that was intelligently lupine. His tailored clothes sat well on his trim figure, while his well-tended mustache and full head of hair were being allowed to acquire a soft sprinkle of gray that sat well, he thought and Kapoor concurred, with his position and responsibilities. He was used to being smiled at and didn't mind smiling back, so he said, "It's a pleasure, Miss Dhingra."

"Please," she replied. "Call me Smita. Everyone does."

"What exactly are you looking for?" she asked, now briskly professional, her young male colleagues watching attentively.

"Well, what I said over the phone. These gangs, the vampires and the werewolves. What do we know about them?"

"What do they have to do with the finger-stealer?" asked one of the young policemen curiously. Kapoor froze him with a look. The DCP didn't even turn around, his attention on Smita, who was tapping away at her keyboard.

"Quite a lot, or not a lot, depending on what you want to know."

"Well, for starters, where can I find them?"

"That's easy. They're all over the Internet."

"Facebook," stated Kapoor.

"Among other places," agreed the young woman, her face still to the screen.

The DCP looked at Kapoor, who blushed and mouthed, "My son."

"Do you know where they're going to be at any time?" asked the DCP.

"It isn't hard," said one of Smita's colleagues. The two older cops turned to him expectantly. "Well, it isn't," he repeated. "We actually circulate e-mails to the local stations when we believe a fight is going to take place. They don't happen spontaneously: they're actually rather well-planned."

"Why?" wondered Kapoor, leaving aside for the moment the question of why the local officers weren't paying any heed to the intelligence this office was providing.

"These are kids, for the most part. The eldest are just about twenty, the younger ones barely in their teens. They live with their parents. If they have to get somewhere, they have to plan it," said Smita.

The DCP nodded. "How do you track them?"

"That's the easy part. They're clever, but not clever

enough to want to clear their tracks. We look for words and phrases, things like *vampires, lycans, rumble*, a random place: you know, like Karol Bagh. Then we put them together and run searches, monitor certain forums, new sites, groups, things like that."

"Lycan?"

"Werewolves, sir," supplied Kapoor. "My son," again, to his superior's wordless question.

"Most of them are just innocent kids. Like your son, sir," said Smita deferentially to Kapoor. "They read these books, *Twilight* and the like, they see the movies and play the games, and they fashion a world for themselves they think they recognize as actually being real, or more worthy of being real, at any rate, than the one they're in. The ones doing the fighting are a harder core.

"I'd be interested in speaking to them," she murmured as an afterthought.

"Really? Why?" asked the DCP.

"Well, I like the books and movies too," she grinned, as did her colleagues. The two older cops couldn't help but join in.

"Do you know where they'll be tonight?"

"We do, as a matter of fact. The metro station in Model Town."

"Model Town," said the DCP thoughtfully, turning to Kapoor, who nodded in turn.

"I have family there."

———— ⟶ ————

Night was well-established in the city by the time the two of them drove by the police lines in the shadow of the newly constructed elevated metro track. Dayal had considered and then rejected the idea of asking the local police for help. His need to be inconspicuous was paramount. Anyway, he pointed out to Kapoor, if the local cops felt that bunches of kids fighting each other in public at night was beneath their notice, he wasn't going to lose any sleep over it either.

Kapoor had wondered why they were coming here. "Call it a hunch," the DCP had replied. They were both content to leave it at that. The bright lights of the Mall Road receded behind them and the shadows lengthened under the elevated track. The citizens of the night were setting up their homes under its spans and Dayal thought, as he had before, of how a bridge's ability to raise you above the water is only one of the ways it shelters you from that particular element. He thought of how a bridge is simultaneously a soaring premonition of a city's future and a weighty anchor tied to the ground it has sprung from. He would no doubt have wordlessly amplified this theme, metaphysical speculation being, as befitted his detective status, one of his primary, albeit solitary joys, but then the car stopped and Kapoor climbed out.

"Up there," he said. Dayal looked up at the expanse of lit-up concrete that loomed above their heads, connecting the elevated track to either side of the busy road below. The way lay up a flight of stairs Kapoor pointedly ignored, heading instead to the lift that was conspicuously marked as being for the benefit of those with special needs. The security man there let them in without demur and they ascended to the level of the ticket counter, where they quietly walked through the electronic turnstiles that another security man beeped open for them, deferentially touching his peaked cap with the other hand.

"So much for being inconspicuous," muttered Dayal.

"Biharis," replied Kapoor nonchalantly, next to him on the escalator up to the track level. "Not the soft kids we're after. Where will they ever have seen a cop before?"

The heavier man stalked onto the platform, looking this way and that. It was empty. Dayal and he walked over to a bench and sat down to wait.

———•—•—•———

Pretty soon, the kids began to arrive. They came in couples and groups, the boys wearing shades, all of them plugged into their iPods and phones, trailing snatches of death metal and electronica and clouds of pheromones. They strung out along the platform affecting boredom and jangling with nerves, and the two cops felt as if it was palpable, the tension of a juvenile riot being birthed. Kapoor was busy on his phone and the DCP was immersed in thought and the noise and strobes of passing traffic on the road below was strong enough to disorient anyone. When the train arrived, its service infrequent at this hour, it seemed as if the kids breathed, inhaling when the doors opened, exhaling when they sighed shut, in time with its rhythm. The two cops stayed put on the platform. The kids finally noticed and one of them, a large almost-man with a turban but not yet a beard, ambled over. "Why didn't you get on that train?" he asked, not very gently.

The DCP looked up at him politely. "Why don't you tell me about vampires and lycans?" he replied.

The boy studied the two of them, the fluorescent light of the platform cold upon his skin, their visages reflected in the mirrored surfaces of his sunglasses. "Dogs," he said softly, then turned and was gone down the stairs. The word was relayed swiftly down the platform and the kids were gone as quickly as they'd come, the ones closer to the escalator descending that way, the ones at the other end of the platform escaping nimbly across the tracks, clambering up the other side and streaming down the stairs. Only one, a young girl, came to hand. Kapoor held her, her shirt clenched in one meaty fist.

"I do hope you're a vampire, sweetie," he smiled. "I want to see how well you fly with my foot up your ass."

She wept and flailed and the few kids left on the opposite platform gestured and shouted abuse. As the DCP looked at them, studying the situation for leverage and clues, one of them, a young man with his face covered with a kaffiyeh even in the hot weather, showed him a finger. Then, quite clearly and still silently, he held up his other hand, showing him two fingers scissoring at each other, which he then brought to the first one, pretending to cut it off. A train headed in the opposite direction hissed to a stop on the other line, wondering faces lining the windows, then the train was gone and the young man with the kaffiyeh and all the other kids as well, and the DCP was left with the thought that his hunch had been right but Angulimala himself had escaped.

So he turned to the girl who was writhing and sweating and crying in Kapoor's grip.

"It's my first time, I swear. I've never come here before. I'll tell you who brought me. I can't go to jail," she moaned. "I'll tell you everything."

"Of course you will, honey," said Kapoor. "Just do me one favor. Promise me you'll take your time."

The girl looked at him first, speechless with fear, then at the DCP, who merely smiled and lit a cigarette. Then they too were gone down the escalator, ignoring the other riders who averted their eyes from the sight of the two men escorting the weeping girl, past the downcast guards, out to their waiting car, parked on the bank of the river of traffic that surged under the fluorescent sterile station above.

———————

The girl, it transpired, was telling the truth. She knew only two of the others, both young women. They'd only come along because they'd been following the conversation across sites and groups of like-minded young people on the Internet. She didn't know the young man in the kaffiyeh, didn't know the moving forces behind the vampire-versus-lycan war, barely recognized her father when he walked into the station to collect her. He was a man of consequence, arrived in an SUV, possessed rings on all his fingers, and didn't bother calling any of the ministers whose numbers were clearly stored in his phone. He thanked the DCP and Kapoor for rescuing his daughter, slapped her once in front of them, then embraced her and cried as well. The DCP was informed by the immigration authorities at Indira Gandhi International Airport that she left for Singapore the next night for an indefinite stay with her maternal uncle. Apparently, she was flying business class.

Records revealed that a few of the young antagonists

had been unwise enough to use their metro cards to gain access to the platform. They were all roused from their scattered sleep before the night was out. Unsurprisingly, they all proved to be models of cooperation, though they added very little to the meager fund of the DCP's knowledge. None of them knew the man in the kaffiyeh. He was known to be solitary, was a vampire, a brutal fighter among a collection of kids who were mostly dilettantes of delinquency, and barely spoke to anyone. He didn't have a name, never corresponded over e-mail, and didn't possess a mobile phone. He followed the conversation and came to the rumbles and that was all they knew.

Tracking an e-mail ID or even an IP address was pointless, Smita told them. "The kids these days change them like you change your clothes."

The two detectives were in her office, their feet comfortably on chairs in front of them. There had been a surge of chatter on the Internet, she told them, and then it had all gone dead. The kids were lying low for the moment.

"You didn't get a good look at him?"

The DCP shook his head. Nothing had set him apart from the other kids on the far platform. Only the kaffiyeh, and plenty of other kids were wearing them that year.

She turned back to her computer. "Okay. I don't know who he is, but I have a fair idea I've read his posts, under various names." One of her colleagues, who'd been monitoring their conversation, nodded too.

"I thought these kids never heard from him," stated Kapoor.

"Most of these kids are hobbyists," said Smita dismissively. "They're told where to go and they show up to see what's happening. A few of them, however, are worth keeping an eye on. This one, in particular, is a dark one. If he's the same guy."

"What do you know about him?"

"We know that he's boastful. He does it under different names, but we can recognize his style," said Smita's colleague. "That he considers himself a vampire is pretty much spot on. He's one of the hard core, a believer. He's not doing it for kicks, or to fit into a crew, or because he likes the hair and the makeup. I've tried tracing him, following him around on the Internet. We've found his signature on underground vampire sites, groups that feed on each other's blood at private parties, things like that. But he doesn't keep the same online persona long enough for us to actually track him down."

The DCP raised an eyebrow. "And?"

Smita picked up the thread. "We know he's convinced there have been vampires in Delhi for hundreds of years."

This time the DCP raised both eyebrows.

Smita and her colleague chuckled in tandem. "That's one of the ways we recognize him. Even in that crowd, this stands out."

"You're an aficionado of Delhi's history, aren't you, sir?" said the young male officer. "What do you think?"

"I think you should tell me what else you know," said his superior officer. "Any noise at all on the finger-snatcher?"

The two cyber-crime officers shook their heads regretfully. They'd been monitoring the chatter, which had of late become a cacophony, but there was nothing to link the vampire to the collector of fingers.

"There is one thing," said Smita. "He's obsessed with the Colonel."

The DCP and Kapoor looked at each other, then at the young woman. "Who?"

"You know, that woman who parties every night. Everyone knows her and talks about her. She's in the silly papers all the time."

"What does he want with her?"

"Photos, for the most part. Information. Posts keep popping up on various forums, asking for either. Her address, where she'll be that night. We're convinced it's him."

The DCP still looked fogged. "If she's always in the papers, surely he can just run a search for her images?"

"That's the point," said Smita with a cagey smile. "She seems to know all the photographers. The writers go on about her, describe her clothes and what she's drinking, but there's never a photo. Practically everyone who goes out at night has seen her. I've seen her. But if you only knew her through the papers, she could almost be a figment of the collective imagination of Delhi's gossip writers."

"A ghost," supplied her colleague helpfully. "Or a vampire. Apparently, some of the stories say vampires can't be photographed. He's offered to pay for her photo. He trawls through the Facebook pages of Delhi's nightbirds looking for camera-phone shots of the night before. He haunts the Flickr accounts of the press photographers. We think he's even hacked the image archives of the dailies. But clearly whatever he's found isn't enough."

"The Colonel," mused the DCP. "Is that really her name?"

"That's what the papers call her," said Smita.

"Alright then," said the DCP. "Where do we find her?"

"That's easy," said Smita's colleague eagerly. "It's Wednesday. She'll be at the nightclub at the Babar Hotel."

Smita nodded sagely.

The DCP looked at Kapoor, who nodded as well and said, "My nephew works there."

"Would you," the DCP formally asked Smita, "be interested in helping me with the investigation into the finger-snatcher case?"

"A table for two," said Kapoor over the phone.

———————

The night saw them heading toward the Babar Hotel in the DCP's personal car. He thought that the young policewoman had hit just the right pitch with her choice of clothes, with the trousers a no-nonsense nod toward what was in effect a working dinner, while the straps on the otherwise discreetly chic blouse were meager enough to suggest that she wasn't entirely unaware of the potential of a night out at Delhi's current hotspot.

She asked him about Delhi's vampires, when she felt the silence beginning to weigh. What about them? he asked back. Did the DCP believe there were such things? she replied.

He told her he'd thought about it all that day and had realized that he didn't really know, one way or another, which surprised him.

Djinns are still invoked in Ferozeshah Kotla and in

other places, he said as if to himself. There are shops in
Dariba that have been empty for generations because the
jewelers believe they're cursed. There are madwomen
on the Ridge and tree spirits in Mehrauli, and during
the Uprising, armies dressed in green silk with their
swords naked to the air were seen and then disappeared.
In daylight.

"This city," he said, gesturing out through the windows of his car at the agglomerations of squat ugly houses
racing by in the land south of Safdarjung's tomb. "It's
a giant necropolis. Entire developments raised on what
used to be graveyards. Old villages gone, fields buried,
their soil used for cement."

The bare bones of householders and thieves, the
spirits of lost cremation grounds, the stories of wander-
ers and village heads and warriors and all their women.
Disinterred and then dispersed back into the dust. But
at what cost? wondered the DCP.

"Would it surprise me that some revenant actually
came knocking? Probably not," he smiled. "Zauq couldn't
leave the streets and alleys of this city. Why should a
ghost or a vampire or whatever be different?"

Smita digested this for a moment. "So what they say
about you is correct? That you're into Delhi's history?"

"It's where I'm from, Smita. Aren't you?"

"I'm from here," she replied, waving outside her window. "From this city that's sprung from your necropolis.
My grandparents were refugees after Partition. These
new colonies are my home. I don't even know who Zauq
is. And I'd be surprised if the streets he's talking about
are the ones we're driving on."

The DCP looked at her in surprise, then inclined his

head. "You're right. Let me begin again. I am interested in Delhi's history. Very interested. And my connection to Delhi predates Partition, as you've probably gathered. Are we . . . cool?"

Smita looked at him and smiled. "We're cool. But who is Zauq?"

"An Urdu poet. Rather famous. He was writing around the time of the Uprising of 1857."

"Really? A contemporary of Ghalib's?"

An eyebrow, raised. "Quite right. But you've heard of him?"

"Who hasn't?" she grinned.

They were pulling into the overly grand entrance of a hotel already famous for its lofty cuisine and tiny rooms and beautiful views of urban sprawl. The way ahead lay off to the side, where the entrance to the nightclub was.

The DCP, while not antisocial, didn't make a habit of going out on the town. His famed incorruptibility militated against a regular enjoyment of Delhi's luxury nightspots, the cost of which was equally legendary. But there was nothing self-consciously austere about his demeanor when he did get out and about, and he looked around, following in Smita's self-possessed and evidently right-at-home wake, with real appreciation. He enjoyed the clubby little bar that also functioned as the entrance, the quite charming way the management had of dismissing those whom it felt were unsuitable, and was impressed with the uniform sullenness of the tight-shirted males who were waiting to get in and the equally invariable smiles of the women who had all, it seemed to his aging eyes, been allowed to escape their homes in their lingerie. It fit together. His innate sense of symmetry was pleased with the way the aspects of this ritual, arcane as it seemed, were being so closely observed.

A beautifully dressed young man detached himself from the bar and hurried toward him, his hand outstretched, just as the DCP was reaching into his pocket for his ID and cards.

"DCP Dayal," he said with a smile, "what an honor. And this lovely lady is your date? It's good to have you both here," he said, leading the way into the temple, past the waiting line of the supplicants, the bouncers one step away from bowing and scraping. Then the older officer didn't have any time to think at all, because the music, hitherto muted by the door, hit him in the chest.

He was glad in those first few moments of Smita's company, of her comforting presence at his shoulder as the lights and the sound and the dense crush of people on the fringes of the dance floor threatened to overwhelm him. Kapoor's beauteous nephew cut an apparently seamless path through the multitudes to the bar, where he set them up with cocktails which, at the DCP's almost imperceptible nod, Smita accepted.

There, over the music, he told them the lay of the land. The first table over there, he gestured, behind the intricately wrought steel and wood screen, was the Colonel's court. "It's the quietest private booth we have. It has an unobstructed view of both the entrance and the dance floor. Would you like me to introduce you?"

The DCP shook his head and took a sip of his drink, raising it in appreciation to the younger man.

"And yours?" he asked Smita. "Is it to your satisfaction?"

"Entirely, sir," she replied.

The DCP nodded and thanked Kapoor's nephew and walked toward the Colonel's table with Smita in tow.

———— + + + ————

She was ensconced on a purple banquette, a stemmed glass in front of her and laughing female acolytes to either side. A lone gent patrolled the outskirts of their party, there apparently to replenish drinks at his own expense. The DCP and Smita walked up to the table where, without preamble, the older officer sat down, inviting Smita to have a seat next to him. By a trick of the acoustic designer's art, the table was a quiet haven, while still close enough to the floor that the officers could glimpse the sweat in the cleavage of the feverish dancers who threw themselves about a few feet away, beyond the almost diaphanous screen.

The Colonel looked inquiringly at the DCP as he made himself comfortable.

He then leaned across and said, loud enough that the young women to either side of her could hear, "I don't know whether to shake your hand or salute you."

The woman looked at him with her eyebrows raised, then smiled. "You can greet me the way you like, Commissioner. I am yours to command."

The DCP would remember that first smile, her perfect even teeth, the warmth in her eyes.

"You know who I am," he said without surprise.

"Who doesn't?" she replied.

"I know who you are, but not what to call you. Colonel sounds awfully formal."

"These girls call me Razia. I don't know why."

"It fits. Delhi's own sultana. Regal, powerful."

"Dead, too, these past eight hundred years."

"A blink of the eye in this city's history, surely."

"Perhaps, Commissioner, but she's still a bit before my time. But if the name pleases you, it is yours to use." She waved her hangers-on away. The young women obediently went off with their solitary male attendant, and the DCP and Smita moved closer to her.

"And you, my dear?" she smiled at Smita. "What's your name?"

"Smita Dhingra."

"A policewoman, perhaps?"

"I am."

"And how," said Razia, "can I be of service to the law?"

"Doubtless you've heard," replied the DCP, "of the finger-snatcher?"

Razia inclined her head.

"Perhaps you've also heard of these gangs of pretend vampires and werewolves who're fighting each other all over Delhi?"

An eyebrow acknowledged that she was indeed in receipt of this information.

Why, wondered the DCP, would a young man who thought himself a vampire be looking for pictures of her? Why, indeed, would a woman such as Razia, an habitué of nightspots far removed from the louche battlegrounds of the angsty undead, have come to the attention of one such as he?

Razia pursed her lips thoughtfully and registered contemplation, and the DCP remarked, as he would again, at how the theatricality of her every movement was rendered with such poise as to make it seem natural. Was it, she said as if to herself, because of the paucity of such material? Perhaps, acknowledged the policeman. Is there a reason for this shortage? he asked in turn. Privacy is a commodity, replied the woman. Like any other, it becomes more precious when the supply begins to dwindle.

"You don't have to come out, you know," said Smita. "If you like your privacy so much."

The woman's soft laugh defused both the acerbity of Smita's response and the rebuke in the older officer's eyes. "In response to your questions, Commissioner. I don't know. But clearly the young man has an unhealthy fascination with creatures of the night. No doubt he classifies me as one."

"Does he search for you because he wants a kindred spirit?"

"Perhaps he wants a candle to light his way out."

"A sign of the dawn, perhaps?"

"Quite right, Commissioner," she replied. "But if he's right, then he's destined to be disappointed, because this candle may be dead as well."

They smiled at each other while Smita narrowed her eyes.

"Ghalib," murmured the DCP. "But surely even he is before your time?"

"Not necessarily," replied Razia evenly. "If poetry can survive the Revolt and the fall of the Mughals, why can't it thrive in a place such as this?"

The lights of the club strobed around them and kept pace with the deejay's efforts on the tables, and the convulsions of the dancers were bright upon the DCP's retinas as he considered what Razia was saying. He thought about her desire for anonymity and how perhaps it wasn't as disingenuous as Smita believed, and whether a club such as the one they were in, with its overt uniformities and hidden alcoves and blandly overpowering sensory assault, wasn't indeed the perfect prescription for such a need. He remembered legends of poetic confrontations in courtyards of homes long abandoned and demolished, the disputants waiting for the candle to be placed in front of them so they could start their recitations, their allies and adversaries cloaked and turbaned in the uniforms of the time and dispersed through the seated crowd, the women watching from behind their screens and curtains in the upper stories, waiting for a new king to be crowned, a new flame to be lit, a new name to be added to the roster to which gifts were to be sent, poems dispatched for comments, love to be made. He brought himself back to the present and found two sets of female eyes on him, one bewildered, the other amused.

"Has this man," he asked formally, "not tried to make contact with you?"

"I don't know, Commissioner," Razia replied. "I'm not on the Internet. I don't normally answer my phone and I certainly don't give my number to just anyone."

The DCP pondered this quietly.

"Would you like my number, Commissioner?" asked Razia.

The DCP nodded his head slowly, fished out his phone, and fed in the number she gave him.

"Bring yourself to my poor house, Commissioner. I'm sure we can find a candle to take turns with."

He nodded again, though he doubted whether his poetic impulse would be up to that or any test.

There was one more thing, pointed out Razia gently. She still didn't know the commissioner's first name.

Sajan.

A fitting name for a man of Delhi, said Razia, inclining her head. "I feel as if I've known many men like you in years past, Sajan. But I fear there are fewer and fewer left."

The DCP and Smita left then, past the screen that shielded Razia's table, past the dance floor and the bar, through the door and up the stairs and out to the hotel's vestibule where, in deference to his position, his car was waiting off to one side. They were in the car and on their way to Smita's home before she opened her mouth.

"She was flirting with you," she said almost accusingly.

"I noticed," he replied drily.

Smita gave him a sidelong look, then laughed, a robustly merry sound that brightened the older man's hitherto-in-free-fall mood.

"So. Do you think she's a vampire?" he asked jocularly.

"I'll tell you one thing," replied Smita. "I was looking at her very closely, and I have no idea how old she is. I hate women like that."

———— ✦ ————

The rains broke with a vengeance that year. The month of Saawan didn't herald the monsoon: it rode in on it. The level of the Yamuna waxed and waned and then rose again and there were dark murmurings in the streets about floods. The watery apocalypse to come was all over the vernacular press and the regional language channels and those Dilliwalas with family in distant places were besieged with phone calls urging a retreat to higher ground. The news that a city as dry as Delhi was to be flooded was greeted with hoots of laughter from Dilliwalas themselves, or at least those that didn't live in close contiguity with the river. Urchins swam in the new streams, infants were beguiled with the unheard sound of the patter of raindrops, vendors of tea and fried snacks did a brisk business everywhere. A city used to associating gray with smog, undrinkable water, and the residue left behind by the dusty air grew to love again the silver light of cloudy skies and falling rain. The monsoon winds swept through the city and cooled homes from the top down and everywhere was vigor and rebirth and brilliant resurgent green.

But Dayal drew little sustenance from the cool and the moistness and the burgeoning trees. He and Kapoor ploughed a lonely furrow through the wet city, on the track of a young man wearing a kaffiyeh who believed he was a vampire. They spent wet afternoons and evenings in the gleaming forecourts of malls in Saket and Rajouri Garden, waiting for young people to grow fangs and beards and engage each other again. Once, as night came to Nehru Place, they ran behind a pack of young boys who exhibited no little athletic skill in climbing up what seemed to be blank walls and who jumped from broken rail to seedy step to dangling grating with an abandonment of physical limitation and fear that seemed otherworldly. The rain fell around them in the dankly dirty plaza and the dark towers loomed around them as they discovered that these young boys were innocent devotees of a new urban sport called parkour and no, they were neither vampires nor werewolves, sorry to disappoint you, but did the two uncles know where they could be found? The last office workers of the evening trudged wearily past in the steadily falling rain as Dayal and his junior worked their way stolidly through the fare provided by the least greasy-looking of Nehru Place's canteens, their faces illumined by the flame under the big metal plate, the dirty tubes above, and the reflected light off the puddles in the broken plaza beyond.

Look at this place, gestured Dayal to Kapoor. "This was once going to be the shining beacon of New Delhi. Its buildings full of the urban elite, its plazas places for its forward thinkers to congregate. Less than forty years ago. A moment in Delhi's history. And look at it now. This is all the time it takes for a dream to disintegrate in New Delhi."

Though he left it unsaid, Kapoor knew that his superior and friend meant it as an exculpation for his own attachment to the cities that had preceded this misbegotten one. Even though he himself was a product of the new city, Kapoor sympathized, as he looked glumly at his plate of forlorn samosas and considered, along with Dayal, how long it would take for the new malls to fall. That he picked up three new Playstation games for free from a street vendor who was closing up for the night was little consolation. My son, he told Dayal, who nodded dolefully as he gazed about himself at the wretched prospect of a business district drowning in the rain.

The weeks came and went, the rain stayed. There were reports of fights all over the city and men continued to lose their fingers to Angulimala and the clouds pulled in closer over Dayal. One evening, after a frantic phone call from Smita, Dayal made his way across the river in the evening traffic. The commuter rush was worsened by citizens who stopped their cars to show their children the unaccustomed sight of the Yamuna actually flowing free and alarmingly close to the roadway. The siren on Dayal's car and the imprecations his driver shouted at their fellow travelers seemed to have little effect. The commissioner settled himself further back in his seat and allowed his mind to wander. The setbacks of the last few weeks, the growing numbers of men missing their fingers on the streets and the city's maddened reaction, the fear of a copycat and the threat that one of these unfortunate men would actually die: all these things and more pressed about him just as the traffic did around his car, and so he, as he always had, sought refuge in abstract speculation.

But today, the expected release failed to materialize. The rain drummed upon the roof of his car and skated off the slick windshield. Through the manic whirring of the wipers he saw raincoated children on the pavement and similarly covered riders on their two-wheelers and impotently honking cars everywhere. He thought of Smita and her laughter and her constant presence over the phone these past few weeks, as he checked in with her for leads and clues. He thought of a woman's beguiling invitation and how he had nothing to offer her, so he hadn't taken her up on it and what did that make him? He thought of the fact that he had nothing to go on, that Angulimala had been the width of a metro platform away and was now gone, his collection growing every

week in the wet night watches while Dayal and his minions foundered in the selfsame dark. The cold wet grip
of failure clutched at him so he told his driver to mount
the pavement and scatter the children, because he had a
riot to disrupt.

They sped along the pavement, their siren and lights
blaring, a posse of civilian two-wheelers following in
their wake, as will happen in Delhi. The driver sought
his superior's eyes in the mirror for confirmation, his
foot poised over the brake, expecting the instruction to
leave the first motorcyclist to hit his bumper lying in the
wet dirt of the pavement as a warning to the others. But
Dayal didn't look up so they drove on, the turgid river
surging below, the supposedly fleet motorized stream
constrained above. Dayal's phone beeped. Smita was
on the line and sounding flustered, not something he
associated with her.

"They're broadcasting," she said peremptorily.
"Those little bastards are shooting their fight and showing
it live."

Dayal nodded. It was only as he expected. "How
many of them? You're recording it, I hope?"

"Of course. No more than three on each side, now.
Perhaps less. Certainly no more. The hobbyists are gone.
Scared off by you. These are the hard-cores."

"Okay. Anything of interest?"

"Your boy in the kaffiyeh is there. He's currently
beating the hell out of one of the lycans."

"Is there any sound?"

"None. It's all silent. Whoever is filming is close to
the action. It's pretty tight. Can't tell where they are,
but I'm assuming it's still in that new bus depot they're

building. There's a lot of open concrete, and there seem to be patches of floodlit ground."

"Where's it being hosted?"

"An open-access web-streaming server. Mainstream, legal. The transmitting address is a ghost. We're working on it. My guess is the source is a smartphone working on a 3G-enabled account. We're working on that too."

"Good," said Dayal. "Very good. Anything else?"

"I suggest you get there quickly, sir. The clip's going to be on YouTube in about two minutes."

The car swept through the intersection that marked the end of the bridge and flew along the raised road that cut through the townships on the other side of the river. Dayal glimpsed towers off to one side and fields interspersed with squat concrete blocks on the other and once he thought he saw a statue of Hanuman, painted and glowering and large beyond belief, but the rain was strong and it might have been an illusion, and before he was really ready, they were there and pulling into the almost-finished bus depot, the security men sheltering forlornly in their little shack to the side. The car sped along the slick surface, its lights off now, the big floods of the bus bays' illumination enough through the steadily falling rain. Off at the far end of the enormous depot, Dayal saw a tight knot of young people dissolving into the darkness. His car raced toward the wraiths, the rhythm of the raindrops and the thwacking of the wiper blades a backbeat to their swift, silent progress.

"Put on your lights," said Dayal quietly. "I don't want you to hit any kids lying on the road." The lights came on and the car swept to a halt. Dayal and his driver barrelled out into the rain—a body lay still on the ground in the lee of one wall, a floodlight tower almost perpendicularly overhead. Dayal motioned his driver to look along the wall, knelt to check the body itself. He turned it over and saw a young man, perhaps in his late teens, with a beaten face that was already turning blue in the watery light. He was alive and breathing but in a bad way. He winced as Dayal moved him.

"Take it easy, son," said the DCP gently. "Help will be here soon." As he said it he heard the wail of sirens and in a moment saw the wash of watery headlights. By and by they were joined by Kapoor and a detachment from the local station, headed by the duty officer. The beaten adolescent lay quietly in Dayal's arms as the men clustered around them. Kapoor knelt as well and felt for the boy's hands. His eyes met Dayal's as he counted ten fingers, then his eyebrows rose as he followed Dayal's gaze to the puncture wounds in the boy's neck. The driver arrived and reported the little gate in the wall a short distance away, and the road on the other side where the vehicles of the fighters must have been parked. Naturally, they were gone. Nevertheless, at a word from the duty officer, the men of the local station took off at a run to have a look around.

Kapoor peered at the local inspector, who picked wearily at the dripping collar of his uniform. "Didn't you know?" he asked, without any apparent heat.

The inspector looked up, then away. "We'd heard."

And so? wondered Kapoor.

"We're a long way from HQ, uncle," responded the inspector. "This rain has caused four accidents already tonight, including one less than a kilometer away on the highway. There's been one building collapse and three evacuations. Up to eleven people might have died in the collapse. And over there, next to that new stadium, the local farmers are up in arms about the acquisition of their land for the parking lot."

And your point is? inquired Kapoor's eyebrows.

"Those fucking villagers are camped out with their sticks and their guns, uncle. If they start heating up, they won't stop at biting each other. Frankly, these kids are a nuisance but they haven't really hurt anybody."

"Till now," said the DCP.

The inspector nodded unhappily.

The DCP's phone beeped. It was Smita. "It's up on all the websites, sir."

"Hmm. How did it end?"

"It came down to the boy in the kaffiyeh, the person holding the camera, and the boy I'm assuming you're hovering over."

The DCP grunted.

"They were obviously in a hurry. The boy in the kaffiyeh pummeled that poor child. Then he knelt over him, with his back to the camera, and appeared to bite his neck. The boy being bitten definitely seemed to be feeling it. Is he still alive?"

"He'll live. Then?"

"The boy in the kaffiyeh let the victim collapse to the ground. Then he turned back to the camera and saluted. Very deliberately. He held up a finger, shook it at the camera, knelt down and drew it across the beaten boy's throat, then stood up and saluted again. Then they seemed to hear something. Probably you. They took off running. The camera was killed seconds later."

"Any progress on the account?"

"We're working on it."

The DCP hung up. At his feet, the boy stirred in the wet slush.

"Sacrifice," he said faintly.

"What?" asked Kapoor.

"Sacrifice. He said I was a sacrifice."

"Who did?" asked Kapoor roughly.

"The boy in the scarf. Our leader."

"I thought you were a lycan?" said the DCP gently.

"No. No lycans. We're all vampires. It was supposed to be my initiation."

Kapoor and Dayal looked at each other.

"I suppose you don't really know these guys?" asked Kapoor with disgust.

"No. They said I was a sacrifice. They said the Colonel would know and understand."

"And that's why they kicked the shit out of you," said the inspector glumly.

"They said it was for my initiation."

"They lied, son," said Kapoor wearily. "They beat you up because they can. I suggest, when you're out of hospital, you find new friends."

The boy was put away in the back of the inspector's duty jeep.

"May I ask you something, sir?" the inspector said to the DCP. The older officer nodded. "Why is Crime Branch interested in these freaks? More to the point, what do they have to do with your task force?"

"That's two questions, inspector. But if you come across anything that might be of interest to me on either front, you'll let me know, won't you?"

The inspector looked at him, the bill of his uniform

hat shaping the flow of the rainwater off his face. Then he nodded in turn, touched his hat, and drove away.

Kapoor and Dayal stood there, next to the latter's car, in the relentless rain.

"That was staged for our benefit," noted Kapoor.

Dayal nodded wordlessly.

"Kids these days. Seriously."

Dayal had to agree.

"I think it's time you called the Colonel."

<hr />

The path to Razia lay through a narrow alley that led off a busy road in south Delhi. There was a bank to one side with a line outside the ATM and a shop selling bodybuilding supplements in the basement. An outlet for Adidas guarded the other flank. The commerce of the main road ebbed and flowed around the parked cars. The pushcarts, cycle-rickshaws, and pedestrians, bent on their own business in the moist night, eddied around Dayal's own car. He stepped out and lit a cigarette, looked one way then another, and moved into the alley.

This was one of Delhi's urban villages and the alley was a tight one, along which ran close-packed houses. They were high enough and dense enough to cut off the sun at noon: at night, every person in these alleys was a ghost. Power lines snaked overhead, the myriad noises of soap operas and cricket matches came and went, and the smoke from the DCP's cigarette floated up into the ephemerally electric night. The air was neon and then fluorescent, and once there was the silver illumination of a lightning flash, the blues and pinks of the streaming homes off to either side starkly vivid. Seconds later Dayal heard its attendant roar. But by then the alley, now meandering through the village, was dark again. A corner store that stocked cigarettes and paan masala and eggs and bread provided a beacon of light where Dayal stopped to ask for directions. The man looked at him, then away, and then looked again, and saw Dayal for what he was. So he pointed, reluctantly, in a particular direction. Dayal bought a cigarette and sauntered through the sodden lane.

The newer houses were built above little parking bays, where Dayal saw scooters and occasionally small cars. Once a cat walked along a boundary wall and sometimes a dog, surprised in his slumber, barked at the policeman. Dayal took no notice. A Northeastern woman hurried past in the opposite direction, her mobile phone at her lips, urgently telling a driver at the mouth of the lane to wait for her, that she couldn't take the next ride because her shift was starting in Gurgaon in less than forty-five minutes. He reached the end of the lane and was faced with a choice, whether to turn right or left. He stubbed out his smoke and glanced around and was pleased to discover that, as with all such places, he was far from alone.

There were eyes on him from balconies and from windows, even from a little set of young men taking it easy on the street. He felt how anonymity and communality can coexist in the same place and time, and knew what it is to be both naked and secure. So fortified, he walked up to the wall in front of him and knocked on the door that he knew was there. It opened quietly. He stepped into the forecourt of a pleasingly large haveli and turned to acknowledge Razia's spare, elegant adaab.

"Welcome," she said simply, leading him through the little gatehouse into the haveli proper. There was a colonnaded courtyard, empty save for the remnant of a fountain. There was a sprinkling of furniture in the verandas off to the sides. She led him to one such alcove, where the mattresses and bolsters were already set up and the makings of both paan and cocktails awaited. Candles illumined their meeting and their shadows played along the whitewashed walls. Rain began to fall again, the quiet courtyard coming alive with the sound of fresh water on ancient flagstone.

"Nice place," said Sajan. "Must be expensive to maintain."

"You've no idea," smiled Razia. "Do you know how hard it is to keep a place like this when everybody else is tearing them down?"

Sajan shrugged and asked her how she found it. She merely said she'd had it for a while. Her neighbors: did she like them? They're good people, she replied. Old families of the area, young people from outside. The way Delhi's always been.

"They look out for you, I imagine?"

"Always."

Dayal nodded and sipped at the cocktail he knew would be excellent before he even tasted it. He closed his eyes and sighed, leaned back against a bolster.

"Long day?" asked Razia with sympathy.

"Long few months," answered Sajan.

"May I prepare a paan for you?"

"In a moment, perhaps."

Then they were both quiet, enjoying the night and the smell and the sound of the rain in the courtyard. But the moment didn't last, for even though the idea of a companionable silence with Razia was a tempting one, and Sajan was glad for the respite, he had work to do.

"You know why I'm here?" he asked.

She inclined her head.

"Can you help?"

"What would you have me do?"

"He'll come to you if you tell him where and when."

"This is true," she acknowledged.

"I'd like you to call him to you. Here."

She indicated her acquiescence.

"I think I'll have that paan now, please."

Later, his head was both on the bolster and perilously close to her knee. She could have been inches away from stroking his hair and he could have been moments away from ecstasy. He thought that this indeed is the reward warriors should expect. The thought crossed his mind that the devious bitch had probably spiked his paan, but he brushed it aside as being of no consequence, for what, in this world or the next, did brave Sajan have to fear from beautiful Razia?

So he asked, in the delirium that follows in the footsteps of a quest fulfilled, why she hadn't yet taken care of this pestilential finger-reliever.

"A number of reasons," she answered as she finally began to stroke his hair, the long slim fingers with their polished nails parting and then bestrewing the strands, now black and further gray. "He hadn't found me. You hadn't approached me. And finally, you hadn't asked. Until now."

Sajan opened his eyes in agreement. "You can't be seen to be involved, I imagine."

"Exactly," smiled Razia, and he noticed the warmth and the candlelight in her dark eyes.

He held her gaze and asked, "Would it have helped if I'd come sooner?"

Perhaps, she replied. But the point to remember was that her Sajan had come. The victims, the young vampire, the consternation of the city: what did it matter?

"Who are you?"

"I think you already know."

"Surely you're not a vampire?"

She laughed, a rich quiet burble both ladylike and real. "What do you think?"

"He certainly seems to think so."

"He doesn't matter. His head isn't in my lap."

"If I thought you were a vampire, my head wouldn't be either."

She smiled at him again and continued to play with his hair.

"I remember," he said, "my father speaking of a home such as this. His own father, my grandfather, must have been about ten when the family left the old city for the new home in Civil Lines. But he told my father stories about it, stories my father passed on to me."

She nodded, waiting.

"What was Skinner like?" he asked.

"Not as Indian as you might think," she replied.

"And Rangila?"

"Not as interesting as you might imagine."

"Ghalib?"

"Exactly as you've ever thought he was."

He smiled at that and so she asked, "My beautiful Sajan has come to my house of his own accord. Is talk all he requires?"

He looked at her, his face inches away from hers, a question in his eyes.

"When you get to my age," replied Razia, "you get choosy. Besides, how many men are going to kiss a woman they think is a vampire?"

He nodded quietly, still looking into her eyes.

"Tell me, Sajan. What are you going to put in my mouth tonight?"

Behind them was the silent light of the moon, un-encumbered now by the lowering clouds. The candles guttered and then went out. The rain returned and then retreated. Everywhere was silence, broken only by the distant sound of thunder and the occasional dreaming dog. The night slipped away in the blink of an eye. The first pale flush of dawn was just beginning to crease the cheek of the attendant sky as he left.

Just once, as he exited the door and heard it being shut behind him, did he feel a moment of disquiet. He felt a pair of eyes on him that didn't belong in that set-ting, so he peered up at the new homes on either side of the alley that faced him. He looked this way and that and shook his head and then looked straight up, but there was nothing there either. He lit another cigarette and was gone down the alley, a drift of smoke the only marker of his passage before he too was swallowed by the almost-night.

"And now?" inquired Kapoor, later that day. They were back in the cyber-crime section, Smita and her colleagues taking them through what they'd found. The matrix of time, location, 3G accounts, and account holder's age had offered up a list of hits which they were currently working their way through.

It's just a matter of time, the two detectives were being assured. That one of the hard-cores used his or her cell phone was the first mistake Angulimala had made.

"He won't get away this time," said Smita confidently.

Kapoor digested this in silence, then repeated his question to his superior officer, whose abstraction had been noted by everyone in the room.

"Sir," said Smita, and the DCP finally looked up.

"No, no," he said. "It all sounds very good. You've all been working very hard indeed."

"We have," affirmed Smita. "None of us went home last night."

Kapoor raised his eyebrows in her direction, and she blushed. "I don't think a roomful of Indian Police Service officers need a chaperone, sir."

"I agree," said Kapoor drily. "I was just thinking how clean you look, after a night spent here."

She shrugged. "A loaded handbag and a lavatory mirror can work wonders, sir."

Her colleagues laughed and Kapoor smiled, while the DCP stared off into space.

"Sir," prompted Kapoor gently.

With an effort, the DCP roused himself. "I'm sorry. I was busy too. Last night."

The others waited.

"I think, with the data you're collecting, we'll have an arrest very soon. Perhaps as soon as tonight."

The younger cops waited for more information to be volunteered, but none was forthcoming. Smita looked at Kapoor for help because nobody had mentioned a time frame for resolution, but the DCP had retreated behind a wall again. Kapoor sighed and waited and indicated, by leaning back and closing his eyes, that the others should curb their impatience and do the same.

Presently, the DCP looked around, felt for his cigarettes, motioned to Kapoor to follow him. They shared a meditative smoke on a balcony overlooking the city. Traffic bristled under them. Off in the near distance, the huge stacks of a thermal power plant lurked over the burgeoning river. Humayun's Tomb, massively red in the cloudy day, lay off to one side. Kapoor watched his smoke disappear and felt the city flow below and heard the dark kites whirl screeching against the sky.

Tonight? inquired Kapoor.

Tonight, nodded Dayal.

"What exactly is going to happen?"

Dayal looked at him, then away. "I'm not entirely sure."

"Does the Colonel indeed have a role to play?"

"It would seem so."

"Has this been a setup from the start?"

"Possibly."

"To what end?"

Dayal looked at his old friend and colleague, the city's gray mass behind him. "I don't know," he said.

"And the Colonel? Who is she?"

"I don't know," repeated Dayal.

Kapoor digested this as he turned to the city, leaning his elbows on a rail almost blackened by soot from the power plant's chimneys and the slow-moving traffic below. And so, to spare his friend the embarrassment of three straight nonanswers, he asked: "Can she end this finger-fucker's roll? Tonight? Really?"

The DCP nodded, a gesture the other man couldn't see. "I think she can. I think she will."

"And you? What are you going to do?"

"I'm going over there to see her. Hopefully he'll be there. Ready and waiting."

"Do you need me?"

"I don't think that's part of the plan."

Kapoor thought about that, then repeated: "And you, boss? What are you going to do?"

The DCP looked at his friend's back, still turned to him as the other man studied the darkening city.

"My father told me," continued Kapoor, "when I was still ambitious and young in the force, that I should know my own limits and choose my friends with care. That the friendship of powerful people carries a price. They don't do favors for free. Not for people like us."

The DCP listened disconsolately.

"He was a small man. Small dreams. Five years of village school. A refugee. My being a policeman was the height of his ambition."

The DCP closed his eyes and rubbed them with one hand.

"I was going to tell you that I hope you know what you're doing. For all of us."

"But?"

"I don't need to. I've been lucky with my friends."

The DCP considered the weight of what had just been laid on him as Smita walked out onto the balcony. Kapoor finally turned to face them both. She stood quietly with her back to the door till Kapoor offered her a cigarette, which she thought about before shaking her head.

"You don't smoke?" asked the DCP.

"I do," admitted the younger officer. "But that isn't my brand. And I don't think I know you two well enough to have a smoke with you." The three of them grinned in unison.

"So tell me, sir," said Smita quietly. "What's going on?"

The two elder policemen looked at her in surprise, then at each other. Kapoor shrugged once, elaborately, then went back to leaning on the railing. The DCP sighed.

"I'll be needing a match from you people by tonight."

Smita nodded slowly. She knew it wasn't a request.

"Will this match be for an arrest, sir, or for confirmation?"

The DCP studied his junior's face for a moment, then nodded without saying anything.

"I see," said Smita. And then, recklessly: "Does that woman have anything to do with this?"

"I really don't see how that's any of your business."

Smita nodded again, a hot flush at her cheeks. She turned to leave.

"Smita," said Dayal. She waited by the door. "You've done well. Very well indeed. You and your colleagues, but especially you. I'd like you to know that my task force couldn't have done this without you."

"Done what exactly, sir?"

The DCP smiled. "I'll be in touch," he said. "We could use someone like you. Couldn't we, Kapoor? Unless of course you're happier here, running a terminal."

Smita looked at the two of them, swallowed once, and quietly left.

"The girl's got balls," observed Kapoor.

"I've noticed," concurred Dayal.

"You're having a tough time with one, boss," said Kapoor. "You really think you can handle both?"

The DCP laughed long and hard with his colleague and friend. Lightning was beginning to play on the horizon when they went in, still chuckling.

———————

The first watch of the next day:

He arrives in the early hours, to give Smita's unit time to do what they've been asked. His quiet knock on the door is immediately answered by Razia. They embrace inside the door, in the forecourt, before she thinks to peek behind him.

"Is Sajan really alone?" she wonders.

"Of course I am," he responds.

"No pet gorillas," she smiles.

"Nary a one," he replies.

"No strong men?"

"Am I not enough?"

"And that rather lovely Punjabi girl?"

"She isn't here either."

She thinks that over for a moment, shrugs, and puts an arm through his, leads him into her home. "I'm glad the men of Delhi have made their peace with the people of Punjab."

"Did we ever have a choice?"

"Perhaps not," agrees Razia, as they walk across the courtyard to their nook in the colonnade off to the side. The lightning, a mere premonition a few hours earlier, now lays siege to the sky.

"Is he here?" Sajan remembers to ask.

She nods, says, "Can we please let him be for a few minutes? He isn't going anywhere."

Sajan is happy to agree and lies back against a bolster, her head on his shoulder and an arm across his chest. The moment is light with happiness and heavy with dread, and he thinks that all life is just this, outcomes irreconcilable with each other masquerading as choices. He knows he isn't here of his free will, but he is happy, happy as long as this head lies on his shoulder and this arm across his chest, and he feels he can hear, with every drumbeat of thunder and in every flash of lightning, the susurration of finite sand running out of its glass.

Happiness and grief, thinks Sajan. They're only to be hoarded and feared so long as we preserve the myth of our own agency. An agency he surrenders willingly as he turns to his Razia in a paroxysm of present happiness and impending grief. He turns to her and kisses her as the lightning plays around the courtyard and throws giant shadows against the walls. He sheds the necessary zips and buttons without losing her mouth, her own hands willing partners in the dance. He forgets the vampire in her house, the shadows across her walls. All he knows is her and the shelter of her arms around him and presently they are done, but still her arms encircle him and they murmur into each other's ears.

"You're going away, aren't you?" asks Sajan.

"Haven't I been here long enough?" she replies. He chuckles quietly and she squirms, the noise loud in her ear.

"Has this always been your home?" he asks.

"In one way or another, it's been very dear to me for a very long time."

"I'm surprised you still have it. How did the builders spare it?"

"They came by. They asked around. My neighbors scared them away."

"Do your neighbors know about you?"

"They suspect, but without suspicion. They've known me, in one way or another, for a very long time."

"How long have you been alone?"

"How do you measure forever?"

"Were you always alone?"

"There were others. They've moved on, one by one. Nobody believed this city would last as long as it has."

"Are you the last one?"

"Not anymore," she replies. Then they're both quiet.

A chik, loose even at night, shifts in the soft breeze, its brass pulls clanking against an arch. The rain falls melodiously against the flagstones in the courtyard and distantly, Sajan hears a man scream.

"Shall we see about your problem?" she asks. Sajan nods dutifully.

They enter the house, dark save for candles here and there, and Sajan, looking about him, is surprised to see how spartan it all is. She takes him through a succession of rooms till they arrive at a staircase leading down to a cellar. The walls are damp and the light is dim and it is entirely appropriate, thinks Sajan, that a creature as crepuscular as Angulimala the vampire should end up in a hole like this. He is attached, loosely, by a rope around his neck to a ring in the wall. He writhes naked in the light of the tapers in the wall, his eyes closed, lost in his delirium. But their coming rouses him. He sees both Sajan and Razia and he spits on the ground in front of the DCP. Razia goes up to him and pats him on the head and he almost purrs with pleasure.

"Here he is," she says.

The DCP nods. He notes the necklace around the vampire's throat and the inserts and tattoos that will, in the days to come, be the talk of Delhi. He goes up to him, risking saliva in the eye, touches the gruesome constituents of his collection.

"Like them?" leers the vampire.

The DCP shrugs. Razia looks on impassively.

"Why," murmurs the DCP to the vampire, "do you want her so badly?"

"I did this for you!" screams the vampire.

"Of course you did," says Razia consolingly. "You've done very well indeed.

"This city," she continues meditatively, the light flickering away from her face, "it has survived so much. Plague, invasions, the vagaries of water. Empire after empire. And all the pretenders. The Gujjars, the Jats, the Marathas and the Persians, the Sikhs in their time, the Rohillas. Taimur and Nadir and Ahmed Shah."

"So much," she repeats. "Eternity's a long time," she says to her Sajan. "I suggest you prepare for it carefully."

Then she puts her hands over the eyes of the vampire and says, "Sleep, sweetheart." So he does.

She looks at her putative pupil, perhaps even tenderly, hanging by his neck from a rope attached to the wall. "He's just a symptom. He isn't the disease, per se."

Sajan can't help but agree so he asks her whether it bothers her that she has so ill-used this twisted young man. And what of the twenty men of this city with only nine fingers on their hands and all the resources of Delhi wasted on this search that could have been utilized elsewhere.

"I've done worse," she says quietly. "I've been around for a while, remember?"

The DCP thinks it over, repeats his question of a moment before: "Why did he want you so much?"

She looks at him, shrugs her shoulders fractionally. "Come. Time to wrap things up."

He follows her up the stairs, and farther, back through the rooms of the old house and up another flight to the roof, where a squat dome sits surrounded by pretend battlements that look both in toward the courtyard and out to the village and the city beyond. The rain is coming down in earnest now, lightning streaks the sky. Razia strips down completely, her clothes lying negligently in a pile at her feet.

They are horribly exposed up on this old dome and Sajan feels naked as well and so he says: "Why me?"

"Who better than you, my beautiful Sajan? Who better to be a bridge? Who better to guard this city now?"

"Is that all I am? A chowkidaar with a taste for history? Is that all this was to you?"

"No," she replies, as she climbs swiftly to the top of the dome, where an iron spike functions both as decoration and lightning rod. Sajan can see its extension snaking sinuously down the side of the dome and the building below to be lost in the cool damp earth. She grasps it firmly, then turns to him. "Come up here, my brave Sajan. Kiss me.

"Eternity is a long time," she repeats. "I want something to warm me through it."

He clambers up as well and embraces her. They cling to each other in the rain, then she tells him softly to step away, because the elements are beyond her control. So he pulls away and climbs down and asks her whether he'll ever see her again and she smiles and says nothing, so he asks her again. She smiles and smiles and motions him away and he backs away, across the roof, down the stairs, still looking, and she keeps her eyes on his and she smiles and then she is gone and so is he to the street and he hears a sizzle and the crack and feels the earth shake and then she is truly, completely gone.

Moments later, Sajan's phone rings.

"We've found him, sir," Smita said quickly over the phone. "He's in that village by the forest. The street address isn't in any database, but the man who did the verification for the bill said he was called to an old house at the end of the last lane in the village. Less than a week ago."

"Really?" murmured the DCP. "Is Kapoor there?"

"I just spoke with him. He's on his way there right now. Say twenty minutes."

"Good. Get over there as quickly as you can, Smita."

"Are you coming straight there, sir?"

"I am."

"He had a rudimentary electronic setup, all done with prepaid cards and the like. Very little paper to link him to this place," said Kapoor later that day. "I know people here. They don't remember him. He must have come here quite recently." He turned to Smita. "Perhaps as recently as a week ago?"

Smita nodded while the DCP averted his eyes. Smita continued: "We found his laptop. His DNA's all over this place. The fingers are there as well. Case closed, I think."

The DCP and Kapoor nodded together.

"Funny thing," said Kapoor. "A few of the villagers swear lightning struck this old house about half an hour before we arrived." Dayal looked at him impassively. Kapoor studied his old friend, then went on, "They're also whispering some rubbish about how this place is haunted. Apparently, some old woman's been living here for hundreds of years. The same woman."

"Imagine that," said Dayal. "Villagers with superstitions."

Kapoor raised an eyebrow, shrugged, and stalked off, knowing he had reports to file. The DCP watched Smita, who seemed to be on the verge of saying something.

"I think you might want these, sir," she said finally, reaching below her chair to give him a plastic bag. He took it from her and saw, hastily folded inside, clothes of a vaguely military cut. His eyes started to brim over so he looked away.

"Does Kapoor know?" he mumbled.

"He's the one who found them, sir. On the roof. There was nothing else."

"Of course he did. Of course there wasn't. Thank you, Smita. Thank you both."

"Is there something you'd like to share with us, sir?"

"Perhaps one day," said the DCP.

"No worries, sir," said Smita in a businesslike tone. "I'm in no hurry."

No hurry, thought the DCP. He savored the words and repeated them to himself.

Smita asked him whether he'd considered the question of just how long Angulimala had been associated with the old house in the village. "I've been thinking of very little else," he replied.

In time, he knew, there would be awards and honors and the long rope of official approbation would pull the likes of Smita up from obscurity as well. That, at least, was in his hands, so he smiled at her and offered her a cigarette, which, after a moment's consideration, she accepted. They stepped outside and watched their city dissolve into the steadily falling rain.

GIRL STORIES

Delhi isn't famous for treating its daughters well. Yet even its well-developed carapace of insensitivity was pierced by the horrors of that year's early winter. A young schoolgirl, raped and sodomized and then abandoned in a ditch to die, was the ember that grew into a full-grown flame when the latest in a line of women from the Northeast was gang-raped in a moving vehicle close to the supposedly secure cantonment of Delhi.

The facts of the matter were familiar enough to everyone. Indeed, followers of the news would have been able to reconstruct the events from memories of other such outrages. The victim was a late-shift worker in a suburban tele-services office. She was left outside the lane to her modest home by a call-center cab, the driver of which had his own roster of clients to drop off. Hence, he couldn't see her to her door. The hour was advanced, well into the small hours of the morning. The night was cold, the streets were dark, her assailants waiting, and her companion fought off from the chase. He didn't even see her assailants' vehicle. They disappeared, he would say, into the fog. As was later established, the police control room vehicle wasn't where it should have been either. The victim's companion, a colleague who lived down the lane from her, wasted precious minutes in a fruitless search for it. Anguished calls resulted in a PCR jeep reaching the site of the abduction a good half-hour later. By which time it was too late for the girl.

It came as no surprise that a task force was formed to combat what one gentleman representative in Parliament called the "growing menace of rape." Dayal, fresh from his triumph in the search for the finger-stealer, was roped in to head it and was given a free hand in choosing its constituents. Kapoor followed him, as did Smita, on leave from the cyber section of Crime Branch.

"She's young. And female," the DCP had explained to his senior commissioner, the one who'd drawn the short straw of having to face the minister, as that good lady cast about for ways to counter the growing ire of her voters and fellow legislators and parliamentarians. The commissioner, having been hung out to dry by his brother officers, was in no mood to argue with the DCP. He'd nodded curtly and told him in so many words not to fuck it up.

"The old lady wants to see you," he'd said the day after the rape, by which time the tumult over the assault and the task force to address it were both well in place. "She wants to know what you think." The DCP had raised his eyebrows, the question implicit. "You know. The crime situation: what are we doing about it; will women ever be safe in this city. The usual rubbish."

"And what should I tell her?"

"What she wants to hear." The commissioner ostentatiously returned to whatever it was he was doing before the DCP had been shown in, and didn't raise his eyes again till the door closed behind his junior.

The conversation the DCP had with the lady minister proved the prescience of his superior. She was courteous, motherly, and registered concern and worry without striking a false note. She didn't forget to fluff his feathers with regard to the successful conclusion of the Angulimala case. In fact, she pointed out what his superior had perhaps forgotten to mention, that she'd specifically asked for him to head the task force. She was pointed in her questions and attentive to his replies and the DCP was left with no illusions as to why he was there.

"You see, Dayal, the city needs closure. Like you provided with that awful finger-snatcher. You do understand, don't you?"

Dayal had nodded.

"I don't expect you to end crimes against women in this city. But I want these men caught. Expeditiously. They will be given exemplary sentences. That will help, I imagine?"

Dayal had nodded again, with less conviction.

"Do you not believe that will help?"

"I don't believe there are too many offenders in this country who're particularly scared by our criminal justice system."

"But you're part of that system, Dayal. And Delhi Police hasn't shown itself in the best light thus far, has it?"

He had nodded glumly, saluted smartly, and turned on his heel as she went back to the flowerbeds and potted chrysanthemums in her enormous garden in central Delhi, the early winter sun gloriously high, a yellow aureole in the inverted blue bosom of the sky. It occurred to him that she was very resolute for a woman who tended to end her sentences with question marks, and was only mildly surprised when she hailed him.

"Yes ma'am?"

"These felons of yours may not be scared of the system. But I suspect they're more than a little scared of the police, hmm?"

———————————

"What does that mean?" asked Smita later that day.

She and Kapoor were facing the DCP, who lounged with his feet up on a little stool in the well of his desk. His eyes were on the ceiling and very far away and his hands were behind his head. Smita knew that no answer would be forthcoming from him.

"Well?" she repeated anyway.

"It means that she knows we'll be using traditional methods to track these guys down," said Kapoor.

Smita still looked quizzical.

"Are you wondering whether the old lady's aware that traditional methods can make anyone own up to anything?"

Smita nodded.

"I think there's a strong possibility of that," allowed Kapoor.

"So?"

"So, you're thinking that she doesn't care whether we catch the right guys, we just need to find someone who fits the bill. Right?"

"You're an old cynic, you know that? Stop polluting her mind with your rubbish," said the DCP from the depths of his reverie.

"Isn't it true, though?"

"What's true, Smita, is that this office doesn't catch the wrong people," pronounced the DCP.

"Anyway," snorted Kapoor, "that particular trick won't work in a court in Delhi. Not with this case. Don't you worry, we'll get the right guys. Tracking rapists isn't rocket science. You know that."

Smita sighed. The depressing truth of that particular statement had been proved in the previous few days, when the schoolgirl's assailant had been identified as her nice young cousin who lived next door.

"We'll run the files," said Kapoor. "Find accused rapists out on bail, recently released offenders, things like that. Then we'll lean on them. Something will come to light."

"Is the victim talking more sense?" asked the DCP.

"She's doing better," said Smita. "I'm going by again this afternoon. I'll take the artist, see if she's ready." She looked at her superior officers. "I wanted to thank you," she added impulsively. "For putting me on this team."

The DCP and Kapoor nodded silently. Gratitude wasn't the wrong response from a young career-track policewoman. The profile of the case, the minister's personal involvement, the strong chance of a quick and decisive conclusion: these were all gilt-edged offerings, to be accepted with grace and humility.

"It's not just this case," continued Smita with some urgency. The DCP opened his eyes in surprise.

"I mean, I am grateful for this opportunity," said Smita. "Don't get me wrong. But there's something you should know. I've been involved in this before."

"No you haven't," said the DCP involuntarily, before feeling the need to explain. "I've looked at your file. You've never investigated a rape . . . Nor reported being subjected to one."

"My best friend in college was a Naga girl. She lived in a hostel near the south campus. It happened to her."

The two men were silent now, looking carefully at their junior.

"It left a lasting impression on me."

"Is that why you joined the police?" asked Kapoor.

"It is one reason, sir," said Smita.

Dayal pursed his lips. "Were her assailants caught?"

"Two of them were. She didn't recognize either. Beyond a point, she didn't care anymore. She left Delhi then."

The three of them sat quietly in the DCP's room, the rays of the afternoon sun slanting in through the window.

"She told me," said Smita, as if in a dream, "that one of the men, the first one, was vile, that he shouted threats and insults in her ear as he was on top of her, and she fought and fought till she couldn't fight anymore."

And then?

"Then," said Smita, "came a quiet, gentle one. He lay on top of her and whispered in her ear and stroked her before and after and told her she was beautiful. That's when she switched off."

The DCP looked out the window and Kapoor looked at his feet and Smita looked at nothing in particular.

"Is it personal, then?" asked the DCP.

"Of course it is. Sir." She got up quietly, collected her things, and left.

———— ✦ ————

The day before had started well. She had been reading the papers and savoring a hot cup of tea on the balcony of her parents' home, enjoying the first pale glimmers of day. While still early in the winter, it was already cold. Her father hadn't yet left for his morning golf game, her mother hadn't returned from her walk. Smita wore a cap against the cold and a shawl over the sweats she slept in, and, as she desultorily leafed through the paper, a magpie robin came and sat by her. She chirruped quietly at the interloper, flicking him a bit of biscuit from the plate in front of her. The trees in the park across the house were losing their foliage, a process that had quickened noticeably in the past week. They wouldn't be bare: they were evergreens, for the most part, and she felt that if she walked under them, she'd still be able to smell the last remnants of the flowering of the *Alstonia scholaris*. But they were hunkering down for the short, sharp Delhi winter, and Smita applauded their good sense.

This is nice, she'd sighed happily, burrowing deeper under her shawl, her fingers wrapped around her tea, a fresh pot snug under its cozy in front of her. And then the phone rang.

It had been Kapoor, tersely informing her of her temporary promotion and the reason for it. She'd gone inside to her own room, where a small TV guarded the approach to her bed. The outrage of the night before was all over the news channels. She'd showered quickly and reported directly to the address Kapoor had given her in the village that had so precariously sheltered the victim. Rush-hour traffic still howled past the gurdwara on the main road. She passed the cop cars and the inevitable gawkers and made her way purposefully down the quiet alley that ran into the village.

She walked past little knots of locals wearing the

look of people everywhere who have been touched, however ephemerally, by infamy. They were confused, delighted to be in the limelight, and hoping to be asked what they thought by a wandering reporter, but saddened that their fifteen minutes were to be forever so tainted. She could feel their eyes on her, measuring her calm poise and her businesslike attire. She wasn't interested in them, wasn't clutching a microphone or a digital recorder, clearly wasn't a reporter. But then what was she? They knew she didn't live here, even though other women her age, who dressed and walked like her—as if they didn't care that their asses were on display, tight in their trousers and propped up on short heels—lived in this village too. She asked a young Sikh boy where the house she was looking for was. He pointed down a street, said she wouldn't miss it with all the dogs hanging around. Smita smiled to herself. She found the house hedged about by policemen as advertised, and ran up the narrow airless stairwell.

The DCP and Kapoor were inside the modest little flat that the victim had shared with three other women like her. Two bedrooms, two girls to a room. A small hall that functioned as dining room, living room, and entrance foyer, a modest bathroom that the two bedrooms shared, and a kitchen. What natural light there was entered from one big window each in the living room and one of the bedrooms. Colorful drapes in front of these windows were kept drawn at all times, so that the women could find a modicum of privacy at least inside their own home.

Smita ran her eye quickly around the room she was in. A small TV, a bookcase with a radio on it and photographs, a few occasional stools, and a mattress with some cushions against the wall. A little table stood by the wall nearest the kitchen. Bright posters, a cross, and a colorful handwoven shawl hung on the walls. Fluorescent lights up high, table lamps closer to the ground. Two Northeastern girls were sitting quietly on the mattress, their arms around their knees. Smita could see the third one making tea in the little kitchen. Kapoor and the DCP cursorily acknowledged Smita's presence, letting her make her own judgments, allowing her to introduce herself.

The two girls on the mattress barely looked at her. The last one came out of the kitchen, a little tray with steaming mugs of tea in her hands. Her eyes were downcast when she stopped before Smita, who took a mug with a smile and a word of thanks that the other woman seemed not to notice. So the young policewoman went and sat down next to the girls on the mattress, who quietly made room for her. She leaned across and shook hands with each one, smiled at them with her eyes as well, and made sure the girl with the tea was settled on a stool next to them. Only then did she look at her seniors, who looked back, on the DCP's part, with quiet approval, and on Kapoor's, with something of the phlegmatic calm of a pedicurist considering a customer's foot.

Our colleague, indicated the DCP. The girls acknowledged his more formal introduction with a wary nod toward him and smiles for Smita who, not for the first time, was brought face-to-face with the fact of the ordinary Indian's alienation from their ostensible protectors, even from one as seemingly amiable and approachable as the DCP. Kapoor and the DCP knew it too and, making their excuses and thanking the girls for their tea, left quietly.

The facts were quickly established. None of them had studied in Delhi, though one of them had been working here for four years now. The others had come, one by one, looking for employment. They were all from the far east of the country, over on the border with Myanmar. They had known each other before they came, but only became friends after they were roommates. One was a senior shop girl in a foreign luxury brand's outlet in a spiffy mall. Another managed a restaurant, while the third worked at a development NGO. They had been in this house for almost a year.

The victim was known to be hardworking, diligent in her job and her duties at home. A good cook, said one of them quietly. They all nodded. She was religious, sang in a church choir, neither smoked nor drank.

"Really?" prompted Smita gently.

"Yes," said one of them urgently. "I smoke. We all like a beer, occasionally. But not her. She didn't have a boyfriend either. Her mother's active in the church back home. She's a believer."

"Are you?"

"Well," laughed one of them embarrassedly, "we all are. To some extent. But living out here . . . The boys come by, the local students. We have a house of our own. It's nice."

"A little slice of home here in Delhi."

"Exactly." All three of them nodded eagerly. Smita could see the scene. A quiet evening of semi-innocent fun, a few beers, perhaps a smoke or two, one of the more daring boys firing up a joint, the stares and remarks the morning after on the stairwell and down the lane. The stations of the harlot's progress, the final scene—a battered young woman lying in a recovery room in a government hospital in a cold alien city.

"I don't know if we can stay here after this."

"Will the landlord throw you out?"

"Even if he doesn't, why would we stay?"

Smita drank her tea and considered this. "What's he like?" she inquired of the landlord.

Quiet enough, was the answer. A Punjabi, not from the village. Bought this building a few years ago, according to those neighbors who deigned to speak to them. Not great with complaints, but not overly concerned with rent payments either. And he never just walked in.

"The people around here?"

There was an old couple who lived on the floor below. The ground floor was kept shut. The owner used it as some sort of storage space.

"And upstairs?"

The girls kept quiet, looking at each other.

"Well?" prodded Smita.

"It's a whorehouse."

———◆——◆——◆———

Kapoor walked up the stairs with his heavy tread and was admitted into the house by the officers already there. A young boy trembled quietly in the corner. Kapoor turned to him, looking him over, asked him whether he worked there. The boy nodded mutely. Kapoor dispatched him into the kitchen for tea.

He ambled into the bedroom with the open door.

He raised the filthy duvet, looked at the dirty mattress underneath, lifted it gingerly with just his fingertips. He saw the napkins and the condoms and nodded to himself. In a corner was a mean little wardrobe. He opened it and scanned the women's clothes inside. Different sizes, he noted. He walked into the other room and repeated his inspection. A religious calendar was on the wall and a few pegs, from which hung the clothes of the young boy making tea for him and his colleagues. The walls were a dirty blue, a cheap wash that had run over the course of the last monsoon. The fitful light of old tubes illumined the house.

"What time do the whores get here?" he asked the boy.

"Madam will be here soon," he mumbled. "The girls arrive after."

Kapoor looked at the other men there. They shook their heads. "He hasn't called anyone. We've checked."

Kapoor nodded and waited. Before too long, a soberly dressed woman who hadn't been young for years knocked on the door and was admitted by the boy. Only when she was at the threshold did she notice there were already men inside who weren't customers. Her face crumpled, but she was pushed into a chair by one of Kapoor's men before she could even begin to cry.

Kapoor looked at her without saying anything. His men stood to one side as the woman waited and began to snuffle. The boy brought a plate with the fixings on it. She looked up at Kapoor, who raised an eyebrow before nodding. She got up slowly, wiped her eyes, and performed the pooja in front of the deity that sat in a corner of the room. The boy closed his eyes and waved his hands through the smoke from the candle and then they were done. Kapoor and his men watched the performance till the woman sat down again.

"Does she service the customers too?" asked one of the policemen.

"Probably not," replied a colleague. Neither of them bothered to lower his voice.

"Why?" said the first one. "I'd fuck her."

The other man nodded.

"She's older," continued the first one. "Probably takes it in the ass too."

"I'd pay for that. This time."

The woman, alone on her chair, quietly cried.

Dayal had made his way up to the roof. He was expecting a call and wanted some time to himself. The brightness of the sun hurt his eyes, after the crypt-like gloom of the narrow house underneath. He slipped on his sunglasses and surveyed the scene. The saffron length of the Nishan Sahib of the gurdwara lay off to one side, the dome of the temple behind it. Houses like the one he was standing on lay all around him, laundry fluttering in the morning breeze. Off in the distance lay the towers of Basant Lok, while the central air-conditioning units of the far posher colonies of Shanti and Anand Niketan loomed closer by. He glanced around, lit a cigarette and then another before answering the phone when it rang.

"I've found what you're looking for," said the voice over the phone.

"Good," said Dayal.

"It took some time, you see. There were lots of local records to sift through. But the house you mean, the village, and the name. There seems to be only one match. It's an interesting one, though."

"Go on."

"The family itself is traceable at least as far back as the coming of the Mughals, almost five hundred years ago, though they claim an earlier ancestry. At various points, they were close to the court and then distanced from it. They acquired grants of land far away, which were later taken from them. They had a jagir closer to Delhi as well. To the south, which they kept. But they always maintained their connection with this one village. Much of their power at court derived from the fact that their ancestral lands were in Delhi itself. They always had revenue at hand, you see. It was useful, especially when the Mughals were in decline."

"Right. Who were they?"

"The early literature refers to them as Afghans, though at least one visitor to the court of Rangila refers to them as Mughals. Anyway, that isn't important. What's funny is that this guy, a young visitor from Hyderabad, wrote very disapprovingly of a young woman from the family. Her name was Razia. According to this provincial prude, she was in the habit of dressing as a man to walk around the city. What's more, she was apparently welcome in the soirees of the time. Grown women didn't go to polite parties, Commissioner. Not if they weren't prostitutes."

"Courtesans."

"Whatever. She went, and was welcomed, and met this guy and blew his mind. Not in a good way."

"Okay."

"So I dug some more. And I found this little nugget. Apparently, since time began, this family always named at least one girl in every generation Razia."

"Hmm. Which means?"

"Which means that every little girl born in the direct line had an aunt by the same name. And that's not the only thing that stands out. These girls were isolated till they reached maturity. And then, on at least two other occasions, I've found mentions of grown Razias taking the public air. Always dressed as men, but still unmistakably women."

Dayal knew this was in direct opposition to what normally happened. Girls were relatively free to wander about till they reached a marriageable age, which is when they were restrained by the demands of purdah. To hear of it happening in reverse was rare indeed, especially in a family of reach and influence.

"Any husbands?"

"Not one mention. It's as if all those Razias died alone."

"What happened to the family?"

"That's another thing. Around the time of the Revolt of 1857, they just disappear. The family was listed in a contemporary journal; they were printed off a few sheets at a time back then. The list was of alleged traitors to the Revolt's cause. It wasn't supported by any evidence, and in any case the journal fell with the rest of Delhi to the British a few weeks later."

"The allegation drove them below ground?"

"Perhaps they were already there. If they'd made their peace with the British before everybody else had to."

"Why didn't they reappear to enjoy the fruit of their betrayal?"

"I told you, sir. It's interesting. One last thing. A minor poet of the end of the nineteenth century devotes a volume of his work to 'Razia who belongs to the night and hurts him then.' Not very good at all. I only know it because he was a man of some importance in what was left of Delhi society."

"What did he do?"

"A lawyer and a businessman. Had the ear of the British and the Indians. One of the first to be comfortable in either camp, and very influential. The old city's littered with his good works."

The DCP digested this. "So that's it?"

"Pretty much."

"Where do you think they are?"

"That family? If anybody's left, Pakistan. That's where most of the old aristocracy ended up."

"Thank you," said the DCP.

The young graduate student at a fine American university made polite noises at the other end. This young man, a promising historian and amateur filmmaker currently in Delhi finishing up his fieldwork, was relieved in turn to hear the commissioner acknowledge his end of the bargain, which was to make sure that a small file, a passing notation of an indiscretion between said young student and a local pusher of feverish weed, was misplaced before it could ever find its way into the legal mill. A promise of further gratis research was made, then Dayal hung up.

Kapoor joined him up on the sun-washed terrace, his own cigarette already in his hand. He coughed and spat and then, looking around, elected to perch on a water pipe that wasn't too befouled by passing pigeons.

"There's a brothel being run on the floor below."

Dayal grunted.

"The madam's in there. She didn't notice all the cops hanging about downstairs, hadn't seen the news. She walked right in."

Dayal grunted again, this time in amusement.

"Poor old tart," said Kapoor comfortably. "Five minutes with the boys and she was ready to sing. Nothing for us, but I'm sure trafficking could use her."

"Make sure you get an officer from the women's wing involved."

"She'll be here by lunch."

"So you're convinced it was strangers?"

"Has to be. No boyfriends, relatives, or enemies. That girl was just in the wrong place at the wrong time."

Dayal grunted a third time, now in agreement. "Let's just make sure, alright? Have the boys check the madam's mobile records. Call the clients who've been here this past month. Breathe some fear into them. Let's see what falls off the tree."

Kapoor finished his cigarette and descended again into the dank building. Dayal began to follow him, then stopped to look one last time at the city laid out below him like a ragged quilt. A lithe shape on the periphery of his vision caught his attention. A young man was standing on a rooftop like his own, a few lanes over. He wore sunglasses as well, and a kaffiyeh. He raised two fingers in an ironic salute and was gone, into the building and then the warren of streets below.

Dayal shook his head and stepped out of the light.

Just then, one floor and a world away:

It's always been personal.

She walks up the flight of stairs into the brothel above. A young woman has followed the madam into the web by repeating the mistake of not noticing the policemen about the building. Perhaps she was on the phone, perhaps she has perfected the Delhi woman's art of always looking at her feet, so that she doesn't notice—or at least doesn't appear to—the avaricious eyes of the men around her. This young woman was dressed in a tight pair of jeans and a jaunty sweater and her hair was up in an elegant bun. When Smita walks in through the unlocked door, she hears the sound of male laughter and spies a young boy standing fearfully in a corner while an older woman stands disconsolately off to one side. She seems to have been weeping. The young woman, meanwhile, is standing in one of the bedrooms. Her sweater is already off, her hair around her shoulders. The shirt below is off as well and her cheap bra is all that separates her creeping skin from the attentions of the male police officer who is in the room with her, his colleague outside snickering gently to himself.

This man notices Smita first and a hiss of disapproval is audible in the room. She gives him a cold look and sweeps past into the bedroom where the officer looks at her mainly with surprise. He wasn't aware that she was on this case and he most certainly wasn't aware that she was in the building. But he, while not in Crime Branch, has spent many more years than her in a police uniform, and the surprise will quickly turn to anger and then, worse, condescension. Or so thinks Smita, but she has already picked her fight and is in the room and bending to retrieve the girl's sweater. The electric moment of decision is past and now the payload of outcomes must be borne, along whichever conduit it may run, whether of present outrage, a future humiliation, or a grudge borne in perpetuity.

It is just as well that Kapoor lumbers in then. He assesses the scene, raises an eyebrow, barks out a word: "Jacket."

The man in the hall, the guard and next in line, looks perplexedly at Kapoor, who then turns his gaze to him.

"Jacket," he repeats.

The man in the hall lowers his eyes and shrugs off his police-issue heavy winter jacket, too warm for the weather outside currently, but more than welcome in the chill environs of this tube-lit walk-up whorehouse. He hands it over to Kapoor, who slowly ambles into the bedroom through the open door, interrupting the tableau in there: the quickly purpling male officer, the pinkly determined female officer, the shivering half-naked slut.

Kapoor hands the jacket to the young woman who accepts it and attempts to thank him. The older man waves it off. He looks his subordinate in the eye till he looks away, then turns to Smita. He peers at her steadily for a moment till she too lowers her gaze.

"I'll be seeing you," says the male officer to Smita, who refuses to even look at him. He tries to shoulder past Kapoor. A heavy hand stops him in his tracks.

"Will you, son? Really?"

"Is that slut her sister?"

"She's someone's sister."

The other man lowers his eyes then and stalks away. The jacketless man outside looks at the walls and seems one step away from whistling to himself.

"Women's wing will be here soon. I want five minutes with the madam. The girl will have to stay. Do you want to stay up here, or do you want to go down and talk to the DCP? He's downstairs," says Kapoor to Smita. She nods.

He considers his young female subordinate, the color of conflict still in her cheeks.

"Forget this," he advises, perhaps a shade too roughly.

"How?"

Then she too leaves, down the stairs, toward the light.

Of course it's personal. She will repeat this the next day in the DCP's office, before she leaves to see the victim herself.

———————

Villages, thought the DCP. How times change.

Even a few decades before, cities here were islands of urbanity in a predominantly rural landscape, bullocks and fields and hoary custom rubbing up against the borders of sewer lines and planning and an intangible yet palpable civic otherness. An otherness that kept the strangeness and the age and darkness of the hinterland at bay, maintaining a fragile equilibrium wrought over the centuries, and respected and furthered by succeeding claimants to the seat of Delhi, whatever they chose to call it by. Now that ancient order was reversed, and cities grew and grew, ravenous for conquest. Delhi encircled its villages, and perhaps the rapine was visited in the opposite direction.

He was born of a long line of city-dwellers, was most comfortable in an urban setting. But this was a village only in name, thought the DCP, as he ambled along in the constant shade of the buildings on either side. The crazy mesh of illegal electric connections webbed the distant sky, if he'd thought to look up. But he, student of criminality and devotee of speculation, kept his gaze on the damp ground, watching where he stepped, through

puddles already filmed with slime, across cow pats fes-
tering in his way. A man smoking his hookah looked up
at the DCP, who happened to catch his eye. The other
man quickly glanced away.

Villages, thought the DCP again, finally raising his
eyes and looking about himself.

He said the word to Smita, who'd fallen in step with
him. She looked at him and smiled. He began to explain
and was perplexed when she shook her head firmly.

"You don't know that the men who did this aren't
villagers," she said.

"You're right," he mused. "All we're fairly convinced
about is that they're not from this village."

"Right. There are plenty of villages in Delhi, and
many more just outside. It isn't as easy as rural versus
urban, sir. These men could be from anywhere."

"You're right," said the DCP appraisingly. "But isn't
that divide part of it?"

"Of course it is. But perhaps it's the wrong way to
look at the question."

"What's the right way?"

"Sifting the civilized from the ignorant. Wherever
they may be."

He raised an eyebrow at her. She raised one too, a
smile still in her eyes. "I saw you looking around, sir. I
know what you were thinking."

He smiled back at her then, and it seemed the growing warmth of the day finally percolated down to the
level of the dank street they were walking down. He noticed the flush still on her cheeks, detected the scent of
recent combat. He asked her what was wrong, but she
shook her head, firmly as before. Kapoor would tell him

the story if he thought it was appropriate. She wouldn't be the one to tell tales out of season.

"What's the plan, sir?"

"I have to meet the minister. You?"

"I'm off to the hospital," she said. "Anything you want me to ask her if I make meaningful contact?"

"Yes," he said thoughtfully. "Ask her if she remembers something about the vehicle itself. Anything. Even its smell."

Smita nodded crisply, slipped on her sunglasses, and stepped out of the village, into the bright sunny New Delhi day.

———————

The day after the DCP's interview with the minister was, in contrast to the clear bright days before, damp, foggy, and cold. It was early in the winter for weather like this, thought Smita as she navigated the drive to HQ, her lights on in what should have been the morning. Her wipers moved intermittently, a gesture against the condensation that sat thickly on every glass surface of her car. She strove desperately to see about herself, noticed people in the cars immediately alongside similarly hampered and wished above all else to be free of her vehicle, to be inside and in front of a heater with a cup of tea in her hand. She ran up the stairs to warm herself when she arrived, rather than waste time waiting for the lift. A glimpse of dirty white through the far doors drew her, however. She stepped out onto the balcony at the end of the hall. Pools of sodium vapor light coalesced and then dissolved. The moving lights of the traffic streams in both directions transfixed her, haloed and incandescent through the fog. Delhi lay as if enshrouded. In the distance, a floodlight pylon swam hazily into view, as if the corpse of the city, in a postmortem spasm, had thrown up a claw. In a moment, it too was gone. Smita shivered silently and withdrew through the doors behind her.

Kapoor and the DCP were waiting, wanting to know what progress she was making with the victim. Smita had now been to see her on two separate occasions.

"Any luck?" asked Kapoor.

"Well. She's beginning to talk. Still traumatized, but the surgeon says she's recovering well."

"I spoke with him," said Kapoor. "He mentioned it wasn't as bad as it could have been."

"I think the distinction is academic, sir," said Smita sharply.

Kapoor made placating noises, while the DCP waved his hands. "Did she mention anything herself?" he asked.

"Not much of any consequence. She said the vehicle was a big truck. It was night. They were careful not to park under a light. She doesn't remember much. It was open. No tarpaulin."

"Were they in the cab or in the bed of the truck?"

"She was abducted in the cab. The act happened in the bed."

"Numbers?"

"At least four. No more than six."

"Language?"

"Hindi. But she's unsure. Like it was a Hindi she didn't recognize."

"Does she speak any Hindi?"

"Enough to get by. She understands it well enough."

Kapoor nodded. "I'll have a couple of the boys try her on the local dialects. We'll soon have a match."

The DCP nodded. "I assume they didn't use condoms?"

"No. Plenty of samples."

Kapoor and the DCP looked at each other.

"Has she been tested?"

"For STDs? Yes. But they'll have to test again in a month. And keep testing for half a year."

"Poor girl," said the DCP, perhaps unnecessarily. "Any chance she might be pregnant?"

"Thankfully, no," said Smita. "She was just beginning her cycle."

"Any features? Anything for the artist?"

"Not yesterday, but he's pretty hopeful about having something for us by tomorrow. She was really opening up by the time the surgeon chased us out."

"Any of them circumcised?" asked Kapoor.

"Why is that important?" replied Smita sharply.

"It narrows the field and helps us look. That's all."

"Since when is religious profiling part of Crime Branch's strategy?"

Kapoor looked at the DCP, who nodded wearily. "Religious profiling has always been part of police strategy. You know that. Besides, this isn't religious profiling. It's penis profiling. Plenty of non-Muslim men are circumcised as well."

"And how will that help us?" asked Smita pinkly. "Will ID parades now be conducted with the subjects' pants around their ankles?"

They stared at each other for a moment, till Kapoor began to laugh. The DCP followed suit, as did Smita, reluctantly to begin with and then with more freedom.

"I don't think it's going to matter, in any case," said Smita. "I'm not sure the victim has any idea of the difference. But I will ask."

"Anything else?" said the DCP.

"Yes. There is. She said the bed of the truck smelled like cattle. Her family owns a farm. It's a smell she knows well."

Kapoor and the DCP looked at each other.

"Cattle thieves," stated Kapoor.

The DCP smiled. "Get on the phone to your nephews," he said to Kapoor. "Tell them to run through their files for cattle thieves with a history of sexual assault."

Smita looked questioningly at her senior officers.

"The police stations in outer Delhi," explained Kapoor. "In Kapashera and Mandi and Kundli and Kanjhawla, and everywhere there are still cows and people to steal them."

"You have family out there?" asked Smita skeptically.

Kapoor just grinned.

It isn't, reflected Dayal, winter: it isn't a Delhi winter till you feel the chill in your bones. Winter, the way he remembered it from his boyhood. Of frost in the city's parks and fires on every corner and a halo of breath around your head as you walked outside. It hadn't been winter till this day, he thought, walking in the colonnades around an ancient mosque not far from his office. Because it wasn't the sun, the winter roses, the smiles in the parks, and the office workers sleeping in the shade that made the season.

This was winter. A dank foggy day as the air, condensing against the earth, carried the taste of precipitation in the distant mountains. A day of marooned cars and diverted planes and crawling trains in the flat plains around the city. A day to sit at home over tea and a heater, there to consider the problems and small mercies of this world. A day to savor your own defeats, to chew them over, cold as the air outside, to wash them down with the bitter realization that winter has just begun, to breathe out the effluvium and to see it again around you. He considered the arches he stopped by, smelled the lingering trace of older sweat overlaid with the more pungent tang of recent urine. These would have been, he'd been told, the cells of visiting scholars and mendicants and the novices who studied with them. The packed cut stone would have been a shield from the heat, but what about the biting Delhi cold? He pictured the scholars, shivering against the chill, perhaps with chiks thrown down against the creeping frigidity, blankets and carpets and sigris deployed. He thought that they may well have shared a cell, spooned together where they lay, perhaps indulged in those activities that were not as proscribed centuries ago as they are today.

The thought made Dayal smile.

He knelt down in the least odorous of the arched spaces and peered about himself. How would a homesick Central Asian have made this hot and then cold little corner of India feel like home, more than half a millennium ago? They had no calendars. No Internet, no phones. No cafés to order in from.

Conversation. Discussion. The lifeblood, then as now, of the intellect and the soul. And who do you speak to when you feel the need, DCP Dayal, sir? he said to himself. That's right. You talk to yourself. The thought made him want to smile and cry, and not for the first time, he wished he could write poetry instead of just reading it. There is pleasure in other people's words as well, but how much nicer it would be to pursue that particular passion as people used to, in knowledgeable crowds, rather than the way he was wont to do, alone, at home. How much better to hear it spoken and then to hear the approbation of the audience as they applauded a particularly deft metaphor, a choice phrase, a play on words unheard before.

So he knelt and thought of Razia, who had walked among men and listened to their poetry and made their world her own. I wish you were here, he thought, only mildly surprised to find he'd spoken aloud. He considered the intervening months since Razia had disappeared. The end of the monsoon, the slow dissolution of mosquito-ridden summer into shorter days and smoky nights. Days spent typing reports and fielding congratulatory calls, nights spent in reading and drinking and solitary thinking. He thought of the approval of his colleagues and the media and the grinding solitude of the small hours as he worried at the jagged meatless bone of his own complicity in a madman's death. For what? he wondered. Did I want closure so badly? Or did I just want to see her again? His jaw clenched as he considered the arithmetic. What did I lose? What did I gain?

What in this world or the next did a creature like Angulimala want with one such as Razia anyway?

The fog shifted around him and the walls and cloisters of the old fortress he was in were revealed and obscured. He leaned his head against a cold stone archway and he tried to still his own breathing.

What spirits are in these walls? he thought with a pleasurable desolation. What stories could you tell me if I had the ears to listen?

Dayal considered the well to which, he'd read, everybody had a rope with a bucket attached; the well from which the stories and myths and tales that unite all men sprang. Could not that water have been used in the erection of these tombs and mosques and homes? Are not these the concrete manifestations of those same stories of love sustained, promises made, confidences betrayed? Here lay a man who thought he spoke with God, there a mosque raised by a king in gratitude to a saint whose body was interred inside. A son delivered, a wife saved, a promise kept. These cut-and-polished stones: were they cut from this earth or did they come from other, older, now forgotten buildings? And what of their inhabitants? If a man of that time were to return to this land, his horizon enclosed by the fog and the walls of this complex: would he recognize the earth from which he sprang? And if the sun were to come up and he were to see the arachnid body of New Delhi looming above, with its cooling towers and windows and antennae: what would he feel?

Is there anything that connects us to the past anymore, beyond these few monuments, beyond these bounded and boarded grounds? Dayal's hand moved with love and compassion over the quiet stones. He caressed the corners, flicked the edges. He walked slowly along the arches, his hand trailing the masonry. Up ahead, a quiet group of men and women swam out of the fog, severing his connection to the building. He skirted the group, their eyes following him silently. They were a mixed bag. City-dwellers sitting on their handkerchiefs, villagers quietly squatting on the ground. The women and men sitting next to each other, unconcerned with impropriety. They were waiting noiselessly, patiently, the fog settling around them like snow.

Dayal knew this to be a place popular with those seeking something of the djinn said to inhabit these walls. Perhaps these people too were waiting for their appointments. He wondered what they had brought along to appease those beings with. The fog spirited them away as he passed on and soon he was at the gate of the complex. He divined with some surprise that he'd made a wish as well.

He looked at the road he had to cross without enthusiasm. The prospect of the short walk down the road ahead attracted him even less. The foggy air collected and cocooned the exhaust of the passing traffic. It felt to him as if his entire face would change color by the time he reached his office. He stepped out into the street to flag a rickshaw down and was almost run over by a motorcycle piloted by a slim figure in black.

The helmet's glass and the gloomy light conspired to defeat the policeman's instinctive look of inquiry. He was mollified by the courteous voice from inside the helmet, a light questioning of whether he was alright in the old language of Delhi. He replied in the affirmative, adding that his office wasn't far. Then jump on, invited the rider, moving forward on the seat. Dayal thought only for a second before he climbed on.

A moment later, they were outside HQ. The rider's

inclined head was a question mark. Dayal replied with a laugh, yes, he did work there.

"How may one address you?" came the voice.

"DCP Dayal. And what do I call you?" he asked, amused at having been given a lift by a black-clad biker.

The biker flipped open the visor.

"My friends call me Razia. But you can call me anything you like, Commissioner. I am yours to command."

Sajan looked at her without surprise. He noted her eyes and the wisp of hair under the lip of the helmet and the strong straight nose and the high cheekbones. He noticed the quiet strength of her face and the warm smile in her eyes. He saw how young she looked and he wondered what trickery of drape and containment and sling had been wrought to conceal her young curves from the public gaze.

"Are you she or her niece?" he remembered to ask.

"Does it matter?"

"I thought you were gone."

"Where would I go without my Sajan?"

"As far as the tank on that bike will take you."

"Only if you come along."

They smiled at each other. It seemed to Sajan as if the sun had sent its rays clean through the coffin of fog.

"Did you come because I asked the djinn to send you?"

"Better them than impoverished academics."

"Wasn't very quiet, was he?"

"They seldom are."

She reached through the cold air to put a warm hand to his cheek. "Look at you," she said softly. "You look as if you haven't slept in months."

"Don't ask of the ruin your passage has caused me," murmured Sajan. "Consider the delights you've laid before me that lead me to it instead."

She threw back her head and laughed. "Ghalib again?"

"Why not?" smiled Sajan. "I'm glad you're here."

"As am I, my beautiful Sajan. But listen. You must be careful."

"Of whom?"

"Cattle thieves, amongst others. Dangerous people. Always have been."

"How am I to be careful?"

"Protect your heart. It is important to me."

She flipped down her visor and rode off into the stream of traffic coursing past them. Dayal watched her disappear. He shook his head, as if clearing it of a dream, walked into HQ and up to his office.

Kapoor and Smita were waiting for him.

"Well?" he asked.

"We've got a match," said Kapoor.

———————✦———————

It transpired that one of Kapoor's nephews had apprehended a gang of active cattle thieves just a few months earlier. While the two prime movers were still incarcerated across the state border in Haryana, the others were out on bail. Of them, at least two had histories of sexual assault, and one of them had actually served time for it.

"They were in Delhi on the night of the rape," said Kapoor.

"How do you know?" inquired the DCP.

"The men inside. There was a wedding here. The local police station just confirmed it."

"Do we have a vehicle ID?"

Smita nodded.

"I suppose they're not stupid enough to have an expressway tag?"

"No, but the toll companies at the borders are already checking their records. And we're circulating the vehicle ID. We know their names, where they're from. We should know where they are by the morning."

"Their local SHO knows to keep it quiet, right?"

"He's the last person we'll tell."

"Cross-border liaison?"

"My nephews," indicated Kapoor.

"Good," said the DCP. He turned to Smita. "I told you it's not rocket science."

She just smiled.

———————✦————————

The road south is a geographic précis of how Delhi has changed, thought the DCP. The clogged arteries to the highway, the Gurgaon Expressway, the fields on either side giving way to high-rises. The tumult of the last few decades, the growth and its issues, the solutions to those problems, the issues those solutions threw up. And then, when you've gone far enough, the fields return.

It was evening of the next day. The Manesar toll plaza was jammed. Kapoor swore into his phone and pretty soon a path was cleared for the DCP's vehicle, through the intransigent snaking lines of obstreperous trucks, truculent buses, enraged cars. The driver breathed through his nose while Kapoor fretted and Smita picked at her nails. The DCP, by contrast, lay with his head back against the seat, his eyes closed. He only opened them when he felt the car picking up speed again. The car turned off the highway onto a quieter, relatively traffic-free road. The DCP surveyed the land outside with some interest. New factories flashed by, joined now by a farm or two and the occasional village. There were signs to golf courses, exclusive clubs that the DCP had heard of but never had occasion to visit. The road was well traveled by dump trucks carrying mining material.

"Illegal?" he asked of nobody in particular. Kapoor nodded briefly. Smita kept quiet, noting the interplay between the two men, Kapoor in front next to the driver, the DCP beside her on the backseat.

The dump trucks went careening by, their big tires raising clouds of gray and sometimes red dust. But the dust itself wasn't able to conceal the beauty of the evening. The setting sun's light now came slanting across the low hills that were nearer and more visible. The rays gleamed off the surface of the young wheat and more mature mustard and turned the latter to burnished gold and the DCP felt an obscure pang, a need never before glimpsed to belong to this older world. His world too was an ancient one, but his people's horizons had been bounded since time began by a city's walls. To see the sun rise and set like this, he thought, no wonder the new men of Delhi build their "farms" and golf courses in such places. He saw old men sitting and enjoying the last of the day's warmth on their beds, their hookahs by their sides. A row of women, their faces veiled, went walking past. A young boy walked a herd of goats along the side of the road. The car honked its way past the most recalcitrant of the beasts. In the near distance, a line of boys raced along a ridge, silhouetted against the setting sun. The DCP caught himself raising a hand to his window, as if tracing the line of their pursuit against the glass, recording it for himself to savor at some future date. He rolled the window down instead and caught the chill of the incipient night against his cheek and far away he thought he heard the crystal fluting of the boys' cries.

The DCP noted that the farms now had stone walls and the villages themselves showed signs of being fortified. They passed an old haveli by the side of a village, around which the road bent. The driver hopped out to ask directions. The other occupants got out as well to stretch their legs. Smita looked at the old wooden doors of the haveli curiously. The house seemed abandoned, or at least empty. But the fact that the doors hadn't been sold suggested someone still exercised a measure of ownership.

She asked a passing man whose home it was. Kapoor and the DCP listened as well.

It belonged, said the man, to a family in Gurgaon. They didn't visit much anymore. But they were big landowners in this area. Had been for generations.

How old was the house? asked Smita.

Two hundred years, perhaps. Maybe older.

The DCP smiled.

The driver returned and started the car again. Not far now, he reported. Kapoor grunted and closed his eyes as night fell.

Smita shook herself awake and found the vehicle stopped. It was completely dark. Kapoor and the DCP were still in the car, waiting for a signal. The driver had the lights off as well. Smita held a surreptitious hand up to her mouth, reached inside her bag for the chewing gum she knew was inside. She blinked her eyes rapidly. The closeness of the atmosphere suggested they had been sitting here, with the lights off, for some time.

"How long have I been asleep?" she asked eventually.

"No more than an hour," replied the DCP.

"Are we here?"

Kapoor nodded wordlessly. Outside lay the closely packed dirt of a dhaba's forecourt. A few trucks were parked there. The dhaba itself was doing a brisk business. The flickering light of a few tubes illuminated the big dishes simmering away. An incongruously gay strand of Christmas lights snaked its way around the façade of the dhaba. Men were sitting at the tables and sprawled on the beds that were strewn around the yard. A few bottles of liquor were visible.

Are we not, thought Smita, too visible here? But then she realized that they weren't, because a man she knew to be one of Kapoor's many "nephews" materialized at a window. Kapoor's window came down and the man smiled at them.

"I suggest you eat, sir," he said to the DCP. "This could take some time. My boys tell me the food here is quite acceptable."

The DCP nodded.

"You've got someone watching them?"

"We're gathering the troops. As soon as they're asleep, we'll know. Give them an hour or so, let them get really addled. Then we go in."

"Any firearms?"

"We haven't seen any, but that doesn't mean they don't have them. One of them is supposedly quite dangerous."

"Your men know to exercise care, correct? This isn't an encounter. We want these men alive."

The other man indicated his understanding and the occupants of the car got out. They walked off their stiffness and the other customers at the dhaba either looked at them curiously or ignored them completely, according to their own dispositions. A few men clustered around a sigri in the middle of the sheltered area. A TV blared forth the match of the day inside. A few beds were turned to it. Out in the forecourt, another truck arrived and hiccupped to a stop.

The two older men, obviously official and probably police, sufficed to protect Smita from the closer attentions of the other men around her, but she still felt their intruding eyes. She, resolved to not look down, stared around her with bright interest and was surprised to find that nobody engaged her gaze. She sank irritably back into her seat and contemplated dinner. A steaming plate of dal, some vegetables with slit green chillies, rotis hot from the tandoor delivered one at a time. She dove in with gusto, matching the DCP roti for roti. Kapoor easily outdistanced the other two, but the fact that she hadn't picked at her food in front of him was a source of some satisfaction to Smita. They waited till he was done and had pushed back his chair with a sigh, then dispersed in various directions to wash up. They returned to the table to find it scrubbed clean, with a selection of cut fruit and a few cups of ice cream waiting for them. The waiter hovered deferentially. Kapoor dismissed him and the offered dessert with a curt gesture, though not without a longing look at the ice cream. Must stay fresh, he pointed out. Then the first glasses of tea came.

Kapoor's nephew arrived in due course. The men they were looking for were holed up in a little building about a kilometer away, where the road curved around a few fields. It was attached to a dhaba like this one and was popular among the truckers looking for a little booze and further action. The man who ran the place supplied liquor and light drugs and turned a blind eye if one of his clients brought a girl along. In this case, there wasn't one. But the men inside had been drinking for hours. "Not much longer now, uncle. I'll let you know." He returned to his own vigil.

"Bring a girl?" asked Smita curiously. "Wouldn't they be available at these places?"

Kapoor shook his head. "The local girls won't do it. Even if they did, these men are from around here. They can't be seen having it off with their own kin."

Smita was unconvinced and argued the point with Kapoor in a desultory way. The DCP watched them debate the relative value systems of the various groups of this part of northern India and let his attention wander. Farming versus nomadic, settled savitris versus roving sluts; the distinctions washed over him in a murmuring flood of ethnic slurs that was distinguished chiefly by Kapoor's catholic ability to slam everybody. The DCP wanted the time of reckoning to come, and soon enough so they could return to Delhi that night itself, so he would have time to rest before the media bombardment that was sure to follow. To say nothing of the paperwork that would ensue from the prosecution of a case such as this.

"You're wearing your bulletproof vests?" he asked suddenly.

Smita and Kapoor looked at him in surprise, their disputation halted in the middle of a particularly exhaustive inquiry into the apparently legendary promiscuity of the minstrel tribes to the immediate south, a character trait matched only by their light-fingeredness.

"I am," replied Smita. Kapoor merely raised his eyes. More tea arrived.

The night around them developed and deepened and soon the TV's sound was muted as more and more men retired to the beds inside. The lights on the façade continued to wink, quietly and cheerily, as a few dogs now meandered through the empty tables, looking for scraps. A truck cleaner climbed into the cab of his vehicle, there to turn in for the night. The men who worked in the dhaba scrubbed their pots and emptied their vats and bowls into the field that lay behind them and pretty soon the scrabbling of dogs could be heard there as well. A man, quietly obsequious, came up to them and asked if there would be anything else, as they were closing up for the night. Some more tea, gestured Kapoor. The other man slunk off and filled their order and then asked, with sudden courage, who they were looking for.

Kapoor merely looked at him over the lip of his glass

of tea. The steam from it rose up into the chill air and around them they could see the wisps of fog settling onto the cooling ground. The region beyond the lit forecourt was now lost to them. The blacktop was a ribbon of ephemeral illumination in the lights of an occasionally passing truck. The field behind them was encased in the vaporous exhalation of the earth itself. Around them were silence and sleep and the half-light of cheap tubes running on the low voltage of a rural line. Smita imagined she could smell the close pack of sleeping men a few yards away. The thought made her flesh creep.

The waiter dropped his eyes, and was gone.

"You think he might call them?" asked Smita anxiously.

"Now he won't," said Kapoor quietly.

"Your parents know where you are, Smita?" asked the DCP.

"Of course. I mean, they know I'm on duty. They know I'm safe."

The DCP looked at her for a space, then looked away. She turned her eyes to Kapoor and found his already on her. He too looked away.

She got up in a sudden burst of irritation and walked over to the edge of the forecourt. The fog was pulling in quickly now and pretty soon vehicles would be crawling past—if any vehicles were still plying on this sleepy little road. The trees to the sides of the road were ghosts now, coming and going with the shifting of the vapors. She shivered and hugged herself, and found the DCP standing next to her, peering out toward the road and beyond. She rejoined Kapoor and saw the DCP still standing, as if waiting for someone, by the side of the road. Kapoor's eyes were closed, so she leaned back in her chair in the light of the tubes and the Christmas decorations and closed hers as well.

The DCP stayed standing. His eyes strained against the fog, then gave up the battle and merely looked at the fog itself. His head moved from side to side in the manner of someone watching a tennis game, but the road divulged none of its secrets. He thought he heard a truck in the distance and distinctly heard a dog howl, a call that was taken up by the dhaba's resident beasts though soon abandoned. He thought he saw the approaching lights of a car but it never appeared. It must be getting late, he thought, but didn't bother to check his watch. He was caught between tiredness and adrenaline, his mind racing and his senses keen. He wished the night to be over. He felt rather than heard the pack of dogs run quietly by him toward the road. They raced past him in a soundless ruffle of noisome fur. Then the fog separated for an instant and he saw a man in a kaffiyeh standing in a field across the road. The dogs were at his side and his feet and he threw them treats and they wished him no harm. The man in the kaffiyeh saw the DCP looking at him and raised a finger, bringing the other hand to it in a scissoring motion. The DCP reached for his holstered weapon, but the fog closed in again and the man was gone.

The DCP pulled his weapon out and stepped into the road and felt the blaring horn of the truck crawling along the fog-bound path and was bathed in its vapor-refracted lights as he jumped to safety. The truck passed on, moving slowly and hugging the side of the road. The dogs returned to their dhaba and regarded the DCP without curiosity as he stood there, trying to reassemble his jangled nerves. A quiet cough behind him caused him to wheel around, his weapon still in hand.

"Time to go, sir," said Kapoor's nephew. Kapoor and Smita stood behind him.

The DCP nodded. They set off on foot to their quarry.

The house itself was unprepossessing. A dirt forecourt dominated by the smell of ancient ordure and recent urine. A truck with an open bed was parked outside, the license plate number matching the one they'd been given. A hint that the sun, when it drove away the fog, would reveal unwholesome pink paint. An outdoor toilet, a closed tin hut that suggested the retail of paan and prepackaged chips, a compressed air machine for tires. A single-story, a veranda of sorts under a lean-to made of corrugated iron, two mean windows. There were no lights on.

"You enter into a hall. There are at least two men asleep there. Then there are two further rooms behind the hall. Behind that are the fields."

"You have men there?"

The nephew nodded.

"I'll lead my men inside," he said. "We'll clear the hall and then the rooms. We're carrying lights. The perimeter is already set. They're not going anywhere."

The DCP indicated his approval.

"Will you be coming in, sir?" asked the nephew.

The DCP and Kapoor both nodded. "We'll follow you," said Kapoor.

Smita looked at the other men anxiously. Kapoor

glanced at her sideways, chuckled quietly. "Don't worry. You're coming too."

The nephew hurried away to confer with his men one last time. The fog was now so thick that conceal- ment was rendered superfluous. The DCP and Kapoor and Smita were waiting barely feet from the front door. No dogs challenged them either.

"Have you done this before?" asked Smita of Kapoor.

"A few times."

"Does the waiting ever get easier?"

"Never."

"You remember the drill, right? We go in behind the active team," said the DCP. "Your weapon out, safety off. Do not discharge it unless you have to. Got it?"

Smita nodded. She peered up at the DCP's set face. "What happened back there?"

"A trick of the light," said the DCP shortly.

Then the nephew was there, five men behind him, their weapons in their hands, two of them carrying emergency lamps.

"We're ready. One minute to kickoff. Give us thirty seconds in the main hall. I'll shout clear. That's your signal. If you don't hear me, don't come in."

"If we hear gunshots?" asked Smita.

"That will be us," said the nephew with a grin.

Smita waited, then found herself walking quickly to- ward the door. She felt the heft of her official weapon in one hand, the other groping toward the door as she'd been taught. She heard the word "Clear" and burst through the door into a world lit by the fluorescent glare of emergency lights and she smelled the rank stench of unwashed men lying on dirty mattresses laid out on a grimy floor. She felt her gorge rise and she didn't know whether it was the smell or the adrenaline, her hand bringing her weapon up in a smooth arc in front of her face as she followed Kapoor and the DCP into the room to the right. She saw the man with the knife emerge from the shadows the emergency light hadn't yet touched, she saw him lunge at the DCP and heard as if in a dream Kapoor's warning cry and heard the knife strike the DCP's protective vest and the cacophonous sonic boom of two high-velocity rounds being discharged in a closed space. She saw the assailant being thrown back and sideways and the DCP on the floor, and then she was kneeling next to him.

"Good job, Smita," said the DCP with a smile. That was when she discovered that one of the bullets in the assailant was her own.

Kapoor loomed over them, a question in his eyes. He looked at the DCP, then walked over to the man crumpled against the wall. He knelt next to him, felt his pulse, turned back to the DCP and Smita, and shook his head. From the other room came the first sounds of the Delhi Police chastising the friends of a man with the temerity to attack one of their own. The DCP decided that the prone position he was in was as good as any to await the arrival of the policemen who actually had jurisdiction here. He looked over at Smita, who had joined him on the floor, though her back was against the dirty wall.

"You alright?"

"I think so. And you?"

"I'll live. I'll have a bruise, but that's about it."

"Good thing you were wearing a vest."

I know, thought the DCP, and closed his eyes. He

opened them to find Kapoor still squatting next to the corpse. The muffled sounds of felons in agony filtered through the now closed door. The DCP watched Kapoor idly, then tensed as he saw what Kapoor was looking at.

"Well?" he said brusquely, sitting up.

Kapoor's bent head nodded. He held up the dead rapist's hand.

Four fingers only.

The DCP glimpsed Smita throwing up in a corner at the periphery of his vision. Villages, thought the DCP. He sighed, slid backward till his spine was against the wall, and closed his eyes again.

COMPROMISE

"It would seem," said DCP Sajan Dayal glumly, "that men don't need all their fingers anymore." Kapoor nodded phlegmatically. Smita Dhingra, recently confirmed member of the standing task force of the Crime Branch, Delhi Police, waited quietly.

"What ails these men?" asked the DCP rhetorically. His question was aimed at the sky to which his face, sheltered behind his aviator sunglasses, was turned. His arms were crossed behind his head, his feet were under a linen-covered table, the sun beat down around the three of them. There was tea on the table in front, an attentive waiter lurked on the periphery of their small group, and around them was that interplay of sun and shade, that warm dappled blanket a gentle winter day drops on a grateful city. But the fineness of the day and the quality of the tea made no difference to the DCP. It was as if the curtain of Ashoka trees that screened their garden oasis from the busy road did nothing to quiet the roar of traffic in their ears.

Winter was now a reality. Dayal's casually well-cut jacket was offset by his wool slacks, while Smita's discreetly chic ensemble was a credit to both her shawl dealer and the younger designers of Delhi. Kapoor's concession to the weather was the sleeveless fleece jacket he sported against the chill. His shirtsleeves were still rolled up in the bellicose fashion he favored. Those rolled-up sleeves had stood him in good stead as he hunted around the dusty outskirts of the capital in the weeks that had followed the conclusion of the gang-rape case.

A plague of nine-fingered men, he'd reported to his superior officer. Tens, hundreds, perhaps thousands. Nobody knew just how many. But they were everywhere, a ring around Delhi, from the Meos to the Ahirs to the Jats to the Gujjars. Even the scheduled castes, men with whom the landlords and herders of Delhi's peripheries would normally have had little to do, shared this affliction. It was an ecumenical epidemic as well: Muslims felt it just as much as Hindus or anyone else.

It had started, as far as Kapoor could gather, about three years before. A small village to the south, amongst the truncated arid hills off the old Alwar Road. An ancient settlement, a dirt-poor populace, water only when the rain fell. "A different world," said Kapoor somberly. "And it's only an hour from Gurgaon." News spread about a deity that promised the riches of Delhi to its adherents and asked only one thing in return. Fealty, attested with the gift of a nonessential digit. It was, to the poor residents of that village and the surrounding areas, a cheap trade. Or so Kapoor had been told.

News spread of this new "god." It was nothing. A village "dev," a stone, a tree, a ribbon in a bush somewhere. No idol, even. Just an idea that took root in the sandy superstitious soil of the region and spread, as things will in places as dry as these, like wildfire. There were nocturnal parties that reached their ludic height with the ecstatic dedigitation of all present. "Drunks cutting each other," said Kapoor. "Can you imagine?"

The DCP's face remained, in its repose, an impassive

urban counterpoint to this tale of rural darkness, but his raised eyebrow indicated that he could, indeed, imagine. So Kapoor continued.

Finally, sometime that year, a visiting and very young development scholar happened on this particular infestation. He was actually there to work on solutions to the region's chronic water shortages. Fueled by curiosity and the nitrous alcohol of the region, he spent a night out with the locals. His mother, a development professional of some repute herself with an impeccable background in rural interventions, would later tell her friends at the India International Centre that she didn't know what to be more horrified by, the fact that her bright young boy now only had nine fingers, or that the bleeding stump he showed her so abjectly the next evening was bound with the dirty end of what was either someone's well-worn turban or his loincloth. She reported it to the authorities. They'd known but had preferred to let sleeping dogs lie, yet were now forced to take cognizance of what was going on, by virtue of the indignant mother's political connections. The tree, bush, beribboned rock, or whatever was burnt, carted off, buried, or whatever.

"But that didn't end it," murmured the DCP.

Kapoor ordered another pot of tea.

"And what of our uniformed cousins? Were any of them so afflicted?"

Nobody currently serving was short a finger, Kapoor told them. However, two men in the intervening period had reported to their stations in that condition. One had since died, apparently of natural causes. The other had disappeared, apparently without a trace.

"Naturally," observed the DCP.

Kapoor added sugar to his already saccharine brew. "What do your nephews think?"

"They think I should stop poking that particular dog to see if it's dead."

"Scared?"

"Unhappy."

"Why? Because of what happened? Or because you're asking?"

"I don't know," admitted Kapoor.

"Really. So we don't actually know anything of the men behind this. Either back then or since."

Kapoor nodded, his head heavy behind his cup of tea.

"It would seem that the intelligence gathered by the local stations has been deficient, then. Are you satisfied," asked the DCP gently, "with the loyalty of your nephews? In this particular instance?"

"I don't know," admitted Kapoor again.

"And the fact that they watched and waited while Dilliwalas were losing their fingers and never bothered to tell us?"

Kapoor looked at him steadily. The pressures of the summer before had melted into the appreciation of the entire city, but now it appeared there had been no resolution. A case they thought was closed was anything but. A man who was little more than a boy had died as well. The DCP was the connoisseur of webs and connections, Kapoor the practitioner of the hard graft of police work. Yet they'd both failed, and neither could yet see what end the boy's passing had served.

The DCP looked away. "The wealth of Delhi," he said aloud. "Is that exactly what you were told?"

"Yes. Rich. Like the men of Delhi."

The DCP smiled and then laughed and glanced around. "Rich like whom? Like us? Like me? My riches are these things. This sun, this breeze, this passing cool, these leaves, these trees, this moment in time. I have them now and I share them with you and then they'll be gone and so will we. Is this not the way of the world?"

That was when Smita had walked in and taken her seat. Kapoor had raised a substantial eyebrow at her and she'd acknowledged it and perhaps they'd both rolled their eyes.

"What ails these men?" repeated the DCP. "Of course, I know what it is. Delhi's always been a beacon to these lowlifes. Like moths to the flame."

"Lowlifes," repeated Smita inadvertently.

The DCP and Kapoor looked at her expectantly.

"Well," she said, coloring behind her sunglasses, "if these men are lowlifes, then what do you think of people like me?"

"And me," added Kapoor with a smile.

"Punjabis," said the DCP with a shake of his head. "You take over this city. You're taking over the police force. Now you want to take on the mantle of lowlifes as well?"

Their laughter was easy upon the sunlit garden. But there was work to be done by the standing task force. While it was important for them to probe why there were still nine-fingered men roaming the vicinity of Delhi even after the ostensible conclusion of that particular horror the previous summer, it was perforce to be done on their own time. It was agreed without being mentioned that there was no future in reopening a case everyone else thought to be closed. The two men waited for their younger colleague to finish her cup of tea, then Dayal summoned the bill with a smile at the hovering waiter. The manager of the establishment, waiting for just such a signal, hurried out obsequiously. The poor tea he had provided, he insisted, was on the restaurant. He just wished he could have given them something more in keeping with their positions and wouldn't they return for dinner? Smita's protests were as air before the emphatic waves of his hand, the DCP a quiet presence behind her. Kapoor had already stalked off. An appropriate few moments later, the DCP and the young policewoman followed, past the windows of the fashion outlets and their old rustic doors, through the recently renovated archway, and into the heaving main road that led toward the ancient settlement of Mehrauli.

"What's it like at night?" asked the DCP.

"Lovely," replied Smita. "Like a fairyland. Lights in the trees and terraces, candles on the tables, soft music."

"Sounds wonderful."

"Well. The food's terrible. And terribly expensive."

"You can't have everything," mumbled Kapoor.

"Why don't you let me bring you? If we're still here when night falls? It would be nice," smiled Smita.

Kapoor and the DCP looked at each other, then at her. "Perhaps some other time," said the DCP with a smile of his own. "But we'll keep it in mind."

Then they were inside the warren of Mehrauli, looking for the house where the dead black man had been found.

It had started, as so many things do in Delhi, with a rumor. Around the same time the previous year, a new mother had come home from her job in a nearby store to find her infant missing, along with the young niece tasked with the child's care. A hysterical and fruitless search followed. An hour later, a party of her incensed male relatives kicked down the door of the African students who lived in the same building. A summary beating was administered, a confession extracted. The two hapless students were on the verge of being drowned in the fetid waters of the Hauz-i-Shamsi when the wondering face of the young mother's niece, her infant cousin snug and asleep in her arms, presented itself at the parapet that surrounded the ancient reservoir. A glad scream and numerous hugs and kisses from the bereft mother confirmed that the child was indeed hers. The niece had merely wanted a change of scene and had taken the child along. She had only just returned. The African students were pulled out and patted down and persuaded against lodging a complaint. But the damage had been done.

Since that unfortunate incident, reports had begun to filter into the Mehrauli police station about the despicable practice, allegedly prevalent among the African residents, of purloining and consuming the newborn babies of the area. Maids swore themselves blue they'd seen the children, whole and in cut pieces, in the freezers of said African residents. As a consequence, they refused to work in those premises.

"The maids say their homes smell," observed Kapoor.

"Well, naturally, if they're not being cleaned," replied Smita tartly.

The DCP just looked around as they walked through the narrow lanes of the old settlement. Kapoor continued apace.

"What's happened, of course, is that the maids who will work in the homes of the Africans can command their own price. They're the richest women in their community."

"Are they seeing babies in freezers as well?"

"Of course. They're rich, not blind."

Smita rolled her eyes again, though there was a smile on her lips. She noticed her own stride lengthening as Kapoor's burly presence cleared a magical path through the bustle of Mehrauli. She felt, as she had before, the presence of that invisible ring that surrounded men such as Kapoor and the DCP. The older, larger man, beefy-shouldered and hairy-armed, rumbling along at his own pace, his eyes seemingly steady but missing nothing in his path. The bear in front, thought Smita, and the wolf behind, sensing the DCP's quietly feral saunter a step or so astern. His eyes turned to the homes above the road, as his deputy's were to ground level, both equally aware of their surroundings. They walked with their arms slung loose by their sides, their feet feeling their own way through the cow pats and occasional puddles, pedestrian traffic no hindrance at all. Did they gain it when they became cops, she thought suddenly, or did men such as this become policemen so they didn't have to change? The demands of that other, more accommodating world, the residents of which moved out of the way of their stately little cavalcade, their eyes cast down; it was as if the men with her didn't even notice them, thought Smita. Neither the demands themselves, nor the legions of men and women who were defined by their acquiescence to those demands.

Perhaps, thought Smita, we are a breed apart. The thought chilled her young heart, in part because she'd articulated the "we" in her own mind. Am I, too, a wolf in the making, she thought. Or was I born this way as well? Then she thought that a line of inquiry such as this would lead her nowhere, and anyway it was more suited to the DCP's mentality than hers. That made her smile again, so she turned to her senior and saw him, beside her now and swinging easily along at the clip being set by Kapoor, smiling back at her.

"Your turn to be gathering wool," he said. "Anything of interest?"

"Only to me," she replied primly. His smile grew broader.

"The maids," said Kapoor. "They see everything. Talk to a few. See what they tell us."

"Will they want to talk to us?" wondered Smita.

"Do they have a choice?"

They turned into a lane not far from the dargah. They'd walked past a few old homes, their wooden shutters and slung-over balconies a stark contrast to the concrete blocks in basic colors that now proliferated here.

"Lots of ghosts," said the DCP meditatively, pausing at just such an old home, running his fingers over the weathered surface of the door, the metal studs a cool counterpoint to the splintered warm wood.

"This area," he gestured around himself. "An ancient place. Parts of it have been around for ten centuries or more."

"Really?"

"Many of the Muslim families that lived here cleared out after 1947. Their homes and businesses were taken over by emigrants from Pakistan. Mostly Hindus from southern Punjab."

Smita nodded slowly, while Kapoor glanced around.

"Ghosts," said the DCP again, his hand still flitting over the cracked and splintered door, the sun now a memory, its rays shaded out by the close-pressed buildings around them. The thin bleats of a preadolescent cricket game in progress down a narrow street filtered through the occasional honks and chimes of the two-wheeled traffic, motorized and otherwise, that dominated these constricted alleys. The day wasn't cold, the hour unadvanced, yet Smita felt a shiver run down her spine. She drew her shawl closer around her shoulders. Then a man they all knew was leaning out a window and beckoning them up the stairs.

"What do we know?" asked the DCP.

The investigating officer, who'd been there all day, consulted his notes. The man had died sometime the night before. The maid had discovered the body that morning. She'd considered just taking off and not saying anything, but better sense had prevailed. You realize, she'd said again and again, that she had nothing to do with either the death of the man or the man himself, besides cleaning his home on a semiregular basis.

"Is she here?" asked Kapoor.

The other man indicated the adjacent room, where a woman who'd clearly been crying sat, her sari's pallu pulled close over her head, a mobile phone clutched in her palm. Kapoor nodded and turned away.

The man was West African and had been in India five years. Originally a student, he had applied for refugee status and was awaiting it still. His visa had run out and he'd been threatened with ejection. Clearly he'd found a way around the system.

The DCP walked around the flat. Two smallish bedrooms, a common bathroom, a nicely set-up kitchen with many empty bottles under the sink. A hall dominated by a leather sofa in front of a flat-screen TV and a comprehensive home theater system. Afrobeat CDs in the tray under the stereo, a bunch of Hindi film music.

"He has an Indian girlfriend," supplied the officer on the spot.

Kapoor looked at him.

"We're trying to find her. She's disappeared."

Kapoor nodded again and kept pacing.

"Neighbors?" asked Smita.

The man looked at her, then at Kapoor and the DCP. They quietly returned his gaze till he cleared his throat.

"Next door, a young Malayali family. Husband's in the government. He's still at work. We've spoken with the wife. She went off to fetch their son from school."

"Then?"

"Across the floor, a Cambodian, Vietnamese, one of those. Seems to be a rotating system. One of them leaves, another one comes. Sometimes a family."

"Associated with the Buddhist center?" inquired Kapoor.

"Perhaps. We're checking."

The older man continued to pace. The DCP, having inspected the couch, chose to sit down in one of the straight-backed chairs around the little circular dining table.

"Anyone else?"

"Downstairs, some more Indians. We're waiting for them to come home. Nobody else, currently."

The DCP nodded. Smita caught the pacing Kapoor's eye and went into the room where the maid sat. She paused, her hand on the knob, as the DCP posed his final question.

"Any word on what he died of?"

"The stab wounds. They're still waiting for confirmation on any underlying issues and problems, but on the face of it, the wounds were enough. Five. Of varying depths. He wouldn't have survived that anyway."

Smita pulled the door closed softly behind her.

———————

She was learning not to be surprised by the perspicacity of Kapoor's seemingly throwaway statements. The maids did indeed see everything, and they remembered it too. This woman wasn't old, but Smita couldn't tell if the years or a hard life had robbed her of the bloom of her youth.

"How many children do you have?"

"Four," replied the maid.

Smita reached gently across the intervening space

and removed the hem of the other woman's sari from her clutching nervous fingers and told her not to bother with it, they were women together and alone and she had no use for her notions of privacy. The other woman blushed, looked up, and finally smiled.

"How old are you?"

"My eldest is twenty."

"Girl or boy?"

"Girl. Then two boys, and a girl again."

"How nice. Is the eldest one married?"

"No." Scornfully. "She's studying. She'll find a job. Then, we'll see."

Smita nodded. "Your family are okay with that?"

"Why wouldn't they be? If a man wants a simple village girl, let him find one in the countryside. This is Delhi."

Smita laughed out loud. The other woman smiled again, this time with more feeling.

"Who do you think we are?" asked the woman archly. "We're not villagers."

Smita nodded again. "Do you clean all the homes here?"

"In this building, yes."

"Tell me about the Vietnamese."

"They're Cambodians. Nice people. Neat, clean. Quiet and polite. Pay promptly and never shout."

"What's their story?"

"They're here for operations."

"What do you mean?"

"It's not a family. Well, there's one man who comes back every three months or so. He's the boss. But the people living there keep changing. They come here with their families and friends. They're not well, they need hospital help. Bypasses, things like that. Sometimes, a transplant. They stay here before the hospital and then after, before they leave for home."

"Which hospitals?"

The other woman gestured vaguely, named some prominent private hospitals.

"Any contact between the African and them?"

"No," said the maid dismissively. "He had nothing those poor sick people would want."

"The Indian family next door?"

"South Indians, but nice. Very polite, very clean. The boy is beautiful. Like a girl. I want to pet him every time I see him. His mother's very proud of him."

"That beautiful?"

"That smart. He's a boy genius. Or so his mother believes, at any rate. I think she shouldn't worry, so long as he keeps his looks."

The two women laughed together this time.

"The couple downstairs?"

"Sweet. Boisterous when they've been drinking. Quiet otherwise. I think he teaches in college. The woman's an artist. They have one big party every year, at the time of the Mehrauli fair. I get a good tip the next day."

Was the African invited? wondered Smita.

"They invite everyone. But I don't think they were friends. Or customers."

"So what was the African doing here?"

"What do you think?" replied the maid.

They leaned against the window frame, the DCP at one end and Smita at the other, mugs of tea in their hands as they soaked in the last few moments of warmth and light before winter's night fell on Delhi. Kapoor, a mug secure in his mitts as well, sat at his ease on a chair close by. A kite's thin cry rang through the alleys, and then they both saw it, wheeling in the narrow wedge of blue sky above.

"A drug dealer."

The DCP nodded. "That's what the Narcotics boys tell me. Never been arrested or charged, but he's been picked up a couple of times. Been lucky so far."

"Not lucky enough," observed Kapoor.

The DCP chuckled. Smita kept quiet.

"How did the maid know?" asked the DCP.

"Well, partly inference. He didn't seem to do anything useful. Watched TV during the day when she cleaned around him. Always had his phones close by."

"Drugs in the house?"

"Never. She swore she looked."

"So?"

"Well. A cousin of her husband works at the airport. In customs. He told them about how the mules bring in the drugs in condoms, which they swallow."

The DCP nodded.

"He had guests who would stay with him, a night or two at a time, pretty regularly. Men and women. She'd been finding the rubbers in the trash for months. It was almost a relief for her to discover that he wasn't sexually omnivorous. Or abnormally active. But she still felt it was a crappy way to make a living."

The DCP and Kapoor burst out laughing. After a

pause long enough to meet the demands of propriety, so did Smita.

"I don't think the boys in Narcotics knew our man was part of the pipeline," said Kapoor after wiping his eyes.

"You'd better tell them," said the DCP. "We're going to need their help anyway."

"Perhaps not," said Smita. The two men looked at her. "He had a friend. A white girl with 'yellow' hair. She was over quite a lot. Spoke some Hindi, seemed friendly. Would come over and sleep in the afternoon sometimes. She told the maid that it was because she worked all night."

"She's a nightclub hostess," said Kapoor.

Smita nodded. "We have her name, phone number, and address. She asked our maid to clean her house. The maid couldn't fit her in, but she kept her name and number just the same. In case, you know."

"Thank god for dumb blondes," observed Kapoor.

———•——•——•———

The blond nightclub hostess lived in Mehrauli as well, though in a neighborhood a ten-minute walk away. The building she lived in looked exactly like the one the dead drug dealer had inhabited. Concrete, on stilts so the cars could park underneath, heavy metal gates and grates. The woman who answered the door was flustered, unsure of where to look.

"Going somewhere?" inquired the DCP pleasantly. The woman stared at them fearfully as Kapoor swept past her into her home.

The house was much more basic than the African's. A small TV, an iPod dock. There were mattresses against the walls to lounge on, a dining table made of cane with two chairs on either side, a steamer trunk in the middle of the room that functioned as a coffee table. On the TV were a few photos in frames. A suitcase lay open on the floor, clothes and books cascading out of it. A cat slept on a rug in the corner.

"May I use your bathroom?" asked Kapoor politely. She gestured toward a closed door, drew her arms around herself.

"You know who we are?" said the DCP, settling in to one of the chairs at the dining table.

The blond girl nodded unhappily.

"You know he's dead," continued the DCP, lighting a cigarette. The woman kept quiet, but her pursed lips gave her away.

"Who told you?" asked the DCP. The woman maintained her silence as Smita sat down on a mattress by the wall. The DCP looked at the blonde. "There's no point in keeping quiet. It's too late for that."

Kapoor came out, shaking his head.

"How much stuff have you flushed, sweetheart?" he asked conversationally. "The cistern's still smoking."

The DCP grinned. The blonde began to cry.

"Why," asked Kapoor rhetorically, "must they always cry? Isn't it obvious that talking is better, easier, more profitable? Why cry? I don't get it."

The DCP shook his head again.

"I mean, it's not as if I've smacked her around. It's not as if I've asked the one female officer in the room to leave. Have I? Why," asked Kapoor of Smita with an expansive wave of his hand, "is this little slut crying?"

Smita watched the performance, her face carefully immobile. Kapoor's eyes stayed on the young officer, watching her reactions. He stalked over to the suitcase, kicked at it, bent down to pull things out at random. A blouse, a pair of jeans, a Hindi grammar book, some underwear, a stuffed toy with a tag still on it.

"You have a child," said Kapoor to the room at large. "Does she know what you do for a living?"

"For my niece," answered the woman in an undertone.

Kapoor tacked over to the TV, studied the photos on it. "This young girl? She's lovely. You want her to grow up to be like you?"

The blonde kept quiet, her red eyes closed.

"You want to see her again?"

She began to cry more openly now, her mouth sobbing as she sank to the floor. Kapoor hitched one shoe around the other chair at the table and pulled it to him and sank his bulk onto it. His feet went on either side of the crying woman, his body a malignant shadow over her.

"You do know," said the DCP mildly, "that if I send in a team to do a thorough check through this . . . house, we will find something. Something that you haven't flushed down the drain."

"But I don't need to do that, do I, darling?" Kapoor's knees were about six inches on either side of the crying woman's face, his crotch not a lot farther away. "The worst thing I can do to you is leave you here. Now, after having spoken to you. How long do you think it'll be before the boys who killed your friend come back for you?" He leaned in more now, his head a few inches from the woman's. "How long?" One hand went up behind his back and beckoned Smita forward.

"We don't have to do it this way, you know," said the young policewoman, rising to Kapoor's side. She put a hand on his shoulder, at which he leaned back. Smita dropped to her haunches, her own face now close to the young blonde's. "I'm assuming you don't want to die."

The other woman continued to cry.

"I'm also assuming you don't want to rot in an Indian jail."

The other woman raised her eyes now, red and fearful still.

"Good. We can take you into protective custody. Take your statement, verify it. Keep you safe while we're about it. How's that sound?"

The blonde nodded for the first time, her crying eyes fixed on Smita's soft brown ones.

"Tell us what we need to know. That's all we ask. That's all we need. We don't need to put you in jail. Tell us everything, and we can guarantee you won't be prosecuted. All that will happen is you'll be asked to leave India. Resume your life, wherever it is you came from. Does that sound okay?"

Kapoor got to his feet and stalked over to the one window in the wall. Smita took his place in the seat. The DCP smoked away impassively.

"What do you think?" asked Smita.

The woman nodded again, more vigorously this time, a smile flickering through the storm. She stuck out a hand impulsively, which Smita took in her own warm grasp.

"My name is Natalya," said the young woman.

"I know," said Smita, with a smile of her own.

"Would you like some tea?"

"We would love that."

The young woman went into the small kitchen at one end of the room they were in. Smita turned around and looked at her senior officers. The DCP's smile was knowing and complicit, while Kapoor's had something she didn't recognize immediately. It was only later that night that she would work out where she'd seen this look before. She was back home now having a cup of after-dinner coffee with her parents. She said something about her day that made her mother sniff and then laugh and she looked to her father and bathed, again, as she had her whole life, in the pride in his smile. It was then that she remembered Kapoor and the light in his eyes.

The woman, as expected, sang like a canary. They didn't even have to get her down to their office. There was nothing particularly sensational in what she had to tell them, but the contents of her phone and her memory of the faces she had been moving drugs to in her night-club would be invaluable. She also impressed the three officers with her insistence that her cat be looked after while she was gone. That animal, a peaceful spayed tom, had already charmed Smita, and she readily accepted his charge.

The facts of Natalya's conversion to the trade were simple. She had arrived in Delhi to pursue her interests in yoga and dance. A friend in yoga class had recommended she meet a man who ran a talent company which provided extras for ad shoots and hostesses for parties. While there were whispers about how his girls also provided other services, Natalya had always found him respectful and professional. He had placed her as a hostess with the nightclub she worked at, where the prospect of a regular salary and a working environment that was conducive to large amounts of time off appealed to the young yogini.

The other girls there were a mixed bag. Some were students, others aspiring models, still others simply in India for their gap years or on exchange programs. There were several who went home with their clients for a fee, but those girls were few and far between and they screwed it up, said Natalya, for the rest of them. As she pointed out, even the ones who had legitimate Indian boyfriends, men they made love to of their own accord, were thought to be tarts.

It was a good living, though, she admitted. Drinking champagne every night with men and women who drove up in Bentleys and Porsches was nice as well. Not the India she saw on the walk home through the cluttered streets of Mehrauli in the early hours, but still a country she was fascinated by. She kept notes. Would Smita like to see?

The African had happened along by chance. She'd met him at a common acquaintance's, an African student who lived in the next house over. The man had expressed an interest in her work, had come to see her at her nightclub, and had impressed her with his charm and the fact that his girlfriend came everywhere with him. When he made his offer, it seemed so simple, so easy, it was hard to say no.

"What did he ask you to do?" Smita inquired.

When the wealthy pleasure-seekers who frequented Natalya's club tired of the bottles of Grey Goose and Black Label on the table and sought her help for something more exciting to keep the party going, she was to point in the African's direction. A name, a phone number. That's it. For which she was paid handsomely.

Before she knew it, a simple one-off favor, that of carrying a packet for him to a regular customer at the club, had become a routine affair.

"And then," she said simply, "I couldn't stop."

"Who were her customers?" Smita asked, as off-handedly as she could manage.

Natalya had looked at her obliquely, a veil dropping between her and the young policewoman.

"Anyone I'd know?" pursued Smita.

Almost everyone, the other girl had replied.

It had been dark for hours by the time the three of them came out of Natalya's home. The girl had been taken in by the women's cell of the Delhi Police. They were charged with her protection. Kapoor and the DCP had already despatched her phone and computer to Smita's old office. Her records would be on their desks in the morning.

"This shouldn't take long," said Kapoor.

The DCP grunted, while Smita looked uneasy.

"What's the matter?" asked Kapoor.

"Well, if her clients are as high-powered as she thinks they are . . . won't it be a problem?"

"Not for us," said Kapoor complacently. Smita raised an eyebrow and the DCP barked unpleasantly.

"He means you two," said the DCP with a shake of

his head. "If there is any political heat, I'll take it."

"That's why you're the boss," chuckled Kapoor.

Smita couldn't help but follow his lead as the DCP glowered in the dark. At that moment, a slim silhouette detached itself from the door behind them and appeared by their sides. Smita jumped, while Kapoor and the DCP lit up again.

"I was wondering," said the DCP, "when you'd come and say hello."

———— ⫶ ————

They had already established that the African next door to Natalya was innocent of any narcotics charges. A phone call with his name, address, and mobile phone details had sufficed to clear him of the weight of Kapoor's interest. He still needed to be talked to, of course. That he'd come across of his own accord had saved them the trip up his stairs.

The DCP and Kapoor made no attempt to put him at ease, but they didn't lean on him either. They didn't have to. Wary though he was, he was also eager to talk.

The girl, he corroborated, was originally his friend. She'd come to a party he'd hosted, met the dead man there. The dealer and he had been close when they were both students. He knew what the other man did and didn't approve. But one can't choose one's friends when one is abroad. If the DCP and Kapoor agreed, they didn't show it.

"We're not all drug dealers," said the man quietly, insistently. "We're not born to this. I've made good friends here. Even though most Indians are racist to the core."

Smita blushed ineffectually in the darkness. The DCP stayed quiet, Kapoor laughed, and the truth of what the African was saying went undisputed in the Delhi night.

"I don't like being called *habshi*. None of us do. *Kala. Andhera*. All those words. But we're not all drug dealers. You need to know that."

"We do," said the DCP. "That's why we're not picking you up."

The other man nodded slowly. "Do you need my help with anything? I want to. Natalya is my friend. So was he."

"Don't leave town," advised Kapoor.

"I have permanent status," said the man with a sudden smile. "I'm not going anywhere."

"What was he like? Your friend?" asked Smita.

"A good man. Then, not so much. You can't do what he did and not change."

"What happened to him?"

"Became boastful. Full of himself. Paranoid, sometimes. Talked of his fancy friends, but almost always with bitterness. Their friendship was of the night. They couldn't help him live here legally, like I do. He hoped they would help, but he knew they wouldn't. They didn't know him in that way."

"Do you know any of them?" asked Kapoor.

"Only by name, and nothing I'd swear to."

"And the girl?" inquired Smita.

"Friendly, sweet. Always nice. Learning Hindi, interested in history. Yoga, dance, a smile for everyone. No more a Russian slut than I am a habshi drug dealer."

"We all have our crosses to bear," said the DCP.

"Stay close," said Kapoor.

The African nodded unhappily. Then he too was gone.

———————————

The sun in the sky the following day was shepherded along its way by a breeze that spun the clouds into cool white wisps. It was a chill breeze that spoke of the Himalayas and Afghanistan and distant valleys where men and women alike wore concealing robes and carried pots of burning coals beneath them. In Delhi, the crisp frigidity of the previous night was a memory dispelled by blue skies and the benevolent sun. Yet to wander from the sun's gaze for a moment was to realize just how unfettered the breeze was between those distant mountains and these cooling plains.

But for all that Smita knew of the day outside, it might as well have been gray. There were phone records to be collated and people to be spoken with, and her old friends and colleagues in the cyber section of Crime Branch were welcome allies. A quick look at the dead drug dealer's phone records had confirmed what they'd suspected the night before: that the great and the good of the city were to be found among his erstwhile clientele. That, or their friendships were more eclectic than breeding and privilege would normally have allowed.

"Any repeat offenders?" Kapoor inquired at lunch, when they met around the DCP's desk.

"Lots of people spoke to him frequently. Or did you mean those Narcotics has already tagged?"

Kapoor nodded mutely. The DCP's arms were behind his head, which was bent toward the ceiling, and his feet were propped on top of his desk.

"Well. One of the guys in the bureau was a classmate of mine. I asked him."

"And?"

"He whistled. Told me to call him later. I haven't yet, but it's obvious they know these names. Do you want to take it up at your level?"

The DCP and Kapoor shook their heads in unison.

"No point," said Kapoor. "If Narcotics has already been spoken with, we'll have to tackle this ourselves."

The DCP nodded quietly.

"Any noise from upstairs?" Kapoor asked the DCP.

"Not yet."

"Will there be?" asked Smita.

The two older officers looked at her, then Kapoor put his hands behind his own head and bent it toward the ceiling.

"Recognize any of the names?" asked the DCP.

"Many of them," said Smita.

The DCP sighed, Kapoor grunted, and Smita seemed mystified.

"Have you not looked at the records yet?" she asked. "Why?" she continued into the lengthening silence.

Later, if pressed, she would have been unable to explain whether it was youth or perversity that drove her further.

"Everyone's going to know that I've seen the records, as has everyone else on this team. The entire cyber section is dealing with this right now."

The ceiling might have sported a fresco, the two male officers were studying it so carefully.

"This isn't going to be a tough one," persisted Smita desperately. "Not compared to the finger-snatcher case."

"That one isn't closed."

"We solved the rape."

"Those guys were poor and stupid."

"Which means?"

"Poor stupid guys always get caught. This dead bastard's customers were stupid, alright. But not one of them is poor," said Kapoor.

"If they don't want this case solved," asked Smita finally, "why give it to us?"

"Are you prepared," asked the DCP by way of answer, "for tomorrow's ceremony?"

He and Smita were being given medals of valor for the parts they'd played in the resolution of the gang-rape case. The ceremony was the next day. The minister herself would be pinning the badges of achievement to their breasts.

Smita nodded mutely.

"The old lady's invited me for breakfast," said the DCP.

Kapoor raised an eyebrow. "The full monty?"

"So it would seem."

"They're famous, those breakfasts," said Kapoor. "Bacon, sausages, fresh parathas, and dosas for the vegetarians. Alcohol for those who want it. Lots of powerful people."

Smita, still fulminating, was interested despite herself.

"One day, Smita, you'll be invited too. Then the rest of your floor will be as green as the other DCPs will be when they hear where the boss is eating his eggs tomorrow."

With that, Kapoor lurched to his feet. Smita watched his exit and turned back toward the DCP to discover his eye was already trained on her.

"What are you doing tonight?" he asked.

"TV. Hot water bottle. Bed."

"Big night."

"Huge."

"Want to have a drink? Celebrate your first medal?"

"Sure," said Smita, before she caught herself. "I mean, yes. That would be nice, sir."

The DCP grinned at her. "I'm thinking that place we had tea yesterday. In Mehrauli. That might be nice, don't you think? You recommended it so highly."

"It's lovely," agreed Smita. "Any . . . other reason?"

The DCP looked at her coolly. "I'm your superior officer, Smita. What other reason would there be?"

Smita colored and glanced away.

"Sometimes being a good officer isn't enough, if you want to make a career in this force. Perhaps we'll talk about that tonight."

———————

Their passage through the honking nightmare of late rush-hour traffic had been a slow one, the beacon of Qutab Minar beckoning to them as it loomed over the snaking river of cars. Then the snake had diverted toward Gurgaon and they were heading into Mehrauli itself, a quick sprint along a stone wall, old buttresses of ancient homes on the other side. They were now inhabited by expensive boutiques and plush restaurants that were a magnet to the city dwellers who lived on either side of Mehrauli.

There was irony in this, thought the DCP. "These people come here and they think Mehrauli's a village."

"Isn't it?"

"Now, I suppose it is. In someone's definition. But it was a city ten centuries ago."

"That's what you said yesterday."

"It was the capital of the Rajput kingdom that preceded the sultanate of Delhi. When the first sultans arrived, it became their capital as well. That's why the Qutab Minar is here."

Smita nodded, her face turned toward the DCP's as it darkened and lightened between the glows of the streetlamps that illumined their passage into Mehrauli.

"Its accoutrements are all urban. It has all the markings of an imperial capital. A Jama Masjid for the people. A reservoir to provide water in bad times. A place for kings to have their graves. Stepwells for their courtiers. Homes for their merchants and their wives and slaves. This was the heart of Delhi before the rest of the world knew there was such a thing."

Smita was transfixed, watching as much as listening as the DCP thought aloud.

"Delhi's first famous Sufi saint lived and died here. The Minar is his namesake, but is it named for him?" The DCP shook his head. "He was the patron saint of kings and emperors to come. The last emperor of Delhi wanted to be buried here as well."

"He isn't?"

"His grave is here. But he isn't in it." He turned to Smita, smiled at the wordless question in her face. "Things don't always work out the way one wants them to. Or as they should.

"And now look at these people," he said, his breath frosty upon the air as he joined Smita outside his car, the valet scurrying past. "They come here for their shi-shas and expensive booze and food and think they're living in the rural past. What do they actually know of this place?"

"They know it's currently cool," said Smita calmly.

"And currently cold," admitted the DCP. "Shall we?" he inquired, as a man wearing a turban held the door to the haveli open for them.

The night was frigid and clear. Smita and the DCP were glad for the heat lamps that cast their red glow on the frosty lawn and carefully bestrewn pebbles and couches on which lounged the new aristocracy of the parvenu city.

Soft music with a quietly insistent beat played from speakers that the DCP couldn't see, while women with bare shoulders looked with interest at what Smita was wearing. They didn't know her escort but clearly some-one at the restaurant did. The discreet hubbub around him of managers and waiters and hostesses marked him as a man of consequence, so Smita was excused her ruinous lack of heels. The fact that she'd deliberately dressed down was not lost on the DCP, nor was the air of quiet entitlement that enabled her to float above the soft scrum around them and dismiss the glances of the other women there, keenly aware though she obviously was of their scrutiny. The DCP approved of both and wasn't discomfited by the attention. He sank into the sofa he was guided to with pleasure, his alcoholic needs noted and attended to, and presently both officers had drinks and hors d'oeuvres in front of them. Smita crunched through the pastry of one such treat to get at the meat within and looked around, her eyes sharp in the dim light. The DCP regarded her with amusement.

"Good?"

"Not awful," allowed Smita.

"And these women?"

"More interesting than the men."

"Why?"

"Well. The men are cutouts. They work hard, or their fathers did. Now they're reaping the benefits of their social promotions. That's pretty much as far as it goes."

"But the girls?"

"Their interests are longer-term. They're thinking of their own dynasties, hierarchies. Even histories."

"Which means?"

"There's nothing so snobby as a Delhi girl with money but no roots."

"You know this from experience?" The DCP smiled.

"Trust me," she said simply. "I know."

"So tell me what they'll do to grow these roots."

"In theory, it's an easy progression. First, you need a home in the right part of town."

The DCP sipped at his drink.

"Your husband has to lose his rough edges. Or make enough money that they don't matter anymore."

The DCP nodded.

"Your children need to go to the right schools. If the money arrives too late for that, they need to go to the right colleges abroad. Even if the son is only going to inherit his father's position behind a store counter: he still needs an MBA."

The DCP was chuckling by now.

"The wife needs to go to the right parties, meet the right sort of women, surround herself with people like herself. Information will be traded, truths obfuscated, lies colluded in."

"Such as?"

"Small things, to begin with. An acquaintance will become a friend. Another friend from college will be introduced to the circle as the granddaughter of one of your own grandfather's closest friends. Your jeweler will become your 'family' jeweler, a position his family has had for generations. A guest at a club will be introduced as a member. A ring on a woman you don't like will be dismissed as fake. The others will agree. Things like that."

"And this builds a bond?"

"This builds dynasties. Come on, sir. You know this. Don't you?"

The DCP smiled again and shrugged and found himself in receipt of a fresh drink.

"Then tell me something I don't know."

"I'll tell you two."

The DCP waited.

"These women fear only one thing."

"Go on," said the DCP.

"Poverty. It's relative, I know. But to arrive in a Ford at a party full of BMWs is to risk social extinction."

"Really?" said the DCP skeptically.

"This city will forgive anything," said Smita quietly. "Your father can make bad drugs, your husband can be a repeat offender with the tax department. Your daughter could be a hit-and-run artist, your family dodgy arms dealers, your son-in-law in jail for bribing government officials to build crap roads. It's all fine, as long as you have money. But if you don't have money, you don't exist. I don't know about your city, sir, but the one thing my Delhi won't forgive is poverty."

The DCP watched her meditatively. "And the other thing?" he asked finally.

"Ah," she grinned. "I'll bet you another drink that one of these women is going to walk over in the next five minutes and ask you where you've met before."

The DCP laughed.

"You watch," said Smita over the rim of her glass.

She didn't need her five-minute buffer. Within about thirty seconds, across stalked a leggy woman of indeterminate age with a shawl drawn delicately over her bare shoulders.

"We've met, have we not?" she asked the DCP with a winning smile.

He shook his head with an equally open grin and said no, he hadn't had the pleasure, for if he had, he would certainly have remembered. She raised a ruthlessly tamed eyebrow and extended a slim hand across the table in a fluid motion. She introduced herself and bathed the DCP anew in another high-wattage flash. Not even at so-and-so's? she insisted. The DCP smiled and shook his head. Perhaps at such-and-such's? she went on, and the DCP said, no, he didn't know them either. She raised her other eyebrow, as if surprised that such socially ignorant creatures still existed in her city. She pushed and probed in her languid way and ignored Smita completely.

"But it's such a pity, is it not, Sajan," for of course she had made the transition to first names, "that one hasn't made your acquaintance yet?"

"Perhaps the fact that we know each other now will

console us both," he grinned in return. At which the lady gave him another smile, nodded in a perfunctory way at Smita, and turned on her heel.

"You don't know who she is," said Smita when she could breathe again, having laughed so hard a bit of her drink had gone up her nose.

"Should I?" asked the DCP.

"It's entirely likely her husband and son are both on those lists you should have been looking at this afternoon."

"Party boys?"

"No more so than she's a party girl."

"Does she suck her husband's earnings up her shapely nose as well?"

"I wouldn't be surprised," said Smita primly. "Not that she'll ever make the call. Women like her have men around who're happy to fill that role."

The DCP digested this. "Well dressed, at any rate," he said eventually.

"Very. Standard Delhi Dior slut."

"I beg your pardon?"

"Every time she gives her husband a blow job, she gets a new dress."

The DCP looked at her open-mouthed. Smita looked accusingly at her second drink, then they both laughed loudly and easily while the lady in question, surrounded by a court of women who looked exactly like her, frowned and then smiled and glanced again with a practiced flirtatiousness at the man whose acquaintance she had just made.

"But isn't it a good thing," protested the DCP eventually, "that women like that creature can have a social life and something to aspire to?"

"I'm not going to argue with that," said Smita simply. "You know why she came over, right?" she asked after a while.

"I'm not such an idiot," responded the DCP.

"Well?" twinkled Smita at her superior officer.

He settled himself more comfortably in his chair and took another pull at his glass, pausing with a grimace to pull some errant mint out of his teeth. "Well," answered the DCP, "clearly they recognized me, or asked the manager why he was making such a fuss over two superficially extremely ordinary people."

Smita nodded, her eyes sparkling.

"Okay. So they know I'm a cop. I'm not young, but I'm not middle-aged. I'm senior enough that an acquaintance with me is useful, in case one's son is caught driving drunk, for instance. I'd be good value at a party. I stand straight, speak without an accent, could tell some good stories when they're tired of talking about last month in London. And I've got almost twenty years left in the service. Who knows? I might make it to the very top. You can't put a price on a friendship like that. Even if it isn't actually a friendship."

"It is now."

"Are you serious?"

"Every time you're on TV. She's going to say, *My friend Sajan, whom I've known for years. Our fathers were friends.* You know she's going to call you home."

"By myself?"

Smita smiled and looked away. "They collect men like you, you know."

"Men like me have always been collectible. In this and every age."

Her eyes flashed as she looked back at him, to find his own fixed coolly on her.

"I'm not being arrogant. So will you be, when the time comes. It's up to you how you decide to take it."

She nodded slowly, then raised an eyebrow in his direction, the question implicit in the gesture.

"I make it up as I go along. In a city as old as this: who knows where the connections are?"

"But everything is connected?"

"Everything. That's what you have to be careful about."

"And once our time is done?"

"After the service? We play golf, bridge. Collect stamps, write petitions. Kill ourselves."

"Fade away?"

The DCP nodded. New drinks appeared in front of both of them. Smita protested, but not too strenuously, while the DCP merely smiled at the waiter.

"And who will remember us then?" asked the DCP rhetorically.

"Only the ones we were actually in school and college with."

The DCP stood and excused himself, set a course across the pebbles to where an attentive steward pointed him. He felt the eyes of the men and women of this new Delhi on him as he strode across the ancient ground and he smiled within at the strangeness of it, that he, a man of the old city, should be the one to feel out of place in such a setting. But it was only natural and fitting, he thought silently, swinging across the pristine yard. Things change, as do people and the cities they live in. Why should this place respect his lineage and his history, when it had turned its back on its own? It wasn't as if he was so out of place here, anyway. He enjoyed the drinks and the atmosphere and the attention of beautiful women, finite as these things were. And when it was all over, he chuckled to himself, he would have his history to sustain him. That, if nothing else, he had regardless.

The restroom was an artfully arranged space with standing sinks and urinals open to the stars yet closeted from view and everywhere was the clean smell of citronella and winter flowers. He stood and unzipped and pissed and thought to himself in a pleasantly maudlin way and realized with some surprise that he was indeed somewhat drunk. Then he felt rather than heard the presence at his shoulder and the cool hand replacing his own and the pleasure one feels when a hand that isn't your own pulls your foreskin back. The last drops fell and the slim body pressed against his and a breath was in his ear, then an expert hand put him away without zipping him up and steered him behind the spiffy little outhouse to a flight of stairs and up them to where the stars were bright and the night cold and clear, the garden with Delhi's new beauties strewn about it on one side, an ancient settlement hulking on the ground like a gray beast in the moonlight on the other, and behind it the sharp clean lines of Delhi's own hard-on, the Qutab Minar, an invitation, threat, and statement of intent all at the same time. So he turned to the form behind him whose hand was still inside the crotch of his trousers and he leaned across and murmured, soft and clear in her ear.

"Where have you been?"

They stood in the shade of the water tanks that flushed the toilets below and the old pipal tree that guarded the garden. Below them thrummed the liquid commerce of the alcoholically active, driven with regularity as the evening progressed to void their bladders. They could see lines of men arrive and disappear back to their tables and occasionally they chuckled as one of them, as for example Sajan or more accurately Razia a few moments earlier, committed the solecism of not washing his or her hands after. They stood close and looked about them and she shivered delicately and he held her closer and the light from the fairy strands in the garden and the tree was such that the world was clear but their own faces and bodies were shadowed, invisible to those on the ground and obscured even to each other.

"Where," he asked again, more gentle even than the first time, "have you been?"

"What does it matter, my Sajan?" replied the well-remembered voice. "I'm here now."

"It's been awhile."

"It's not like you missed me."

Sajan saw the fine head nod subtly at the waiting policewoman in one corner of the garden.

"Is she nothing for a woman like me to worry about?" wondered Razia.

"A woman like you has nothing to worry about from anyone."

"She is lovely, though."

Sajan could only agree. That Smita drew attention hadn't escaped his.

"These Punjabi girls," continued Razia. "Such a bloom when they're young. But do they age as we do?"

He felt rather than saw her eyes on his, so he bent and kissed her, slowly at first and then with more intensity, and presently they disengaged and so he asked:

"Who are you? The aunt or the niece?"

"You've asked before. The answer remains the same."

"Is it a question I shouldn't ask?"

"It's a question that wastes time we could well be using in other ways."

So he leaned in again and kissed his love deeply and wondered how a stranger could taste so familiarly sweet. Then her busy hands were shucking him effortlessly out of his trousers, her own supple form bending against the wall. Her hands pulled him to her and guided him under her casually lifted skirt and he was simultaneously cold and warm and present and transported and he could see over her shoulder and arching neck, as through the peephole of a kaleidoscope, a world that turned and twisted and shaped itself anew around falling, trailing lights and musical notes and he was as happy as only a man getting laid on a cold winter night can be. Then he was done, a sheen of sweat on his body and hers. He leaned to her neck and tasted it and the salt of her was on his tongue as she commenced to writhe anew and he was surprised to discover there was life in him yet.

"I'm finished," he half-protested.

"I'm not," she said over her shoulder, grinding against him.

"Have some patience," he pleaded.

"When you're as old as I am," she chuckled, "you'll learn that patience is the most overrated quality there is."

"My cock," observed Sajan, "is going to fall off."

"Better that than it atrophies."

He laughed into the hollow of her neck and cupped her breasts, her nipples hard and aware through the material of her dress as he rubbed his crotch against her ass, their union still unbroken. "What makes you think I'm not getting any other exercise?"

"What makes you think I care?"

"Don't you?"

She reached between her legs and his and cupped his sack and pulled him closer to her and suddenly he was completely rigid again, turgid as the lit-up monument that glowered above the scene in the bilious luminescence of its many floodlights.

"Don't you?" he asked again, more urgently, as her hips rocked back against his.

"More," she gasped, "than anything else in the world."

They took it easy this time. It was awhile before the lights strobed again for Sajan Dayal. He felt the rich fabric of her skirt and the cool tingle of her panties pulled to one side and he wondered why she wasn't wearing tights against the cold though he was thankful, that was one impediment to their current position he was happy to do without, and pretty soon he wasn't thinking of anything at all as his breath condensed in the night against her hair and then mingled with her own as she turned, finally, to him.

"I want a cigarette," she said. She was in his arms and they were still against the wall and the blood was still pounding in Sajan's head. He lit one for both of them. They listened idly to the roar of the flushes below and the tinkling of the music, and occasionally outside the boundary wall there was the passing of a bus or late-night celebrant. They passed the cigarette between them till it was done and still they clung to each other.

"Don't you want to clean yourself off?" he asked.

She twisted around and looked at him. "How?" she asked. "Why? I like the feel of you between my legs." She inclined her head to his crotch. "And you?" she asked demurely. "Won't all those people downstairs notice the stains on your trousers?"

He shook his head negligently, then suddenly remembered, his eyes opening wide. He rose as best he could, Razia protesting but still in his lap, and peered over the edge of the terrace to see an empty table where, a few minutes, a lifetime ago, sat a young policewoman with a drink in front of her. He sank back down against the wall. Razia sighed happily against his chest and he closed his eyes again.

"Every time I see you," he said softly, "something bad happens to me."

"Really? How so?"

"The first time you left, I thought it was forever. Did you ever consider what that did to me?"

The woman thought it over. "And then?"

"The next time, I almost got knifed."

"And now?"

"My junior officer is going to think I'm either mad or a complete idiot. Probably both."

"I wish I could tell you the disapproval of your underlings is the worst you can expect."

He thought this over and shook his head and asked whether she knew anything about a dead black drug dealer. She was quiet and then shook her head as well but it wasn't a negative, more a clearing of the air around her and inside herself.

"What about these finger-stealers?" he asked. "You knew there were more of them, didn't you? And what do they want with you?"

His arms were still around her warm body. The back of her head rubbed against his face in a soft cloud.

"Why didn't you tell me?" he whispered. "Why don't you tell me?"

"That was a miscalculation," she said. "We wanted you, Sajan. I wanted you. That creature was a means to an end. Now it seems there are more of them. Many more."

"Who is we?" asked Sajan, but there was no answer. "Should I be worried?"

She rose off his lap and composed herself against the lit heft of the Qutab Minar and her shadow enveloped him, her face utterly, completely dark.

"I want you to know how much I care for you. I always will." She paused and he waited and she said, "They want the same things everyone does. I want you to think about where your loyalties lie."

Then she was gone and a few moments later so was he. He returned to his table where the manager met him, jacketed and solicitous and carrying the tale of how Smita, after a wait of about twenty minutes, had finally left. He made no mention of her state and the DCP didn't ask.

"I met someone," said the DCP carelessly.

The manager waved his hands and told the DCP to come whenever he liked. The bill? inquired the DCP. The manager waved his hands again, his smile even more brilliant than before. The lady at the table across the yard had been waiting for him to reappear and she flashed a smile at him which he returned. Then the pebbles crunched under his feet, he was outside and in his car, and Mehrauli, frigidly entombed in the winter night with the Minar as its gravestone, was a receding speck in his mirror.

———————⬩———⬩———

It was, reflected the DCP, a mark of the minister's position that her seat behind the coffee service didn't detract from her authority. She dispensed good south Indian coffee and advice and the occasional nugget of gossip to her appreciative breakfast audience with the air of a society matron. Someone who didn't know her would have been forgiven for believing that was exactly what she was. The chrysanthemums were in their glory in the immense garden and the sun seemed as if it had been ordered up for the occasion. Her gardeners had been awake before dawn, she had confided to Sajan, to run their coarse brooms over the grass, so the dew was dispersed and frost didn't form to subvert the warmth of the winter sun into a burnt lawn. The gaily covered swing was currently occupied by the ex-editor of a daily paper and a lady friend, and here and there among the tables and chairs were spread various notable citizens of Delhi.

She presided over the assemblage with a quiet élan, her uniformed staff alert to her signals with fingers and eyes, filling a cup here, clearing a plate there. It was all superficially casual, a buffet breakfast with people told to sit where they found room and converse with those they found of interest. Jackets and sweaters for the men, knee-high boots for the younger women, sheltering sunglasses on everyone: the democracy of expensive fashion rendered everyone equal. But she was after all the minister and this was an invitation people fought over, and to be seated, as Sajan was, at her own little table with only a silver coffee service between them was to be exposed to the jealous glare of Delhi society as her current favorite.

"Some more to eat?" she asked in her well-bred voice.

The DCP shook his head with a smile and wondered when she'd get to the point.

"Coffee?" she inquired.

The DCP extended his cup and saucer with a word of thanks.

"I believe," said the minister, "you met a friend of mine last night."

The DCP raised his eyebrows politely and waited for more.

"Come, Sajan. Don't be coy. Don't you remember?"

"This city's full of your well-wishers, ma'am," murmured the DCP.

She favored him with a smile. "And what of those who don't wish me well?"

"That's why you have us."

This time she laughed, a girlish chortle that transformed her white-haired visage. "A nice place, I'm told. Such a lovely owner. He's been here himself. Last week, I think."

The DCP waited.

"Did you enjoy yourself?"

"Within the bounds of the law, yes."

"Yes, the law. I believe that charming young officer,

Dhingra, she was there as well? The girl I'm going to be meeting later?"

"She was," admitted the DCP.

She sipped at her coffee. "I'm glad you've found her. Her youth and background are assets, don't you think? She knows the new city in a way that your other colleagues might struggle with, hmm?"

"Perhaps," allowed the DCP.

"Yes. You must hold on to her. I often think that a good subordinate is like an attractive woman. You leave her alone for any length of time, someone else will come along and claim her."

The DCP looked straight at her. The kindly brown eyes looked back at him calmly, betraying absolutely nothing.

"Someone else," repeated the older woman. "Come, Sajan. Walk with me."

He extended his arm to her. She took his elbow with a smile and a word of thanks and they wandered into the garden, where the revelers talked and watched and waited.

She nodded to a man with a loud voice and a booming laugh who greeted her familiarly, using her first name. He held court at one table toward the center of the gathering, a few men and women as plushly appointed as himself draped around it. He made a joke loud enough for the minister to hear. She smiled politely and he brayed in response, the table following suit in close harmony. The DCP noted his heavy gold watch, the yellow metal in his ears and in the frames of his sunglasses and in the cuff links he exposed to the sun. The logo on the car keys in front of him wasn't lost on the policeman, nor the

clutch of phones his hand hovered over. The accoutrements were the same around the table and the lawn, and
the man who had been raised in a uniform wondered
with the irony native to him whether the other men and
women there knew just how rigid their own dress code
was.

"I can't bear that man," said the minister to the DCP.
She peered up at him and smiled at his astonishment,
then laughed again.

The DCP could feel as if it were palpable the envy of
the watching crowd.

"Such a climber. He really is obnoxious."

"He seems well connected," ventured the DCP.

"He certainly seems to think so. Now he's convinced
a few editors and a few businessmen and a few society
ladies."

"Which means that he is now, in fact, actually well
connected?"

"Indeed. What he actually is, is an ass. A loud one.
But he has his uses."

The DCP kept quiet as she guided him along her
famed rose beds. The bushes were bare, but in a week or
so would be aflame. He noted the thorns on the bushes
with interest. She noticed him looking.

"Local varieties. It isn't just about the look, for me.
The way a rose smells and feels is important too, don't
you think? I have beds for the fancier hybrids. But I pre-
fer these, the ones our ancestors would have smelled
when their time came every year. Thorns and all." She
bent to one and looked at something that caught her
attention, then straightened again, her hand still upon
the DCP's arm.

"Thorns and all," she repeated. "Like our city. We know its drawbacks and its failings and we're still loyal, are we not, Sajan?"

He looked away from her then and into the sky. He felt her eyes on the side of his face so he, by and by, composed himself and smiled down at her and said, "That man is going to have me over for dinner, isn't he?"

"Your number's already on at least two of his phones."

"I've never met him."

"He's seen you here. That's enough."

They ambled along her beds, her beagles now strolling at her ankles, clad in red coats with white paws stitched across them.

"This is the currency of this city, Sajan. It always has been. Influence and its peddling are the marks of a capital. Wealth is new. Power isn't."

"There were merchants in this city before."

"They knew their place."

"The new ones don't?"

The minister considered this. "Perhaps you're right," she allowed. "Money and power have always been close friends."

"So what exactly is new?" asked the DCP.

They were now at the farthest reach of the garden, her dogs the only auditors of their conversation.

"People like us prosper, Sajan, because we protect the interests of people like ourselves. Is this not true?"

The DCP waited.

"I'm a politician functioning in a democracy. I keep my voters happy, they keep reelecting me."

The DCP nodded.

"Except we both know it isn't that simple. I have to pick and choose the people I represent. I simply can't guard every single person's interest."

The DCP nodded again, though with less conviction.

"It isn't in their interest for me to spread myself too thin. It isn't in my interest. And if it isn't in my interest, well, it isn't in *our* interest. Is it?"

The DCP turned his shaded eyes to the watching crowd. They all seemed suddenly very far away.

"It's very simple, really. It's a question of alignment. Whose interests do you serve, Sajan?"

"This city and its citizens'."

"Exactly. Yet do you sometimes feel the wrath and ire of those selfsame citizens when you're helping them, hmm?"

Sometimes, nodded the DCP.

"But you continue."

The DCP nodded yet again, like a snake before its charmer.

"Why, Sajan? Why do you continue? Because you were trained to? Because you were told to? Or simply because you feel you know better? Because you're better placed, oftentimes, to know some poor illiterate's interests better than he or she does?"

The DCP waited and the minister, alive to his discomfort, laughed lightly and touched his arm again.

"You don't have to answer that," she said with a twinkle. "All you have to do is remember how long people like ourselves have been doing this. We've run this city, in one way or another, for centuries. In all that time, over all those years: don't you think it inevitable that our interests and this city's would become the same?"

Who is *we*? thought the DCP, shivering in an emerald

garden under a blue sky in a wintry, contested city. He didn't name his question, though his silence proclaimed it. The old woman with the kind eyes looked at him shrewdly, and then coquettishly away.

"A long time," she said, savoring the words. "People like you and I, Sajan. Dilliwalas to the core. This new Delhi too will fade away, and people like us will be watching over its demise and preserving its future."

"Quite a responsibility."

"It's one I'm glad to bear," replied the old woman. "Are you?"

The DCP looked away again across her immaculate garden, where the man she couldn't bear was announcing his mirth to his circle again. She saw what he was looking at and her expressive mouth came together in a moue of disapproval, dissolving almost immediately into a smile.

"My grandson taught me the most lovely word yesterday," she said.

The DCP waited.

"He's twelve, quite aware of everything around him. He reads the sillier papers. He saw a photo of that man and said he was a *player*. Do you know the word?"

The DCP indicated his possession thereof.

"Then the boy looked at me and smiled and said, *But that's only what he thinks, isn't it?* So we both laughed. His mother walked in and demanded to know what we were chortling about. Of course we said nothing at all."

"Of course," agreed the DCP.

"*Player,*" mused the minister. "Do you know what the problem is with men like him? Publicists, marketing gurus, social climbers, and the like?"

"They all look the same?"

She laughed again, a genuine gurgling that ripened in her belly and shook her slim frame.

"Aside from their ridiculous watches and cars and overly made-up tarts, yes. The other thing that bedevils them is that they're all successful. Really successful. They're so successful they're blind to what it is they've mastered."

The DCP waited while the minister gave him a sidelong glance.

"The present, Sajan. They're men of the moment. That's all they are, all they'll ever be. They'll have their cars and cigars and they'll finally get their club memberships and it will be as if they've effaced the past and recast their futures. But it isn't true, because they have no understanding of the past."

She touched his arm again. They walked back toward the waiting court scattered amongst the china-strewn tables on the carpet-like lawn.

"Every tyrant who came here thought his words and deeds would endure. The smart ones knew they'd fail, but they fought and raged and tried anyway. We fade away, my dear. It is part of our condition. Yet even my enemies think I'll never go away." She chuckled quietly. "What an absurd idea. Women who won't die. Where else but Delhi would people even think such a thing? If you don't know your own history, then how in heaven's name can you know anything of the future?"

They reached the waiting assembly, the minister casting a word here, a smile there. "Such players . . . how nice that they think they're in charge, or close to it. When we both know, don't we, that they are in fact in the game only to be played. There is most certainly a game afoot. Men like you, men of vision and integrity, with an ear to the past and an eye to the future: men of Delhi, my dear Sajan; you must decide where your loyalties lie."

The sun beat down without any warmth on the embattled DCP. His head ached with the echoes of what Razia had said the night before. A wrinkled but still soft hand came up to his face, in full view of the incandescent throng. He bent his head to the woman's as she looked deeply into his eyes.

"This dead drug dealer. It would be unseemly for our players to be inconvenienced by one such as him. And these nine-fingered men, these vampires and werewolves and women who won't die. Let them remain what all Delhi thinks them to have been. Closed cases. Games for young children. Stories." She smiled up at him in the glittering light. "You'll handle this for me, I trust?"

She turned away. The DCP felt as if they were coals, the eyes of the watchers. He wondered whether the braying player's number was in the dead dealer's call lists, the dealer's name in the player's mobile phone. He heard the man laugh his raucous laugh again and felt himself flush in the heat of the watching crowd's attention. Who else had been spoken with? he wondered. Who else so completely compromised?

He thought of the way he'd been led to Angulimala, the fact that the minister had personally asked for him to address the gang-rape. He thought of the accolades his team had received, the patronage they were seen to enjoy.

"We" had reeled him in effortlessly.

He waited a moment longer, nodded to the men and women he knew in the crowd, and walked outside to where his car was waiting to take him to the awards ceremony. The policeman at the gate threw him a smart salute, then the DCP was outside on the shaded roads of Delhi and the red beacon atop his official white car was no comfort at all.

———————

The open parade ground where he and Smita were to receive their medals wasn't far away. He arrived there with plenty of time to spare. He knew from past experience that the minister wouldn't be perfectly on time, but she wouldn't keep them waiting too long either. The entire ceremony, with press photos after, would only take an hour. It was slated to be over well before lunch. Fine by me, thought the DCP sourly. Enough time for me to burrow under some paperwork at the office and mull my options in privacy and solitude.

The sun was, if possible, even more brilliant here. The marquee set off to one side was an improbably festive color, the big red sashes on the chairs and the flowers in the vases in front of the first-row sofas gay accessories to the smiling visages of the soon-to-be-honored cops. The entire space reeked of esprit de corps and smug Delhi officialdom. The DCP wrinkled his nose. He felt in his pocket for his cigarettes, considering the advisability of lighting up in such close proximity to his senior officers, glancing around distractedly for someone from his team. He was momentarily blinded by the sun as he turned this way and that and smelled Smita's fresh perfume and shampoo before he saw her at his shoulder.

"Congratulations," she said archly, "for becoming the light of someone's eyes."

He squinted at her as his eyes adjusted to the glare.

"So close to that person," she continued, "that you're lost to everyone else."

He laughed shortly. "I didn't think you even knew songs of that era."

"My father used to sing it to me when I was a baby. When I grew up, I remembered the tune and used to hum it. YouTube showed me the full song and the full message."

"Rather a sour message, don't you think?"

"Why? Weren't you happy last night?"

The DCP looked at her steadily, then turned away.

"'Ajeeb dastan hai yeh,' written by Shailendra, sung by Lata. Lovely song. You know he was barely older than me when he passed away?"

"May heaven save you from such a pass," replied Smita demurely.

"Indeed. You remember the first verse?"

Smita's eyes were invisible behind her sunglasses.

"The singer is sitting on a boat with her love, who of course is with someone else. She asks why smoke always accompanies the light and she wonders whether she is in a dream, or whether she has, in fact, woken from one to find herself in this position."

"Jealous, perhaps," said the young policewoman, in the smokeless light of the brilliant sun.

"Certainly unhappy. If she is jealous, then I wonder

if that particular emotion has ever been more beautifully portrayed."

"Smoke helps. And dreaming."

"No doubt," said the DCP. A burst of sirens and a cloud of dust announced the arrival of the minister's cavalcade. "Still, a lovely song. Shall we?"

———————

The minister departed as she had arrived, in a cloud of bonhomie and goodwill and expensive perfume. The senior officers of the Delhi Police lingered after her departure in the healingly dense fog of self-congratulation that settles in and after such events. The regulation tea was supplemented by cigarettes and invitations to each other's homes that evening to celebrate such medal and that citation, and the city at large was reckoned to be lucky to have such a committed and fearless corps of defenders. Smita laughed and smiled and wondered whether one of her superior officers would take a loving fumble at her in such an inappropriate place, while the DCP stood off to one side and accepted his congratulations in his own fashion.

They were both entirely unprepared for the call.

Kapoor had brusquely informed them that the drug dealer's girlfriend had been found in Sanjay Van, a remnant of the old Ridge Forest that stretched from Mehrauli to Jawaharlal Nehru University. The body was cold, the voice on the telephone frightened.

The DCP and Smita were in his car and on their way, the beacon flashing.

"Who found it?"

"An old woman. Probably gathering firewood. She was scared."

"Who did she speak with?"

"One of our boys."

"How did she know to call him?"

"She called emergency. Smart operator on duty; he put two and two together and routed her to us."

"One of your nephews?"

"He will be."

The DCP grunted. "The local cops?"

"Haven't told them. I don't want them spoiling the scene. It was just phoned in moments ago. If you're lucky, you'll get there first."

"We'll be there in less than five minutes."

"I'll see you there. I'm already on the way."

The DCP and Smita entered the park from the north side. Their car made its way to the wall through a shaded area of calm roads and quiet offices bathed in the soft light of official patronage. A Tibetan monastery guarded the gate.

Inside, the park was a verdant dream, well-marked paths close to the wall disappearing into thickets of old trees. The traffic noise of the busy roads that bordered it was hushed. It seemed to Smita that she could hear things she never would have with the normal amplified volume of the city outside.

"How will we find the body?"

"Good question," said the DCP.

The woman on the line had given the officer she spoke with a landmark, the resting place of a saint of centuries past whose tranquil gravesite was a magnet for those wandering about in the forest. Smita, her eyes now more attuned to the sun up high and the earth-level gloom, noticed broken bottles by the side of the path and the debris of encounters both psychedelic and carnal. A bird chirped in her ear as she reached a tumble-down fragment of wall. She glanced over at the DCP, who grinned at her and waved as if to say, *After you.*

She sighed, hitching up her dressy sari and hoping the crumbling stone and masonry would support her heels, and started up the slope. Her glossy black hair gleamed in the sun and the silk of her sari glinted and the DCP, starting up the wall in her wake, watched the curve of her ass and the slim waist above and wondered without guilt at how happy he would have been if she'd been wearing a skirt. Her shoulders shook as if she could read his mind, her hair tossed as she paused, searching for a true foothold, the sun and the warmth and clear blue sky smiling down all around them. The DCP chuckled to himself. His junior officer, hearing his good humor, looked down over her shoulder at him.

"Nothing," he said airily. "Just this wall. It dates from when Delhi was still a Hindu kingdom."

"Really?" said Smita, resuming her ascent.

"It was tended to and added to by the sultans who came later. When the new cities were built, this one's fortifications became part of the new grid. Just imagine. You're stepping on something men have been climbing up for a thousand years at least. It's something to behold, isn't it?"

Smita reached the top and peered at the DCP, wondering if he was pulling her chain. Then she looked up and saw the forest and the quiet buildings where their car was, the new city beyond, here and there minarets old and new, and the new towers in the distance, the hills to one side and then the Qutab Minar, and she was struck by the sudden beauty of her difficult city. She stood quiet and shining on that ancient wall while the DCP clambered up beside her.

The cry of a kite was the only sound. A jetliner drew its vapor trails across the crystal sky and then there was another one and still they stood there, and if an arm that belonged to the DCP went across his junior's shoulder who could have blamed either him or her? He didn't, though, her silk blouse and pashmina shawl still strangers to his touch. But he could feel the goose pimples on her arms as if they were on his own.

"Wow," she said eventually.

The DCP nodded. Then they heard the voices from the dargah below them, a quiet site nestled against the wall with a view of green trees. A trio of men in prayer caps waited amiably for them to make the trip down the flight of steps.

They exchanged pleasantries, the DCP asking whether they knew of an incident worthy of the police being called in.

"Here?" asked the eldest of the three men good-naturedly. "Young people and drinkers come in and do their business all the time, but they have the good sense and taste not to do it here. This is holy ground for everyone."

The DCP smiled and left a currency note on the cheerful cloth spread before the saint's resting place. The men acknowledged the gesture and bade them both farewell. The two officers ascended the wall again, this time steering their footsteps in the direction of Mehrauli. A pack of dogs sniffed around them, then disappeared. Pretty soon the dargah was out of sight as well.

"Well, now what?" asked Smita. "Where's this bloody woman?"

"The wood-gatherer," replied the DCP mordantly, "or the corpse?"

"Either," sighed Smita. "These are good shoes, sir."

The DCP looked at her feet and beckoned to her to stop for a rest. The younger officer sat down on the edge of the wall, her back to the carpet of trees below. She leaned down and massaged her ankles and then, with a muttered curse, took one of her shoes off. She rubbed at her foot gingerly, then with more vigor. The DCP lit a cigarette and tried not to notice her stockinged feet.

"I'm sorry I disappeared last night," he said eventually.

Smita kept rubbing, now focused on the other foot.

"Perhaps you felt abandoned."

"I felt like a bloody fool."

The DCP nodded, his eyes on the path before them, which lay along the top of the old city wall.

"We're not so far away from there, you know. The restaurant."

Smita raised her eyes.

"Only about a kilometer as the crow flies."

"Do you want to go back there?" asked Smita quietly.

"I'd like to find that dead woman," said the DCP. "But I wouldn't mind a chance to have a drink with you. Again. If you feel up to it."

"Would that be appropriate, sir?" asked his junior officer, her eyes now back to her feet.

The DCP considered the top of her head, then turned away. He heard her slip her shoes on and rise.

"It's amazing how far a kilometer can seem," said her voice at his shoulder.

She looked around them, the trees, the broken but still belligerent wall, the silence and the distance of the years, and then she smiled, and the DCP smiled as well. They resumed their journey along the wall. A group of young men were kicking a ball around a little open area where the wall suddenly dipped. The DCP reached for his phone, noted the strength of the signal, and was about to dial Kapoor to compare notes on the nonappearance of the body when he heard Smita's call. She ran across the little clearing to where a strip of cloth covered what was revealed immediately to be the body of a young Indian woman who was utterly naked and clearly dead. The DCP followed more sedately in her footsteps, noticing the cessation of the kicking of the ball behind him, and he remembered what he'd seen right before he'd reached for his phone: a woman of advanced years squatting right by where the men were having their game and there seemed to be no pile of wood anywhere near her. He dug deeper as he walked, without turning his head, and noted with clarity the kaffiyeh under the upturned lapel of the winter jacket one of the young men wore against the cold. His hand pressed the call button, dialing Kapoor's number, waited a second or two, and hit *End*. He noticed the absence of goalposts and the proximity of better grounds outside the park in Mehrauli itself. He thought with a pang of self-reproach how utterly composed this pack of young men was in the face of a beautiful woman in a sari discovering a dead woman wearing nothing practically next to them. He felt his hand searching uselessly for the weapon that wasn't where it should be due to the security protocol of the awards ceremony that morning and he knew the young woman officer in front of him carried no gun either. Smita was kneeling next to the dead body, her hands searching for her phone in her dressy little bag. He reached her side and one hand went gently to her shoulder, the other still tight around his phone. She looked up at him with surprise and heard him say, quietly and clearly, "Run."

She looked into his shaded eyes and past him, then down at the corpse. Then she was gone, a shimmer of silk and a clatter of heels, her hair a glint in the hard sunlight.

The DCP watched her go from the corner of his eye as she skirted the edge of the clearing, back toward the path to the dargah. The phone rang in his hand. He answered it and said, "Past the dargah. Five hundred yards. Find the girl."

Then he dropped it on the ground to free his hands and the pack of young wolves was upon him. He swung and spun and raised his guard, and presently measured his length on the ancient ground, on the hitherto safe side of Delhi's oldest surviving wall. Built to keep generations of barbarians out, he thought inconsequentially as he slipped away. But what of the killers within the city itself?

He felt the jab of the needle, heard the shouting on the periphery. He saw a man wearing a kaffiyeh pull away from him, a finger cocked against his head. He thought he saw Kapoor, Smita behind him. Then he saw nothing at all.

Kapoor had found Smita running toward him on the wall. His weapon was already in his paw. He brought it up over her shoulder as she ran into his burly arms. His phone was at his ear as he ordered up an armed team from the police station in Mehrauli. He disconnected, watched Smita's face, his arm still outstretched beyond her shoulder.

A gentle finger came to her cheek, his gun arm now resting on her shoulder. "You alright, girl?" he asked in Punjabi.

Smita nodded, blinking quickly, then turned back toward where the DCP was. "Hurry," she urged.

"Wait at the dargah," he said.

She looked at him and then his gun, said, "Thanks, but I'm safer with you," and started running back along the wall. The bear lumbered after her, the trees sliding away to one side, the hill to the other, the Qutab Minar beckoning them on.

A young man in a kaffiyeh stood in their path. He was about fifty yards away. Smita stopped to the side, Kapoor dropped into a shooting crouch. The man seemed to smile, threw them a two-fingered salute, and was gone over the edge of the wall. Smita ran to the edge and saw a pile of scree and a man scrambling down it and then he was in the trees and lost to her. Kapoor cursed and they resumed their sprint. They came around the bend in the wall, the decline and its clearing in front of them. They saw the DCP's body lying off to the side, by the cold girlfriend of the just-as-dead drug dealer. The soccer players and their elderly female mascot had melted away.

Smita ran to the DCP's side, knelt, and felt for his

pulse. Kapoor huffed up next to her, his weapon still in his hand. "I'm about ready to stop seeing bodies," he said between laboring breaths. She nodded with relief, reaching for her phone. Kapoor stopped her. "Who are you calling?"

"Medical backup."

"He's alive, isn't he? Leave him be. If they wanted him dead, he'd be that way."

She gazed at him, long and wonderingly, before putting her phone away.

"How long," asked Kapoor meditatively, "before the local cops get here?"

"Five minutes. Maybe. You told them to hurry."

"Okay. Lucky for us those idiots left his phone. Help me," said Kapoor, bending down to the DCP. With a muttered oath and a push from Smita, he hoisted the senior officer onto his shoulder, after pocketing his phone. "I'll be at the dargah. You're in charge of this body. The uniforms won't question your authority. If they ask, say it was phoned in, and the woman who made the call took off. The DCP was never here. If they probe any further, ice them."

The bear lumbered off with his sack on his shoulder. Smita collected her nerves and a cigarette from her bag and smoked till the local cops arrived in a fuss and a flurry, their weapons out and their dicks hard.

"Who's in charge?" said the oldest one, peremptorily.

Smita looked around exaggeratedly, then back at the uniformed cop, taking a drag and exhaling slowly. She kept quiet, as she'd seen Kapoor and the DCP do, merely watching the other man. He wilted and turned back to his colleagues, who were looking this way and that.

"Where's Kapoor sahib?" asked one of them suspiciously.

"He'll be along soon," said Smita coolly. She watched one of the new arrivals edge toward the body of the dead woman and stopped him in his tracks.

"Watch the scene, please," she said pleasantly enough. "I'm sure Kapoor sahib wouldn't want people trampling around."

"He wanted us armed and here at once. What's the problem?" asked the suspicious one.

"A dead body in the middle of nowhere isn't problem enough?"

The others accepted this without any apparent fuss and, having searched the periphery of the clearing, started lounging around. Smita finished her cigarette, pretended to examine the body, and when that was done walked over to the wall. She saw Kapoor's head appear over the lip of the path, then the rest of him. She heard the word "bitch" as she passed a group of the uniforms. Smita didn't even try to hide her smile.

———— ✦ ————

"The phone," said Kapoor, "was key. If they'd taken it, we'd have been screwed."

A few days had elapsed since the DCP's assault. Smita had fallen in line with Kapoor's thinking unquestioningly. She felt herself to be part of a game the parameters of which she could only dimly glimpse, and his was a support she desperately needed. So she did as she was told and felt with a sense of comfort that to trust as she trusted Kapoor was a sign of strength and not weakness. She knew that she may well have been rationalizing a particularly bad choice to herself, but she couldn't disregard the way he seemed, quietly and unobtrusively, to have taken charge of both the situation around the DCP and her.

"Clearly we were set up," said Kapoor.

Smita nodded.

"That young operator who transferred the call to our task force—I'm checking on him. Perhaps I was too quick to think he was up to being part of the family."

"What do you think they hoped to achieve?"

"They didn't want him dead. Or you, for that matter. They didn't even pursue you. Perhaps all they wanted was a finger. Perhaps that's all they ever want. Stupid fucks. No imagination. No ambition."

Smita kept quiet. They were in Kapoor's unmarked personal car, headed somewhere on the western edge of the sprawling city. The airport lay to their left as Kapoor swung toward the west.

"Perhaps they just wanted to shake the tree. See what fell out. Prove they can strike wherever they want. Whenever they want. Scare us. All of us."

"And?"

"Leaving the phone screws the last part of that plan. Nobody knows the DCP's gone."

Smita nodded again. Clever management had restricted the number of people who knew the DCP was missing to a mere handful, who all thought he was unwell. His official driver was the only person who knew he'd actually disappeared. Kapoor had set him straight that same day.

"Perhaps," said Kapoor slowly, "it was a test."

"How so?"

"To see how we'd react."

"Who wants to know?"

Kapoor gave her a sidelong look. "Take your pick." He thought for a moment, then continued, "In a situation where you have no cards, and we have none, remember; in a situation like that, you bluff. Folding isn't an option. These guys are smart. They're well informed. They knew I'd call you in and not the local uniforms. They knew you were close by, and unarmed. How'd they know that?

"They knew you'd be first on the scene. The phone they used was reported missing only that morning. The owner is legitimate. They knew how long the uniforms would take. Even if they didn't, they probably had someone there who'd warn them when they were en route. Then the dead girl. Stab wounds, just like the boyfriend. What's their problem with her?"

"There's no proof they killed her. They could just have found her."

"Correct," said Kapoor. "There's nothing to connect these fools to either dead body. Who wants them dead is the question. And what do they have to do with these fucking finger-snatchers?" He rolled down a window a bit and lit a cigarette. "You know why I kept the DCP's situation quiet, right?"

"It didn't help us for anyone else to know."

"Exactly. In fact, if someone came sniffing around, that would help us."

"But nobody did. Not to me."

Kapoor nodded glumly. "Nor me."

They had come out of a tunnel underpass and were

now climbing a long flyover. Old villages brimming with new construction hurtled past. Gurdwaras, mosques, gyms, and homes: all mere inches away from the flyover, their commerce a flash in the corners of the officers' eyes. The wind through the chink in Kapoor's window was icy, cold enough to bring an ache to Smita's head, but she was glad for it. She wanted clarity, and that particular commodity was in desperately short supply.

"So," said Kapoor. "This is what we know. There's a gang, a cult, a sect of nine-fingered men on Delhi's peripheries. What's the worst thing about them?"

"That we know so little?"

"Correct. Then. There's that woman."

"Razia."

"Right. She's the key, or so the DCP thinks. But to which lock? And what did that dead freak want with her anyway?"

"Was it just him?"

Kapoor thought that over.

"What do they want?" asked Smita desperately.

But Kapoor didn't know the answer to that one either. "Do you know where we're going?" he asked eventually.

"To see the DCP, I presume."

He nodded. "The dargah keepers were very helpful. I'll have to find a way to reward them for keeping the DCP till I could have him picked up."

Smita waited for him to continue, but Kapoor smoked quietly and drove.

"What were you chatting about when that whole thing happened?" asked Kapoor after a while.

"God knows. He was probably lecturing me on the history of that broken wall. You know how he is."

They both laughed.

"Wait. Remember I told you he'd taken me for a drink the night before, and how he'd disappeared?"

Kapoor nodded.

"He tried, I think, to apologize. I told him not to bother. Or something. What I wanted to tell him is how humiliated I was. I can't remember if I did or not."

"That's not humiliation, girl. Not even close."

"To be left alone in a bar while twenty overprivileged Dilliwalis bitch about you? Really?"

Kapoor laughed mirthlessly. "I suppose you're right. But there are plenty of women in these places who'd die for your problems." He gestured outside the window of the car, where new towers had sprouted from the dusty ground, interspersed with the bastis of the men and women who worked for their inhabitants.

Something in his tone arrested Smita. He could feel her eyes on him so he glanced at her, a measuring gaze, before turning his eyes to the road again.

"I have a . . . niece. She lives here," he said quietly. "She made a wrong turn. Got mixed up with the wrong man. Something like that. You understand?"

Smita waited.

"She fell out with her family. They . . . We'd like to see her. Her child. Be part of her little family and her little life. But hard things were said. Then we couldn't help her anymore. You understand?"

Kapoor's profile was dark against the glare of the clear cold day outside.

"It's so easy to fall through the cracks in this city. A wrong choice, a harsh word. Help denied and then, when it arrives, turned away. You know?"

Smita shook her head, for in truth she didn't know. Kapoor looked at her and smiled.

"A child. Rent. Food. The wrong friends. An absent family. Who knows how it happens?"

Smita looked away then.

"I'll tell you what this city does do," said Kapoor. "It makes it really easy to survive, provided you're willing to compromise."

———————————

The hours after his beating passed in a hallucinatory haze for the DCP. The trauma of his punishment coupled with the narcotic he'd been injected with rendered him incapable of any physical or mental exertion. At best, he'd remember later, he collected impressions.

A cotton mattress that was lumpy. A duvet that wasn't quite clean. Cheap plastic emulsion on the walls that gleamed in the light of the fluorescent tubes.

He couldn't remember the color of the walls. Or the time. Or when he slept.

He remembered the door not being far away, but his legs couldn't get him there.

He remembered a child. A young girl. She sat next to him on the bed. There were no other chairs. No furniture save the bed he was on. A cold wall next to the bed. No heater in the room.

She read. She talked. She ate.

She slept. Next to him.

He would remember her presence, her toes up against his under the duvet, her gentle snores.

At some stage he would wonder what time it was.

A cheap curtain drawn across the window in one wall. Day. Night. Always drawn.

He slept.

He was walked, he would remember, to a bathroom whose floor was wet. He was held up as he pissed into the squat toilet. Next to it lay a plastic bucket full of water in which a giant immersion rod bubbled away. A tiny window at eye level with a view of pigeon shit and pipes. He finished his pee. He threw up.

He slept.

He woke up and the girl was gone. To school? Was it day?

She returned and did her homework. There was a smell of dal and then he was fed too.

He threw up again and fell asleep. He woke up and the girl was asleep next to him.

There was a man. A big man who helped him to the bathroom. He brought him his food and soothed the girl to sleep.

There was a woman. A quiet pretty thing who read to the girl and helped her with her homework and disappeared periodically when the bell rang.

Once, a man he didn't recognize came into the room. Sit here, said the first man. On the bed. The DCP moved his feet to make room. The new man averted his gaze from the quiet eyes of the young girl. A few minutes, said the first man. Don't worry.

A TV blared. A man walked quickly past the open door. The stranger got up just as quickly and disappeared into the other room.

He slept.

At some stage the DCP knew what was going on.

He saw the man answer his phone and the bell and the woman leave the room when she had to and the girl on the bed turn her face to the wall. He saw the quiet rhythm of the day and night, the dal and rice and the oatmeal in its time and the getting ready for school and the coming home and the homework and the reading and the sleeping and the eating. He saw the expectant faces of the men who walked in, the quick steps of the sated as they walked out with eyes averted.

He saw something familiar in the face of the young woman but he couldn't put a name to it. He saw the arm of the man around the young woman's shoulder as they sat over the sleeping figure of their child. He'd hear the blare of the TV from the other room and he'd know another man had finished.

He studied, he'd remember later, the father in the bright light of the tubes when he knew he was otherwise occupied. He knew the father's name was tattooed on the woman's arm. He'd seen it. He'd seen their laughter and their bond, he'd seen the man leave to pick up the guys from the main road and seat them next to his sleeping child as they waited their turn.

Finally, he managed to keep something down.

He slept.

———— ·—·— ————

They pulled up outside a nondescript three-story house in a dirty lane of a crowded basti. The streets were full of small traders selling biscuits and brooms to each other. Every other storefront was a beauty salon. Every woman in this mean little colony wore bright nail polish.

Kapoor took a deep breath. "Ready?"

Smita nodded, and they ascended the stairs.

A man opened the door to Smita's knock. He smiled at her, then saw Kapoor's granite eyes. He dropped his own and let them in. A young woman walked out of a small room to one side. She ran to Kapoor and threw her arms around him. He kissed the top of her head as he hugged her. A hairy paw came up, the back of one finger delicately stroking her cheek.

"You alright, girl?" he asked in Punjabi.

The woman nodded and smiled up at him and Smita saw his eyes were warm and full of love. Then she was gone and he looked at the man, his eyes hard again.

She came out leading the still groggy DCP. He smiled at the woman, shook hands with the man, took Kapoor's offered arm. Smita wanted to hug him but contented herself with a smile, which was tiredly returned.

"We told people you were unwell," she ventured.

"I'm glad you didn't have to lie," was the dry reply.

He switched his support to Smita, while Kapoor turned back into the house. The DCP and Smita made their slow way down to the street and the waiting car.

"Is that woman actually . . ." started Smita.

"They're certainly alike."

"How does something like that happen? I mean, she's a policeman's . . ."

The DCP looked away. "She isn't the first. She won't be the last."

"Where do you find a crack that large to fall through, sir?"

"In this city? Everywhere."

Smita flushed and thought of humiliation and its

variants and degrees. She imagined a place where the police didn't know where the whores lived and she knew Delhi wasn't that city. She thought with a shudder that perhaps they were lining up for their freebies knowing the poor woman's bond with Kapoor. She thought of the daily weight of being Kapoor. She wanted to scream, but she remembered his warm eyes, the finger to the young woman's cheek, the quiet question in Punjabi.

"He wants to say hello to the child, I think," said the DCP.

Smita wasn't finished. "Why doesn't she stop? He can help her, if anyone can."

"Maybe it isn't that simple. Maybe she doesn't want the help."

"Why in the world not?"

"Why not indeed," murmured the DCP. "Can it be true of this city that a woman only accepts a man's help if it is on her own terms?"

Smita looked away, her cheeks aflame.

"I take it he's got things well in hand?" asked the DCP quietly.

"Such as they are, yes, he does."

"He trusts you. I've seen that."

Smita nodded.

"Every man deserves a second chance," said the DCP, lighting a cigarette he'd just taken from the man upstairs.

Smita looked at his carefully averted face, then up at the sliver of sky visible through the dense lanes where Kapoor's connections had their lives.

"So many nephews," continued the DCP. "A man like him needs a niece or two as well."

A stray dog gamboled about them, was chased away by a pack of kids who ran past in a burst of good cheer, the tails of their winter jackets flying gaily behind them. Kapoor came out of the gate, his face a mask.

"Shall we?" he asked, climbing into his car.

The DCP was in front with Kapoor. Smita was in the back.

"We're working on the dead girl," began Kapoor.

"Not too hard, I imagine?"

"She's a druggie. The signs are all over her. It won't be difficult."

"And the Russian girl?"

"I put her on a plane back to where she came from last night."

The DCP nodded.

"What's going on, sir?" asked Smita from the backseat.

"I don't know," answered the DCP with a shrug.

"Can't the girl help?"

"No. What she knows is something none of us can control. Better that we get rid of her. Before someone else does."

"Permanently," added Kapoor.

"So the drug dealer and his girlfriend, their deaths are just going to be swept under the carpet?"

"There's plenty of room," observed the DCP.

Smita laughed bitterly and looked out the window.

"We can't solve every case," said Kapoor softly. "There will be others. We all know that."

"But what about this one?"

"It isn't going anywhere," said the DCP tiredly. "The players are still here. You'll get your chance again. Soon."

"We're just going to let this one go?"

"Nobody wants this case solved. I suggest you try and understand that."

"Compromise, girl," said Kapoor. His eyes met hers in the rearview mirror. "Sometimes you have to. It's only this difficult the very first time."

His car accelerated up the long bridge. The bright orange disc of the sun was huge in the winter sky, but it seemed to Smita that there was neither light nor warmth to be had in her city, so she slumped back into her seat, drew her coat around her, and waited for the journey to end.

CHILDREN IN SPRING

Spring's light touch was upon the populace and flowers bloomed in the parks and roundabouts of Delhi. The days were warm and sun-filled, the nights cool enough for wool. The temperature of the breeze, warm from the south and east and cold from the north and west, alternated, it seemed, only to bring smiles to Dilliwalas everywhere. The first silk-cottons of the year were thinking of springing into bloom and the kachnars had already done so. There were beds of sweet williams and rows of hollyhocks and snapdragons and daisies of all varieties competed for the wanderer's attention. The roses were in bloom in the better class of garden, there were dahlias in pots and ice cream in the streets, and if you looked up the clouds sported gaily in the empyrean.

Yet the markets of bourgeois Delhi were chilled and empty, and the carts of the ice cream vendors saw little custom from the families they depended on. Fear stalked the day-lit streets of the city. The DCP and his team from Crime Branch, still smarting from the defeats of the previous few weeks, were called into action again to quell the increasingly querulous demands of a restive citizenry.

It had happened, as chroniclers of those events would henceforth remember, because of the bitterly contested admissions to the primary schools of the city. Parents of little emperors-in-waiting were desirous of getting their absurdly talented progeny into the best possible private schools. These were not only incubators of talent. It was taken as a given that the other parents there would be "people like us," with the same goals and education and taste in footwear. Thus the little baba and baby would be gaining not only a good education, but also like-minded friends for life, the best possible hedge against an uncertain future. Daddy would retain his weekend four-ball with men he'd known his entire life and Mama's coffee circle would grow, and when the time came, in twelve years, to organize Junior's Ivy League admission, the stamp of this school on his transcript could only help.

This process repeated itself down the line till it reached the level of the fly-by-night private schools in the bastis and villages of the city, where even those sorry establishments with their nominally English-proficient tutors were seen to be superior to their counterparts in Delhi's sclerotic government school system. Advances were taken at ruinous rates of interest from loan sharks so that a treasured child could be given a precarious shot at a better existence a dozen-odd years down the line. Schools across the educational firmament were rumored and proven to be taking money and favors of all kinds to guarantee admissions to the children of stressed-out parents. Temples and counselors saw massive footfalls and Valium was sold freely. The pushing and pulling of an anguished city finally drove the government to action. A points system was established, which included proximity to the school in question and the education of the parents as criteria. A quota was put in place to ensure a good percentage of every inducted class would be children from disadvantaged backgrounds, injecting both diversity and reality into hitherto cloistered classrooms. The results of these processes would then be posted publicly and on the Internet to guarantee maximum transparency. We care, said Delhi's education minister emphatically, about the common citizen: there is nothing as important as the schooling of the children of this city.

The result of all this caring, muttered Kapoor, was that the rich and privileged were now competing for even smaller numbers of seats. Thus the price for each one had just gone up. The lists on the school websites threw up an intriguing fact. Say there were a hundred seats. Forty were given to children who qualified under the points system. Another forty went to the economically underprivileged, who had their own points system to navigate. That left twenty seats for the "management" to distribute as they saw fit. "How," he said heavily, "do you think they see so fit?"

The DCP rolled his eyes and Smita snickered, while the older policeman assured them that what they saw as his cynicism was only a realistic appraisal of the facts. Those were, he pointed out, indisputable.

A stellar local school, much beloved by politicians, industrialists, and others who saw a need for bodyguards to accompany their prodigies to school and back, had been beset the previous week with a serious problem. The admissions roll had been released, along with the supplementary one that included those waitlisted for admission, should any of the original allottees forgo their turn. Auditors of this sort of information had noted the presence of many notable surnames in both the admissions and waiting lists and had sighed with envy. It should be remembered that the academic year started only in April. All these children were still in their respective preschools.

The day after the release of the first list, a child whose name figured on the admissions roll had been kidnapped in broad daylight while being led across the road to his preschool by his maid. That young woman had been clubbed on the head from behind and remembered nothing. The driver had seen nothing as he had gone ahead to find parking. The people driving on the busy street had passed by. The watchman of the school had been questioned, as had the people who were regulars on that stretch of road. But finally, it wasn't the profile of the child's parents or the notability of the preschool outside which the outrage had taken place that had convulsed upwardly mobile Delhi.

A note had been pinned to the preschool's wall: *Take your child off the list. Tell your friends.*

The child was three years old.

The outrage had been immediate, but even at its swiftest it had followed on the coattails of terror. A child's future is contingent upon his being alive to see it. Is anything worth this? asked petrified parents of each other.

The thing we need to worry about, Delhi's commissioner of police told his junior officers, is copycats. The joint and additional and deputy commissioners nodded, conferred, and quietly called home to ask whether their own little princes and princesses were safe. The commissioner's warning had been a sage one. Two more kidnappings were reported from outer Delhi, one from as far away as Aligarh. Those were quickly solved, the miscreants thrashed for their pains and handed over to the police. One would-be kidnapper actually lost his unlamented life due to the summary justice of the enraged relatives and neighbors of the child he'd sought to ferret away.

There were police pickets outside the preschools and policemen outside the offices of the principals of the better class of private school. But the damage had been done. Fewer and fewer children left their homes. Ayahs reported sick and stayed away. Drivers found new excuses to not come in. The price of bodyguards went up, overnight, by 100 percent.

The schools were in ferment. The principals called in favors to meet with ministers and commissioners and bureaucrats of all stripes. The head of the school in question—the one to which the kidnapped child had been admitted—was beside himself.

"It isn't," he claimed loudly, "that our reputation will suffer." Of course it would, if people who mattered chose not to apply.

"It isn't," he protested further, "that we're worried about our future as one of the elite schools of this city." If people stopped attending his school, then there was no future.

"We're worried," he stated with palpable sincerity, "about the well-being of this poor child. We will do anything to ensure his safety and we assure his parents his seat is secure with us."

His parents were quick to make their views on his assurance public. The day after the abduction, Delhi woke up and logged on and discovered that the child's name had been taken off the list. Most people thought the parents had acted thus, or their agents. The parents themselves were careful to avoid the media. The sight of the mother, her eyes behind sunglasses, hiding her face behind an upraised hand as she exited her home while her husband glared at the assembled cameramen, shamed even the most hardened journalists of the city.

Letters poured in to the dailies, panels of experts were assembled by the TV channels, prognostications made as to the safety of the child, the date of his delivery to his parents, the state of his mental health. The blogs were as busy as the schools were silent. Three days after the event, the DCP was called in and put on the case.

"What," he inquired, delicately as he could, "do you want me to do? Find the child? Soothe the parents? Stop the copycats? Handle the press? What?"

"All of that," said the commissioner, the only one who didn't carry a prefix before his title.

The DCP nodded, saluted, and turned on his heel.

"Dayal."

"Sir?" said the DCP, turning back to his senior officer.

"The old lady asked for you. Again. There's going to be some political heat."

"I'm aware of that, sir."

"The child may already be dead."

The DCP nodded quietly.

"The fear won't go away."

The DCP stayed silent.

"Nobody will win here, son. I hope you realize that."

"Is that why she asked for me?"

"Proximity to power is always a negotiation," answered the commissioner. With which oblique reply the DCP had to be content as he left to assemble his own expert team.

———————•————•————•———

They were on their way to the preschool outside which the boy had disappeared when Kapoor launched into his discourse on the facts of life regarding admissions.

"If enough kids on the first list have their names removed, the ones on the waiting list get in," he said.

"Easy, then," replied Smita. "We start with the people on the second list."

Kapoor looked at her while the DCP communed with himself.

"What?" asked Smita.

"Have you looked at the surnames on the waiting list?"

"Yes."

"Anything strike you as odd?"

"Not really. Two politicians, a cop, and a bureaucrat each, a couple of media types. The rest businessmen."

"Any of those businessmen stand out?"

"They're all connected, obviously. Two of them are real estate developers. Both bent. One of them's a land shark from Uttar Pradesh. Everyone knows he's a gangster."

"So he's our suspect?"

"Frankly, yes. These guys all think they're invincible. It may well be him, but they're all suspects."

Kapoor looked at her owlishly, then at the DCP, who dragged himself to the present.

"You want to tell her?" Kapoor suggested.

The DCP sighed and took over. "Firstly. Our gangster and his friend, the other developer. You know who they front for, right?"

"Sure. One's got the chief minister of UP in his pocket. The other one's a blind for a cabinet minister."

"Of India. Exactly. And they're on the waiting list. What does that tell you about the weight of the parents who actually got their kids in?"

"What does that have to do with us?" asked Smita pugnaciously.

Kapoor sighed in his turn.

The DCP continued phlegmatically: "You'll grant me that our 'suspects' have some political heft in this town?"

"I'm damned if that's going to stop me this time."

"Fair enough. However, I suggest you start by actually doing a bit of research."

Smita raised an eyebrow suspiciously.

"We got called in today. The kid was taken three days ago. The day after, his parents, or somebody, took his name off the admissions list. Correct?"

"Right."

"Have you checked the lists since?"

"No. Everyone knows the lists have been pulled off the Internet."

"I mean the lists of the other schools. The ones like this one."

"They've all been removed."

"Correct. But before they were taken off. Did you look at them?"

No, said Smita's face.

"That poor kid was on four first lists. Four different schools. Four waiting lists of potential suspects, Smita. All with connections to cabinet ministers, both in India and in Delhi's neighboring states. How many rich, powerful people do you want to piss off today?"

Kapoor spoke through the hand with which he was massaging his face. "The note just said to take the kid's name off the list. Which list?"

"I assumed that . . ."

"You assumed, like everyone else, that the school whose principal's been shouting himself hoarse was the one the kidnappers meant. We don't know that."

"The education minister's been calling every newspaper and channel in town," said the DCP. "Do you even know the scale of the fire-fighting the government's doing? Why do you think those lists were yanked so suddenly?"

"Why've they thrown that particular school to the wolves?"

"Because the principal opened his mouth before he could be told not to. Apart from him, have you heard a single soundbite from a principal of a school you'd actually want to send a child to?"

"Or maybe the education minister phoned him on behalf of someone's child, and the principal didn't take his call. Politicians remember these things."

The car braked to a stop outside the preschool where the child had been taken. Sundry rubberneckers congregated on the sidewalk outside the school, while a uniformed guard made sullen ineffectual attempts to disperse them. A pinched face peered through the gate at them, motioning them forth peremptorily. The gate opened just enough to admit them.

"One thing more," murmured the DCP in Smita's ear. "Your friend the gangster. His daughter got into two of the same schools the missing kid made it into. She was waitlisted in the other two. Does that make *our* list shorter in any way?"

Smita looked up at him.

"And another thing," continued the DCP, glancing about himself at the preschool world of plastic toys in the garden and paper cutouts of animals that they found themselves in. "His child came here too."

———————·——·——·———————

The lady who ran the preschool was a nice woman of indeterminate age who wore her hair up in a bun with a pencil through it. The yard of her home, for she lived above the school, was cluttered with the accoutrements of her vocation. There were playsets and little wooden tables and chairs. Wherever one looked there were posters with numbers and letters and the imprints of little hands. A few other women, her teachers, sat disconsolately on the veranda, quietly working away at their mugs of tea. They seemed of a piece with their employer, women past their first youths who had found this way to fill their mornings now that their own kids were safely in school and beyond. All capable, all kind, all utterly unprepared for the storm that had engulfed them.

To Smita's eye, it seemed as if one had been crying. Three days after the event. The principal of the preschool saw Smita's look of inquiry. She nodded, sympathy and exhaustion competing in her face. "The little boy was in her class."

"Sweet child?"

"They all are, at that age. We're not supposed to have favorites. But that child's a doll. Polite, good in class, just a joy to have around."

Smita nodded. "May I speak with them?"

"Of course." The principal led the DCP and Kapoor into her sanctum. Smita accepted her own cup of tea and joined the group of teachers keeping lonely vigil over the ghost of their hitherto noisy school.

The women were quiet and then expressive, and misery and anger and bewilderment stewed nicely in their conversation. They were scared for the child, fearful of the fallout, and mostly they just wanted it all to go away. They liked and respected their employer, and said she'd been a rock. They expressed, furtively and then collectively, gladness they weren't in her position.

But how, poor thing, was it her fault anyway? How was it theirs? The child had been lifted from the street. He hadn't even been in their care at the moment of his abduction. How could the whole world hold them responsible?

A panel of "experts" on a private news channel the previous night had castigated their school for its slipshod security. There had been broad hints that in its zeal to extract as much profit as possible from the children, the school had been remiss in providing the basic level of safety to its wards.

How dare they, said one woman. Do they teach here? Do they ever come here? Do their kids study here?

How dare they question our commitment? Do we love these children less because they pay fees?

Do they know, they chorused, the parents give us presents when their kids leave, because they know how much this school means to these children?

Smita listened and sipped her tea.

"I can't believe he's gone," said the woman who'd been crying, eventually. "That's all that matters. Of course we feel responsible. How could we not? We're all mothers too."

The other women nodded somberly. They'd seen the images of the mother on the news and in the papers and they'd cried as well. The teacher who taught the stricken woman's child had called her even. It hadn't been returned.

What, inquired Smita gently, were the parents like?

Nice enough, was the consensus. The father was from a prominent Delhi family. Good-looking enough, polite enough. Played golf, was a businessman, came to all the school's functions with cameras, both still and video. The mother was quiet, had her friends amongst the other mothers, enjoyed coffee with them while the kids were playing in school. More sensible than some of the others. No stilettos and short dresses for her when she came to get her child, though her sunglasses were designer and there were real diamonds in her watch. They brought cake for everyone when their son had his birthday and their party at home wasn't unreasonably ostentatious, according to the gossip of the maids who accompanied the children to school.

Old money, clearly. Or as old as New Delhi demanded. The father wasn't old enough to pull the sort of strings that had gotten his child into all those schools, but his own father was still alive and kicking, and obviously the family's access went all the way to the top. The child's future had already been mapped out for him. And now he was gone.

Just shows you, doesn't it, said one of the teachers quietly. You can have everything in this world. And it still isn't enough.

The others looked at her as if she'd been caught giving the gardener a handjob in the children's restroom. Then they noted the absence of an interlocutor who would judge such an utterance, shrugged, nodded, and returned to their tea. Smita finished her second mug and waited for her senior officers to emerge.

⁕

"That woman's scared," was Kapoor's verdict.

"Why?" asked Smita.

"Her school is closed. Who knows when it will reopen? This isn't the sort of thing that makes young mothers line up at admissions time."

"Anything else?"

"She knows the people involved. The victims, the suspects. Not the kind of people you want to piss off. In any way at all."

"Do you think it's her fault?"

"Not at all. But the scrutiny isn't going to help. There are already people who want to know why a school was operating from these premises. Did they have the right clearances, certificates, a release from the fire department? I'd be surprised if it opens again."

"This isn't the only school in Delhi to be derelict."

"It's currently the only school which has managed to lose a child."

"Currently," said the DCP soberly. Kapoor grunted. They were back in the car.

"I'll tell you one thing," said Kapoor. "Those teachers, these last few days; they'll have found out who their real friends are." He cracked a window, a tendril of cool air sneaking in to the stuffy vehicle. "And that note," he continued.

"What about it?" asked Smita.

"Why leave it at all? The smart thing would have been to take the child and call the parents. Change the lists that way, instead of having them taken down publicly. Why make this fuss? How does it help? And who?"

"Whoever did it wants publicity," said the DCP. "But why?"

Kapoor sighed, patted the driver on the shoulder.

"The parents."

———————

The parents of the missing child lived in a cozy apartment overlooking a park in one of Delhi's most desirable neighborhoods. The flat wasn't huge and the staircase was steep, but the living room was lined with books and there were two terraces lined with plants. The art on the walls was a mixture of names that drew an inaudible whistle from Smita, while the silver-framed photographs artfully bestrewn across the living areas were proof that the young family traveled across many continents. The carpets were beautifully aged and among the photos were the markers of a prosperous and connected lineage: the wife of a visiting American president, an Indian politician or two, the obligatory Nehru corner. The furniture was worn but comfy, the living room warm and inviting, and even in this moment of the family's despair, there were fresh flowers in vases everywhere. In front of the hearth lounged an ancient dog.

Old family, thought Smita, with not a lot to prove. The right education and accents, wearing shahtoosh shawls that were actually legal. Effortless taste, the sort that upwardly mobile residents of the newer districts paid millions to achieve. But where, she thought mordantly, would they find the old photos and carpets? These people had been born with these things. The dog was of a piece with the other furnishings: he probably had a backstory too.

A door swung open and the three officers had a glimpse, fleetingly, of a woman lying on her side on a disheveled bed. Then the door closed and the man who'd opened it strode across the living room, his hand outstretched.

Young enough, thought Smita dispassionately. Good-looking enough. Of a sort she recognized, member of the Delhi Golf Club and the Delhi Gymkhana, possessed of a low handicap and a sense of humor, a bit of a lad when surrounded by his friends. In a previous life, she thought, waiting for the DCP and Kapoor to murmur their platitudes, she would have admired one such as he. Even now, his jaw was shaven and he smelled good. And why shouldn't he? thought Smita. Should a moment such as this reduce you to sackcloth and ashes? If cashmere sweaters are all a man owns, in other words; but it still, obscurely, grated on the young policewoman that even such a pass in his affairs hadn't compelled him to break type. Then his hand was in hers and she was saying how sorry she was but he should rest assured and his other hand was waving it away.

"Please," he said, gesturing to the sofas and chairs. "Sit . . . Coffee?" he asked. "Tea?"

There was tiredness in his eyes, noted Smita, confusion in the way he ran a hand through his brushed hair. She thought with a rush of sympathy of the woman lying on her side on an unmade bed in the afternoon while the spring sun bathed the children playing in the park outside in its warm glow. An old servant placed the tea on a table in front of the man, who poured and passed the cups around.

"I've spoken at length with the other officers," he said after a space, a saucer and cup securely in his own hand.

The DCP and Kapoor nodded.

"I'm not sure there's much to add," he continued. "Though I'm glad to make your acquaintance," he said with a smile. "You all have quite a reputation."

Smita saw how easy his manner was. It can't be easy, she thought, being married to a man like that. To charm people is like drawing breath for him. Even now.

"There's been no contact with you aside from the note?" asked Kapoor. The father shook his head.

"There was some talk of private investigators," said the DCP.

The father shook his head again. "My wife," he said by way of explanation. "She wanted to explore every opportunity. I . . . we, my family and hers, we've convinced her that it would only muddy the waters. We don't want to endanger our child in any way."

"May I speak freely?" asked the DCP.

The father nodded wordlessly.

"We're going to try our best. You know that. But every day that passes . . ."

The father nodded again, his gaze fixed on the DCP. Smita could feel as if it were sweat the distaste melting away from her as she looked at the quiet suffering in his eyes.

"We will find who did this. Rest assured of that."

"But you can't guarantee the safety of my son?"

The officers looked at him quietly. The father got up and stalked over to the French windows that gave on to the larger of the two terraces.

"I'm not deaf," he said to his own reflection in the glass. "We're not blind. We hear and see what people are saying. That people like us live in bubbles. It's sad that our child is gone, everyone agrees. But it's a lesson. That even people like us can and should suffer . . . What do you think?" he asked of the room behind him. "Even if it's true: why not me? Why not my wife, instead of our child? Why must everything be us versus them?"

Smita saw his form outlined against the rays of the afternoon sun. She noted his slim back through the thin sweater and she felt his anger and his question and she was moved to anger herself, a blind rage that a man such as this, with a life charmed as if by an auspicious planetary conjunction, with a pretty wife and beautiful home and a future secured against every possible vicissitude, should feel such self-pity. She wanted to shout to him that nobody chooses to be born poor and unconnected. She knew his answer, sophistic and solipsistic, would be the quick one that he didn't ask to be born rich. A man unconnected to the world around him by virtue of his bubble will founder exactly like this when it intrudes upon him and he will question this unmet world and its ways. She thought all this in the time it takes to raise a cup of tea to one's lips and suddenly the anger was gone, again, as she remembered why they were there. Kapoor got up, heavy and quiet, to put a paternal paw on the father's shoulder. The younger man glanced around in surprise, saw the look in Kapoor's eyes, recognized something there and smiled back. Then Smita's notebook was in her hand and patiently, firmly and without haste, they took the afflicted father back through the last few days.

At some stage, the tea was cleared away and then reappeared. Then dusk came and the lamps around the living room were lit. The ancient dog went downstairs, then came up again and laid his languid head on the knee of first one officer and then the next. Night arrived and still they asked questions. Finally the mother appeared, a cigarette in her hand as she stepped to the balcony doors.

"I wish you wouldn't smoke inside," said her husband.

"Why? Because of our child?"

He looked away. The mother smoked defiantly for a minute, before opening the door fully and throwing out her still burning cigarette. She came and put her arms around her husband.

"I'm sorry," she murmured against his back. Her hair, expensively colored and highlighted and now clearly unwashed, cascaded around her shoulders. She wore a comfy old cardigan and sweats inside the house and on her feet were carpet slippers. Smita had no doubt that professionally applied polish still lay on her hidden toes. But the pain in her posture was real as she clung to her husband. There was nothing fake about the way he caressed her hands. She was surprised to see her two senior officers decorously looking away.

"I want a drink," announced the mother. She sat down on a chair to one side and crossed her arms and legs and looked at her husband, who raised an eyebrow. "Just some white wine. Whatever's open in the fridge." Her eyes flickered over to the officers. "Will you join me?" she asked, attempting a smile. The DCP and Kapoor mumbled their regrets. Smita found a servant at her shoulder with a tray in his hand.

"And you?" asked the mother. "Will you make us drink alone?"

"No," said Smita, surprising herself as much as everyone else. "A glass of wine would be lovely, thank you."

The servant went off to reappear with two glasses of wine and a strong-looking whiskey and soda. Another minute produced some wasabi peas and assorted nuts and cocktail napkins. The wife watched with amusement as Kapoor sampled the green peas with his glass of water and the look in his eyes as the flavor hit the back of his throat and climbed to his nose. It struck Smita that the woman had already been drinking, that she had possibly been drinking all day, and if your only child has disappeared and may never appear again then perhaps drinking is the only thing to do. She watched the other woman take a draft of her wine, sigh, and stretch her shoulders and relax even further into the saggily contoured seat, her legs now crossed at the ankle over one cushioned arm.

"Is there anything you'd like to ask me?" she said to the room at large, her eyes closed.

The DCP and Kapoor looked at Smita.

"Who," asked Smita slowly, "do you think did it?"

"Apart from the people behind us in the admissions line? Aside from all of Delhi? Nobody in particular."

Smita flushed. The husband flashed her a look in which sympathy and an apology were nicely mixed. But our circumstances, said the look: our missing child; please don't judge my wife on this performance.

"The particular is what I'm interested in," persisted Smita gently.

"Everyone's talking about this builder."

"Right," said Smita encouragingly.

"He's my father-in-law's neighbor. Their farms have a common wall. We've met him socially."

"And?"

"I can't bear him. And his wife, poor thing. He drags her along to these parties, when we all know she doesn't want to be there. She tries so hard to please. But she can't."

The wife opened her eyes, peered at Smita over the rim of her glass. "She's not one of us, she never will be. There isn't enough Valentino in the world. I hate that he makes her try."

Smita nodded, her eyes on the wife.

"What possesses these people to want to be like us? Do they think our lives are so perfect? God knows he's got enough money, he can have any life he wants. Why does he want mine?"

"They're our neighbors," said her husband quietly.

"They're not mine," flashed his wife. "It's fucking excruciating watching her struggle with the cutlery and hoping she doesn't drink out of the finger bowl. And him with his rings and reeking of cologne and that fucking tika on his forehead. Like that will set him right with his god for all the thieving he does." Her voice rose almost to a scream. "Who are these people?"

"They didn't take our son," said her husband without heat.

"How do you know that?" asked his wife desperately.

"Because he told me."

———+———+———

A woman dressed in the street version of the mother's current outfit had marched in, sunglasses atop her head, sneakers on her feet, an expensive shawl completing the ensemble. She'd ignored the police officers, brushed aside the servant's offer of a drink, given the husband a quick peck on the cheek, and huddled next to the wife. They were obviously good friends. The visitor had led the wife away to an interior room without a backward glance. The entire procedure lasted about thirty seconds. As if, the DCP would remark drily, we weren't there.

The husband was quietly informative. The woman who'd walked in was indeed a close friend. He'd been in school with her husband. The wives had been associated since their youths as well. She was almost, no, she was family.

And the dodgy neighbor? Smita asked.

The neighbor had been one of the first people to call.

The afternoon of the kidnapping, when the family had taken refuge at the patriarch's farm, he'd walked across, his hands clasped in sympathy, his brow furrowed. He had known that day itself which way the wind would blow and he'd come across to make his case.

"The man has resources. He placed them at our disposal."

"And your own resources?" asked the DCP.

"My father?"

The DCP shrugged, his lips pursed.

"My father has moved heaven and earth," said the younger man. "As I'm sure you know," he added with a tired smile. "We're still minus one son."

"If . . . your resources turn something up, you'll let us know, won't you?"

Of course, indicated the father, his eyes averted.

"What will you do when your son returns?" asked Smita before she could stop herself.

"Leave, I suppose," he replied, sparing Smita the embarrassment of questioning her assumption of the child's well-being. "God knows we don't want to live here. Not anymore."

"Where'll you go?"

"Singapore, perhaps. Somewhere safer. Anywhere."

From inside a room they heard the muted sound of voices raised in argument, a crash, and a female scream. A servant ran past, a grim look on his face.

"Is there anything else?" said the father tiredly. "My wife needs me."

The officers collected themselves to leave, the man walking them to the door.

"One thing," he said.

Smita was behind the combined bulk of Kapoor and the DCP.

"If you find the people who did this. If there is nothing else to be done. I'd appreciate it if you called me. To be there."

Smita strained around the human wall between her and the man, but she couldn't see him. It was as if the wall itself moved to deny her. All she heard were his words.

"I'd make it worth your while."

She neither heard nor saw a response. A moment later they were descending the staircase to the dark street below. The men fired up their cigarettes next to the car, puffing away and avoiding each other's eyes. Smita gathered her strength to pose her question when a woman's voice, clear as a bell through the glass and the curtains and the intervening walls, rent the air. "I want my child!" she wailed. She cried with an absence of embarrassment foreign to her tribe and Smita felt the hair on her arms rise. She looked at her male colleagues in disbelief as they quickly, quietly finished their cigarettes, the glowing ends spiraling through the air as first one and then the other flicked them away, and then all three of them were gone through the fractured night.

———•—————•———•———

The next morning was bright, beautiful, and wasted on the combined bad moods of three dispirited police officers. The DCP was more abstracted, if anything, than usual. Smita felt exhausted from the day before while Kapoor just looked hungover. The DCP gave Kapoor a questioning look, extracting an ursine grunt in response. Smita rolled her eyes behind her shades, settling back against her seat.

They were en route to the fancy farmhouse suburbs of Delhi, where the richest citizens had their mansions, complete with lawns and pools and occasionally stables. The grandfather of the missing child had already been spoken with. His neighbor, the man with the suspect past and the shining present and future, was their prelunch appointment. The city gave way to villages and still Bentleys and BMWs flashed past. There were occasionally mustard fields to be glimpsed through the windows and tractors amongst the SUVs and once a bullock cart held them up, the cops huffily quiet in their white car.

"I hate people like that," said Kapoor finally. "From last night."

Silence greeted this pronouncement. He didn't seem to mind.

"I hate being the one who has to wait to be seated. It's as if the whole world is back to front."

Dayal and Smita considered this and finally began to laugh, slowly at first and then with more abandon.

Kapoor looked at them owlishly, then repeated himself in Punjabi. "Back to front. How do they expect us to do our work when people aren't scared of us?"

He watched Smita from the corner of his eye, waiting for her to take the bait, but she knew better by now, so she just smiled sympathetically. "Don't worry, uncle. I'm sure you'll find someone to scare the piss out of where we're going."

"In this place?" moaned Kapoor. "These people's

servants live in palaces." He turned to the DCP. "Solving cases, boss. This is where it gets us. Rubbing shoulders with people who don't know who we are, and don't need to."

The DCP laughed again. He rolled down a window, tension evaporating through the crack. A high wall with fantastic terra-cotta figurines embedded in it flashed past, then they were there. Uniformed and inconspicuously armed security men waved them through an imposing gate. Their car made its way down a paved driveway laid through a lawn bestrewn with expensive shrubbery and flowering trees. There was a swimming pool to one side, another in front. Statuary of vaguely Grecian aspect dotted the vista. They pulled up at the house, a tribute to the architect's long-distant and dimly remembered acid trip through the Georgian terraces of Bath. A pair of tree pies flew across their path as they exited the car. Overfed koi swam in the reflecting pool past which they walked to the entrance. Smita knelt to study one, a particularly confused-looking specimen who gaped at the surface. I know how you feel, she thought to herself. This place is completely mad. Then the master of the establishment was at the door to usher them in. She rose, her hand outstretched, only to find his own hands pressed together in greeting.

"I thought you'd enjoy the sun," he said, leading them to a loggia to one side, under whose capacious and currently rose-encrusted lattice lurked a bar, a grill, seating for ten, and a foosball table. Coffee arrived before they were even comfortably seated and Smita could begin to comprehend the foosball table. She remembered what the mother of the night before had said of the man she was sitting across from and she strained to catch his scent but it seemed unobjectionable enough, this early in the morning. There was no tika on his forehead, though perhaps he hadn't had time to visit his favorite temple, and his clothing was quietly casual. The only ring he was wearing was a gold wedding band. He was, she noted through her sunglasses, even attractive. A full head of hair going quietly gray, a well-trimmed mustache, a shaven jaw. Brown eyes, soft now with crinkles in the corners that hinted at a warm smile.

"So, sir," he said to the DCP, "what will you have?" The DCP indicated his preference and the builder turned to Kapoor. "And you, Kapoor sahib? Madam?" He handed them their cups and offered sweets and savory snacks and waited for the meeting to be called to order.

"You know you don't have to call me sir," said the DCP.

"I wasn't born in this house, sir," said the other man with a smile. "Old habits die hard."

The DCP smiled back mirthlessly. "You know men socially I have to call sir."

"Perhaps one day you'll do me the honor of entertaining you. Sir."

The man was on the edge of insolence, but his charm was such that the smiles the DCP and Kapoor wore were real.

"Uncle won't remember this," continued the man, "but we've met before."

"When?"

"Two decades ago. When I'd just arrived in this city. You were in the Seelampur station across the river."

Kapoor's teeth bared. "How did it go?"

"Not well for me."

Kapoor waited, his smile still in place. The other man laughed and raised a hand.

"I deserved it. Learned a good lesson that day. Two, actually."

"Which are?" inquired Smita.

"Well, ma'am," said the builder, his smile roguish, his warm eyes now a crueler shade, "firstly, if you're doing something illegal, don't get caught."

"And second?"

He looked at her, shrugged his shoulders elaborately.

"Whatever I did to you," said Kapoor, "did it scare you straight?"

The man looked about himself at his palatial home and began to laugh. Moments later, the male officers joined him.

"You understand," he continued when the mirth had died down, "you'll find no record of our little meeting all those years ago. I didn't have to tell you. But I did."

The DCP nodded without speaking.

"I had nothing to do with this child's disappearance. Am I the only man with a past in this city?"

"Your child stood to gain."

"I stand to lose. Everything. There is no gain for me in this. No offense, sir, but I know how to account for gain and loss at a deeper level than any of you do."

He got up and pulled a rose closer to himself, inhaled deeply, oblivious to the thorns. Smita noted his hands, callused by hard use in a way she didn't see in the men around her. This man had known thorns and familiarity robbed them of their sting, and she knew, obscurely yet clearly, why the woman of the night before had lied so blatantly about this man's appearance. Despite what he is, she fancies him too. Too?

"I have more money than I can ever spend, more money than my child will ever need. I waited for her so I could have everything exactly the way I wanted before she arrived."

His hands were still busy among his roses.

"She was on the waiting list because I wanted her there. To have her accepted immediately would have raised eyebrows, so I kept her on the waiting list. I knew she'd get in. It was all arranged. That school was going to have five new seats from this year because I'd donated enough money to make it so. And that was on the off chance that we decided to send her there. She'd been accepted to two other perfectly decent schools, where her parentage wouldn't have raised hackles. Her mother's quite happy for her to go to either of those. She'll end up in a Swiss boarding school anyway; let her have a normal childhood, says my wife, in an average school."

"What do you say?" asked Smita.

"I did all this so she could be like those other kids raised to think this city belongs to them." There was a shark's smile in his hard mouth and eyes. "I didn't have the minutes of our meeting removed from my back, uncle. I could have, but I chose not to. They remind me of where I started and how far I've come. I don't carry them today so my child can go to an average school."

His face softened under the shade of his roses.

"You have to believe I didn't do it. I'm not that arrogant. I'm not that stupid. I have the most to lose."

Smita excused herself. She ignored the builder's offer to show her to the changing rooms of one of his pools, opting instead to head into the house itself. Partly she wanted to nose around; mostly she just wanted to see what it looked like inside. She expected a wedding cake. What she got was a surprisingly tasteful resort, with overtones of Delhi baroque. A large lobby with a winding staircase at one end, expensive if characterless art to either side, and ceilings well in excess of twenty feet. Lots of air-conditioning, she thought irrelevantly. And a spa in the basement with a resident masseur. Definitely.

She ducked into the powder room and chuckled when she saw the moldy old soap in its dish. There's only so much the interior decorator can do for you, she thought acidly. A wrong turn outside led her to a living room in which a family party of sorts was in session. A gigantic woman of irascible demeanor presided over an overstuffed couch, out of which her own cushiony exterior protruded as if organically. In front of her was a pile of savory snacks. To either side of her cascaded a feminine wave, those closest to her wearing saris and salwar kameez, those on the peripheries sporting dresses and trousers and designer sunglasses atop their bare crests. They all looked inquiringly at her as she walked in, conversation coming miraculously to a stop. Hindi, noted Smita dispassionately. Of a sort that was spoken in the vicinity of the capital. A nonmusical rendering, coarsened further by the aspirations of this current pack. Bags

and dresses emblazoned with the logos of their designers. At least two pairs of high-heeled shoes with red soles.
Red lips, red nails, the younger set studying hard to be
well set-up Delhi tarts, their husbands and personal train-
ers on speed dial and Porsche Cayennes waiting outside.
She smiled pleasantly. They looked back quietly, waiting
for a lead from one of the older ladies.

It came from a pleasant-faced woman dressed incongruously in designer sweats, the maker's name spelled
out on her capacious backside. "May I help you?" she
asked politely in English. Smita introduced herself to
a murmuring from the crowd, in which welcome and
dismay at the circumstances of her arrival were evenly
mixed. The matriarch sniffed and looked away, but the
woman who'd spoken walked quickly over to Smita's
side.

"You've met my husband?" she asked. Smita nodded.
Of course: this was the lady of the house. No cigarettes
and glasses of wine about her. Not this early or in this
company, at any rate. She looked like what she probably was, a nice middle-class woman with a comfortable
education and a young child and another two or three
probably on the way. Twenty years ago, twenty kilome-
ters away, she'd be sitting in a courtyard with her sari
over her head. But she's here now, thought Smita. With
sequins on her ass.

The other women sensed their dismissal and turned
back to their own conversations. Smita and the builder's wife exited the room. "My mother-in-law," she said
with a vague wave of her hand. Smita inclined her head,
acknowledging the matriarch. "She doesn't approve of
the police coming to our home," continued the wife.

Smita shook her head, still in agreement. "She's old-fashioned," said the wife with a small smile. Smita shrugged with a smile of her own. "I know who you are. It's nice to meet women who actually do things."

They walked without haste to where the men were sitting. Smita asked the other woman about the art on the walls. A consultant. The furniture? A designer. The servants and kitchen? The mother-in-law. They came outside, to where the gardens were in riot. Smita asked her about them. The other woman loved the gardens, but was uninvolved in their maintenance. The gardeners took care of that, under the direct tutelage of her husband. What is it she did, then? inquired Smita, gently as she could.

The other woman looked at her directly, perhaps for the first time, then away again. The sitting group of men, laughing in each other's company in the wary, overly boisterous way of athletes on opposing teams, glanced up at their approach. Smita took her seat, while the other woman went and stood behind her husband's chair.

"My wife," he said to the male officers, who stood, their hands together in greeting. She nodded and returned the gesture and looked toward her husband, who remained seated, his back to her. He bent his head back toward the house. His wife lowered her eyes, turned, walked away. Smita felt her own face flushing as if from the sun and she felt the builder's eyes upon her, so she forced herself to meet his gaze, thankful for the glasses which obscured her eyes. She saw his amusement at her anger. Then he turned away, not, she felt, to spare her the humiliation, but because he'd tired of the sport.

She pulled herself together. "Did I miss anything?"

"He was refreshing our memory," murmured the DCP, "about his history with Mr. Kapoor."

"A painful subject, perhaps?"

"Only when it's cold," said the builder, the shark's smile still firmly in place, eyes back upon the female officer. "Have you witnessed uncle at work, madam?"

"A bit before my time."

"True," grunted Kapoor. "I was much younger in those days. Warm blood. I'm more gentle now."

"It's worth seeing," said the builder. "Not something you'd learn in your classes. That expertise comes on the job. With practice. Uncle has had a lot of practice. Wouldn't you like some practice, madam?"

"She doesn't need any practice, son. Not while I'm around," said Kapoor.

The builder's eyes flashed as he heard the familiarity in Kapoor's voice. He turned to the older cop only to see steel there, and in the DCP's eyes as well, so he smiled again and then laughed, shaking his head.

"Anything else I can help you with?" he asked pleasantly.

The officers stood up then, the males shaking the builder's hand, Smita returning his namaste with one of her own. "There is one thing," said the DCP. "Rather silly. But a man like you, with your far-flung interests . . ."

The builder inclined his head politely.

"Have you noticed any men recently with missing fingers? Nine-fingered men?"

The builder had slipped his glasses on against the sun, now that they were out of the bower. His eyes were opaque, but his mouth smiled.

"How strange that you should ask, sir," he said.

"A driver showed up last year with a finger missing. Claimed it was an accident."

"Really?" said the DCP. "And where is he now?"

"Dead. Had a heart attack some months ago. We found out he was a drinker. Just as well he died at home and not at the wheel with my family in the car."

"Anyone else?" asked Kapoor.

"No. But this is the strange part. A lady I know asked me the same thing just last night."

"Did she?" said the DCP.

"Yes. I told her I was meeting you today, and she told me you'd be asking that very same question. She knows you too."

"I'm very well known," said the DCP, looking away.

"Her name's Razia," continued the builder. "Young woman. Pretty. Accommodating. A good friend."

The DCP turned his own shaded eyes back to the builder, taking out a cigarette, lighting it. "Known her long?"

"A month. Maybe six weeks. Certainly no longer than this winter."

"What does your wife think of your good friends?" asked Smita unwisely.

"My wife knows her place."

"Thank you for all your help," said the DCP easily. The builder waved it away, his hand a light weight on Kapoor's shoulder as he walked them out.

"Take care," said the builder.

"You too," replied the DCP.

The car slid away.

"Excuse my language, but what an asshole!" exploded Smita.

"Not to everyone's taste," agreed Kapoor.

"Do you remember him?" asked the DCP.

"I remember every man I've ever bamboo'd," said Kapoor comfortably.

"And?"

"Well, it was only after he reminded me, of course. Then I remembered him. I have to confess, I'd lost track. I can't imagine why. When my victims graduate to better things, I try to follow their careers. Partly out of fear. Partly paternal pride."

Smita rolled her eyes while the DCP chuckled.

"What did you do to him?" asked Smita.

Kapoor waved the question away. "While you were gone," he said, "I stepped away and made some calls. He got married about ten years ago. Then, it was a good match. Respectable, educated girl. The same community, a family untainted by crime."

"Now?"

"She bores him. His sights are set higher."

"But?"

"People like him don't get divorced. He knows that, she knows that. They'll come to some arrangement. In the meantime, poor thing, she'll have to try."

"What else?" asked the DCP.

"The minister he's fronting for may be in trouble."

"What kind?"

"Money. As in, he's not passing enough of it along to his cabinet colleagues."

"So?"

"So his colleagues have done this to embarrass the builder. And through him, his patron."

"The minister?"

"Exactly."

"A conspiracy theory."

"A baroque one," sniffed Smita.

"The good ones always are," smiled the DCP. "Besides, you missed what he told us when you were gone."

"What?"

"That public note," said Kapoor. "It doesn't fit."

"What does that have to do with this guy?"

"If the child isn't the point, then what is? Who has the most to lose?"

"What did he say?" Smita asked.

"That there would be a dead body at the end of the chase. But it wouldn't be the child's."

Smita shook her head again dubiously. They halted at a crossroads, held up by a tractor involved in a disagreement with an SUV.

"This woman, sir," said Smita cautiously. "Razia."

Kapoor looked away ostentatiously. The DCP said nothing.

"What's the deal with her?"

"As in?"

"As in this case, sir. What does she have to do with it? And what does she have to do with a bunch of nine-fingered men?"

The two men were silent as the car started to move again in the bright spring day.

———•———•———

Kapoor's investigations into the plague of nine-fingered men had continued apace as the weather had turned milder. The warmth of the days hadn't gentled his hands

as they coaxed information out of unwilling felons and
their associates in Delhi and its immediate environs. His
nephews in the outlying station houses of the city had
slapped the usual suspects till their hands bruised. Veg-
etable vendors, domestics, rickshaw drivers, pushers of
handcarts, sellers of bootleg DVDs—they'd all felt the
brunt of Kapoor's zeal. But it had all added up to nothing. Even the ones they found with missing digits knew
little save the amorphous promises of riches to come.
Some of them actively regretted having so cavalierly sac-
rificed parts of their bodies. One of them plaintively informed Kapoor's representative at their discussion that
he wished it had been a kidney. At least that way he'd
have been paid.

Razia, on the other hand, had been a constant presence, even if only on the other end of the line, and always from a private number. After the first few times,
Sajan had wanted to tell her that she was safe and so
was her secret, he wasn't going to waste his time tracking her down. It was enough for him that she stayed in
touch. If the price for this was that it was on her terms,
it was one he was willing to pay. The nights had turned
warmer, the trees fuller, the days longer, yet she'd remained in the shadows. "Words," he'd been provoked
to remark one night as he lay in bed, gently stroking
himself, "may be enough for you. But they're not enough
for me."

She'd laughed and flirted and refused to let him
know how to reach her. All she'd say about the larger
world was that things were coming to a head. When it
was time, she implied, he'd know whatever there was to
know about her. Not before then.

That the builder had known her had thrown him. That the two of them had discussed him made it worse.

———•———•———

"I wish I knew what to tell you," he replied, not bothering to lie. "But I barely know more than you do."

Smita bit her lip and looked away. Kapoor, in front, punched the driver in the arm.

"What's the story with your son's admission?" he asked severely.

"Stuck, sir," replied the driver.

"Well?" The two officers in the back listened with interest.

"He got in, sir. But now there's no clarity. Even the Internet lists are gone."

Kapoor rolled his eyes at his colleagues, who were looking mystified.

"His son got into the same school as that missing kid. Under the poor children's quota. Now he's stuck too, wondering what's going on."

"The same school?" exclaimed Smita. "But you never told us."

The driver looked at her in the rearview mirror. You never asked, said his eyebrows.

She glanced in embarrassment at the DCP, who was staring thoughtfully at the back of his driver's head.

"Yes," he said. "Of course. I wrote that letter for you."

The driver gestured in agreement.

"Tell me," said the DCP. "What do you think?"

"I think it's a shame, sir. That poor child disappearing. But, if you don't mind my saying so . . . ma'am?"

Smita nodded in annoyance.

"It's a nuisance to people like us, more than anything else. My son getting into that school is the best thing that's ever happened to my family. God knows what will happen now."

"That school isn't going anywhere," said Kapoor quietly.

"You say that, sir. But sitting where I am, I don't know that."

"Which means?"

"Sir, you know the ways of this world. More than I do. The height of my ambition was to educate my child right. So he'd know this world as you do. But I don't know what the upshot of all this will be. Begging your pardon."

The DCP leaned forward and patted his subordinate's shoulder, a gesture that was as heartfelt as it was surprising to everyone else in the car. "Don't worry," he said. "That school won't falter because of this. Too many fancy people already have their children there."

The driver smiled into the mirror. "Thank you for saying so, sir. My wife tells me the same thing. But it just feels like it's what we want to hear, not what we know. To hear it from you is heartening."

The DCP smiled again as did Smita and Kapoor, and they all left unsaid what they were thinking, that the fancy people of that particular school would pull their kids out if the wind shifted and find them spots at other good institutions. But the poor kids in the class, the ones who'd fought their way in via the special quota, would be left high and dry. Perhaps the driver knew it too, but the reassurance he'd just received was enough and exactly what he wanted so he didn't press it further.

Kapoor and the DCP hopped off en route as they passed under the metro line, there to take the train to their next port of call, a lunch in Gurgaon they had committed to the previous week. Smita and the driver continued on their stately way into the city.

"Why," she asked, more to pass the time than anything else, "is it so important?"

The driver looked at her in polite inquiry, his eyes framed in the mirror.

"This school, I mean. I don't understand the need. Surely there are other schools?"

"There are other jobs too, ma'am," said the driver. "Why the police?"

Smita acknowledged the hit with a chuckle.

"But if," she continued, "the objective is to have equality. Surely it makes more sense to push for more good schools, so that everyone can attend one. Don't you agree?"

"Have everyone go to the same schools, you mean? Even people like yourselves? Eliminate the private schools?"

"Exactly."

The driver was quiet.

"Go on," urged Smita. "I want to know. Speak freely."

"Ma'am, I want my child to be a sahib one day, to have someone like me to drive him around. We're Indians. These are relationships we know."

"But isn't equality of opportunity the issue here? For everyone?"

"Equality never works downward, ma'am. It's only attractive when the move is up."

"So?"

"I don't want your children to be like me, ma'am. How does that help anyone? I want my son to be like you."

Smita sank further into her seat. Around her pressed a city on the move, traffic hobbled by scooterists aspiring to motorcycles, the riders of which dreamed of cars that made their way from humble domestic four-bangers to the most luxurious foreign models. There were pedestrians on the streets, vendors on the sidewalks, beggars at the windows of the adjoining nonofficial vehicles. There was a world outside her little cocoon that fought its little wars for its paltry triumphs and piffling defeats, and at its heart were ambition and its fickle twin, opportunity, before whom snarled and drooled the supplicants of Delhi. She knew that a lack of ambition was the surest sign there was of privilege in this city and she knew her privileges gathered around her like a pheromone to which nobody was immune. The traffic lights came and went, then there were roundabouts with flowers in them and they were in peaceful central Delhi where there were bauhinias in the parks. Yet the sight of them gave Smita no solace for she knew she was in the quiet eye of the racing storm and just because she didn't hear the engine didn't mean that it wasn't whirring away, fed on the dreams of an unfulfilled populace in a grasping city. The homes of billionaires and cabinet ministers and Supreme Court judges flashed past, a traffic policeman saluting the officer he assumed sat inside the official cop car.

"Don't worry," she said slowly, softly into the void. "We'll take care of your son."

The driver's soft eyes studied her for a moment in

the mirror. There was a smile in them and then they were gone.

———— ·—·—·—· ————

The DCP and Kapoor had clocked in later that afternoon, the worse for wear after what had clearly been a sodden meal. They lolled and avoided Smita's eye. Kapoor was taciturn and watched his hands and feet. The DCP had his feet up on his desk and studied the ceiling with a casual intensity. She sighed and went outside to have a smoke and was joined by the two other officers five minutes later.

"Nice lunch?" she asked.

Kapoor grunted. The DCP made no reply. The sun was brilliant. The blue sky and bright light carried the beautiful barb of spring—that summer's unremitting misery was just around the corner. Even the breeze up on their balcony was warm. It seemed to Smita that perhaps the next day she wouldn't have to bother with a sweater or a shawl. Below them scurried the citizens of the city on their cacophonous ways, while around them wheeled the kites, calling out to each other in the still cool air.

"Oh look," murmured the DCP. The two others looked at him expectantly. "Up there," he pointed with his cigarette.

A bird with a fantastic wingspan hung motionless on a thermal, riding the invisible wave, a moment of uncommon stillness in a clangorous place. Then it tired of the sport and swooped gracefully to a tree whose crown reached close to their balcony and stood, revealing itself to be a vulture, its ungainly head looking this way and that.

"So beautiful in flight," remarked Smita. "So ugly otherwise."

"So rare," observed Kapoor. "Haven't seen one down here in years. Have you, sir?"

"No."

"They've been gone?" inquired Smita suspiciously. The two male officers nodded at her, slightly superciliously. "Why?" asked Smita in her direct way.

"I'm not sure," responded the DCP. "I'm just glad to see one again. It's been almost twenty years."

Kapoor nodded and blew rings, watching the huge beast in the tree below. "Maybe he knows something we don't."

The DCP's phone rang. He answered it without looking. "Hello?"

"Good afternoon sir," said the well-mannered voice at the other end.

"Good afternoon," replied the DCP. "Who am I speaking with?"

"A vampire, sir. Surrounded by nine-fingered men. Isn't it time we spoke?"

The DCP's eyebrow rose. He looked at his colleagues, his cigarette quietly smoking in his hand.

"By all means, put me on speakerphone, sir. I'd like Kapoor sahib and Miss Smita to hear this too."

The DCP's eyes swung around his city, from the dome of a fabled mosque at one end to the cooling towers of a power plant at the other. The air itself swam with the coughs and bleats of traffic and the shrieks of the kites and there were people everywhere, on the roads, in buildings, on roofs and corners and even on the ancient battlements across the road. His finger flipped the call to speaker while his eyes continued to scan the city even as his mind told him he hadn't a hope of tying a location to the voice.

"Good of you to call," he said drily.

"Pleasure's mine, sir. A nice day for it too, don't you think?"

There was a question in Smita's eyes and Kapoor's were narrowed.

"Please don't bother trying to locate me," said the voice conversationally. "If one of you leaves your balcony, I'll hang up."

"Only reason I'll be leaving this balcony is to hang your balls around your throat," said Kapoor pleasantly.

The voice chuckled.

"Such stories one hears about you, uncle. Some of my friends, these past few weeks. When will you realize we're not the enemy?"

"Clearly you're not our friends," said Smita shortly.

"Why do you say that, miss? Because we ran around and played games with foolish kids last summer? Because my friends and I collected our due from men who reneged on their commitments? All we ever did was take one finger. The same one those fools promised us when they were drunk and took their oaths."

"That's all it was?" asked the DCP.

"That's all it's ever been. The fingers were nothing. A symbol. A penance. A price."

"What about the drug dealer?"

"We didn't kill him and you know it."

"His girlfriend?"

"We knew where she was. By the time we got to her, she was dead."

"Who killed him?"

"He had a long client list."

"Do you know?"

"We may. But do you care?"

"Why should we believe you?"

"Why would I lie?"

"Why call us there?"

"We wanted to talk."

"Why beat me up?"

"That was a mistake. Some of our number still resent what happened with my brother."

"The one who died?"

The voice laughed. "Don't bother trying to connect the dots. We're all brothers."

"He wasn't missing a finger," said Kapoor suspiciously.

"Neither am I."

"A caste system," murmured the DCP.

"Exactly. We're *for* the brotherhood, sir. Not of it. What do I have in common with a ragpicker or a village cobbler?"

The police officers assimilated this in the bright afternoon, new cigarettes smoking in their hands.

"Why didn't you talk to me when you had the chance?" asked the DCP.

"Miss Smita ran away. Quite a feat, miss. Especially in those shoes. You looked lovely."

"You're the one in the kaffiyeh," said Smita.

"Quite right. I'm wearing it now."

Three sets of eyes turned involuntarily to the city. The voice laughed out loud.

"You seem very sure of yourself," said the DCP.

"That's because we know quite a lot."

"Such as?"

"We know where you went to ground." Kapoor's eyes flared, then dropped. "Handy place to hide, sir. But now we know where she is."

The police officers waited.

"We know about Miss Smita's personal interest in the rape case you solved so spectacularly."

"Really?" said Smita sharply. "Did you know that one of the rapists was missing a finger?"

"We're not a religion," said the voice levelly. "We don't expect our brothers to conform to a higher morality. I'm not a rapist. I'm glad he's dead, frankly. But him being a rapist has nothing to do with me."

"Were you there that night?" asked the DCP suddenly.

"I might have been."

"Why didn't you warn your friend?" asked Kapoor.

"Pay attention, Kapoor sahib. I said I'm glad he's dead. Do you think your nephews are loyal only to you? How do you think you found the rapists so quickly?"

Kapoor laughed, uninhibited, unexpected. "There are more of you than I thought. I'd like to meet you one day, son. Just you and me."

"I'm sure you would, uncle. You don't mind if I do my best to make sure that never happens?"

Kapoor laughed again, this time joined by the voice at the other end.

"What do you want?" said the DCP quietly.

"What does anyone want? A better life. A place to call home. A car with leather seats."

Smita laughed in her turn, bitter on the afternoon

air. "That's all? That's the extent of your ambitions? You're just another gang of petty criminals."

"Perhaps, Miss Smita. But we hope to be in a position where that won't always be the case."

"My god," she said. "With your web, your connections. What changes you could unleash. But you don't want change, do you?"

"Of course not," said the voice, the shrug audible in his tone. "We just want a slice of the world as it is. You must see that. We're beginning to understand this world and its workings. Why would we want another one?"

There was a pause, a moment where he seemed to be marshaling his thoughts.

"It started as a game a few years ago. On the Internet. Some like-minded friends. That's what you disrupted last summer. But it had already grown of its own accord. We never knew it would take root that quickly, and to that extent. Now there are legions of nine-fingered fuck-ups on the fringes of this city run by men like myself. We're not a political party. We're not a social organization. We're not vigilantes and we're certainly not criminals. Not yet."

"So what," repeated the DCP gently, "do you want?"

"From you? Not a lot. Respect. A listening ear. Razia."

The DCP exhaled slowly. "Why?"

"She's of interest to us. We can work out everyone else involved. But she's a mystery. She has everyone's ear, but nobody knows who she is. Even in this city, sir, don't you think that's odd?"

The DCP thought about Delhi's nooks and shadows and the creatures within them, born of darkness and bred on percentages, ephemeral ghosts of buried contracts and barely acknowledged deals.

"My brother lost his way, sir. Perhaps he was lost to begin with and all she did was take advantage of the opportunity he presented. Maybe it's a good thing for everyone concerned that he's dead. But he wanted the right thing."

"Which is?"

"Who is Razia, sir? What is she?"

"Anything else?" asked the DCP by way of reply.

"We just want to be taken seriously. Can you make that happen for us? Make your friend the minister take us seriously? And everyone else?"

The DCP rubbed his eyes and turned them to the sky, a passing helicopter beating a throbbing tattoo against the cloudless firmament.

"What can you tell me about this missing child?" he asked softly.

There was a chuckle from the other end. "I thought you'd never ask."

———

The child had been sequestered in a quiet middle-class locality just south of the Outer Ring Road. There were vestiges of older cities amid the jutting appurtenances of newer villages and the baroque and neogothic shadows of builders' flats. But in the shady lanes of that particular enclave, facing parks which would be dotted, later that day, with dozing seniors and retired teachers, sat old single-story homes with peeling paint and laundry on lines outside. The bare skeleton of the special task force had kept vigil outside one such home that evening and night, monitoring presence and activity. Nobody had been spoken with, nobody informed. There was, it was noted, at least one adult male, who left the house for the shopping. There seemed to be one woman of uncertain age, spied only through a window. A radio played quietly through the cracked window. A TV had come on at night, tuned to the same bland fare that consumed the rest of the city. There was no hint of any other life or activity, certainly nothing to indicate the presence of a child.

The entry was planned for the next morning, as soon as the adult male left the house. A group of three officers was instructed to apprehend him on receiving word from the DCP or Kapoor that the child was secure.

The adult male exited the house nice and early, the air still cold and the sky pink. He wandered away, hawking and spitting, toward the nearby market. On his arm jingled a vessel for the milk he was clearly off to collect. The DCP waited for the amount of time they'd agreed on beforehand to elapse, then walked across to the door and rang the bell. The TV was abruptly switched off. The DCP nodded at Kapoor, who ran across with Smita to either side of the door. The DCP waited and rang the bell again. He took a deep breath and aimed a kick at the door. It buckled beneath his foot and a moment later, the three of them were in, their weapons in their hands but the safeties still on. There was no point, Kapoor had noted, in delivering a dead child.

The frightened woman inside put up no semblance of a fight. She was young, minimally literate in Hindi. Her eyes flicked to the room she'd just been in, a darker space behind an open door. The DCP was there in three strides, his weapon scanning for threats. On the bed lay a child with its eyes open. A glance at him and the DCP knew their search was at an end. Kapoor was past him in a moment, a paw snatching the child to his breast. Then Smita was behind them. "Clear," she reported, a catch in her breath as she saw the young boy in Kapoor's arms.

"Drugged," said Kapoor. "Seems fine otherwise. His breathing is normal." His weapon was already holstered, his hands busy about the boy. "No fever. Warmly dressed. Not cold at all. He's okay."

"Secure the woman," said the DCP to Smita.

She nodded toward the far wall of the outside room, where the woman was already handcuffed and cowering next to the window grill to which she was attached. Then they heard the gunshots, percussive against the quiet early morning. Then, inevitably as the night follows the day, the screams. First a feminine howl, then a mixture of masculine yells, and finally a thin continuous wailing from the handcuffed terrified woman behind them. The DCP swore as Kapoor swung to Smita, handing over his burden. Smita cradled the drugged child and ran out to the car where the driver already had the engine running, his finger poised on the siren. She dove in with the child, the car in motion even before the door slammed shut. The last thing she saw before they turned the corner was her senior officers crouching, their weapons at the ready, this time presumably with the safeties off. Around them were two dogs, an elderly morning walker, a couple hand in hand with their spare hands to their mouths, a child in school uniform with his hand in his mother's. Birds startled by all the activity shrieked by. A peaceful morning tableau, she thought to herself, before we came along.

———————⟶——⟶———

"What the fuck is going on?" inquired Kapoor, reasonably enough.

A man, the single adult male of a few moments before, lay at his feet. His blood mingled with the milk from the fallen steel vessel by his side. An inclination of the head from Kapoor and one of the men kneeled at his side, feeling for a pulse. He shook his head. The DCP, now holstering his weapon, swore again. He squinted up against the quickening sun, searching for the source of the screams. A useless search, he discovered, as the previously mono wail was now in stereo mode, as the mothers and wives and domestics of this quiet enclave registered that violent death had stopped by. The DCP squatted by the corpse, noted the wounds, looked up at the unit of men who'd so let him down. They stood there, sullen defeat in their shoulders and backs, their fingers still on their trigger guards till Kapoor told them to put their weapons away. The DCP went back to his examination. His hands worked away at the man's pockets, taking things out, sifting for information.

Kapoor turned to the colony at large and said the magic word: "Police."

The dogs had already disappeared, though the mixture of blood and milk was a rich one they'd be back for. The mother had dragged the child to the periphery of the scene and was now bawling. The child wasn't, its eyes wide open and absorbing everything. The couple were pressed against a wall. The elderly walker was the only one who strode up to Kapoor.

"I saw everything," he said.

Kapoor flipped open his notebook, took down his particulars. He thanked him, advised him to stay at home till he'd been spoken with. One of the other men had already called and set the wheels in motion. More officers were on their way, a forensics unit, an ambulance which they all knew wouldn't be required.

The old man wasn't going anywhere. He was lurking, his mouth working, his eyes jumping about. He couldn't hold it in.

"In cold blood!" he shouted. He pointed to the trio of police officers who were now patrolling the perimeter, keeping walkers, students, and other pleasure-seekers away from the thrill of watching a man's lifeblood drain away. His finger shook and so did his voice, but there was no uncertainty in him as he pointed at the men he'd so implicated.

Kapoor walked him away, a gentle arm around one skinny shoulder. "I know," he said soothingly. "Go now. I promise I'll take your testimony. I want the truth too."

"I served in the army," said the old man determinedly. "I know what's right. I won't be scared. I'll testify."

"I can believe it," said Kapoor admiringly. "Now go."

The old man walked away, his eyes still on the scene. The men he'd pointed at looked after him, their sunglasses now on against the brightening light; nobody could see what was in their eyes.

Kapoor turned back to the DCP, who was looking

at the meager trove in his hands and on the road before him, oblivious to the blood and the milk that were now pooling against his boots.

"What was that about?" asked the DCP.

"The old man saw it."

"Clearly. Will he testify?"

"Seems so. A bit early in the day. Testosterone, adrenaline. Says he served in the army."

"When?"

"The Mutiny, by the look of him. I'll get a statement before he changes his mind."

"The local cops?"

"I called the SHO. He should be here any moment."

"Talk to the boys. Before they have a chance to talk to each other. We all know what happened just now."

Kapoor lumbered to his feet. The DCP's fit frame could bear to squat, but Kapoor's older bones were a different story. His grimace didn't go away as he ambled over to the nearest officer.

"Who shot him?"

The officer looked away as the cops from the station poured in. They took over the perimeter, talking to the people who were lurking on the scene, hitting doorbells and quieting screamers. The sobbing woman from inside the building that had housed the child was led away to the charge of the women's wing. The other two members of the special task force, the remaining men who had been at the scene, walked over and joined Kapoor, who lit a cigarette and sat down on the hood of the nearest car. The three men took their positions in a quiet line before him.

"Who shot him?" he asked again, without heat.

"I did," said one of them finally.

"How many times?"

"Twice."

"I heard three shots."

"The last one was mine," said one of the others.

"Why?"

"He was walking back from the market. We heard a commotion from the house. A woman screamed. I thought I saw him quickening his steps."

"So?"

The first shooter took up the story: "He reached for his weapon. I shouted to him to stop. He didn't. I had my gun out."

"How far were you?" Kapoor asked.

"Ten feet. Maybe less."

Kapoor looked at the second man. "You?"

"About the same. But behind him."

Kapoor eyed the third man, the one who hadn't squeezed off a shot. "Where were you?"

"To the side. Perhaps twenty feet."

"The man didn't notice any of you?"

The three of them stayed silent.

Kapoor waited, smoking quietly, the hubbub of the investigation picking up around him. The four of them were conscious of being the center of attention of a hundred pairs of hidden eyes. One of the men was beginning to sweat despite the chill of the morning. If Kapoor noticed, he gave no sign.

"Three bullets," he said with a shrug. "Head, chest, and back. Ten feet or less. I suppose congratulations are in order."

The three of them shuffled silently.

"He didn't have a weapon. No gun. No knife. Not even a set of keys."

They danced from foot to foot as Kapoor smoked and watched.

"Ever kill anyone before, son?"

The first man shook his head.

"You?"

The second one shook his head as well, attempted to say something. Kapoor silenced him with a wave.

"Was it worth it?"

"He was a criminal, sir," insisted one of the shooters sullenly.

"How do you know that? Did you see me exit the house with the child? What you saw was a man with a milk can in his hand."

"You could have been in danger!"

"With my nephews around me?" laughed Kapoor mirthlessly. "Whom I trust above all else? How, why, would I ever be scared?"

The three of them looked at Kapoor, then at each other, then at nothing at all.

"Which one of you took the contract? Was it both? All three, and the third just lost his nerve?"

They were all sweating now as Kapoor's affable voice droned on.

"Or was it just the one man, and you panicked and fired too? And now you see your chance, you know what happened, you were there, and you'll have your hand out as well when the payout comes? Are you even telling me the truth? Hmm? Can I trust my nephews? Or not?"

"I've been with you for three years, sir," said the last one, the one with no bullets missing from his chamber.

"Yes, you have," said Kapoor meditatively. "I suggest you men get your stories ready. Lord knows you'll be given the chance to fuck them up."

The three of them dispersed unhappily.

"One more thing," added Kapoor as an afterthought. "It doesn't matter how stupid that woman inside turns out to be. You know this man wasn't the last link, right?"

They all turned back. He grinned at them.

"You are."

⸻

The third officer, the one with all the bullets still in his gun, had come up to Kapoor, as the older man had known he would. He'd claimed his innocence, first quietly and then strenuously, oblivious to the two other officers standing sullenly to one side. It was, he claimed, an execution. The first man had stepped up to the milk-bearer and challenged him, provoking him to flight. The next second, he'd pulled his weapon and shot him. The other one had been quick to shoot as well, but he wasn't prepared to swear that the second man was in on it. Perhaps the adrenaline of the moment had led to his joining the party. What was a fact was that the first man's bullets had been entirely unprovoked.

Kapoor thanked him and told him his troubles were just starting, but if he kept his head and story straight and told the inquiries that would inevitably follow exactly what he'd seen, he'd be fine. He owed nothing to those trigger-happy assholes, Kapoor was at pains to point out. If anything, he owed him, Kapoor, and his patron the DCP, whose benevolence had led to the glamour and perks of Crime Branch. And they, said Kapoor, were on the side of the good guys, did he understand? The other man nodded unhappily.

"Nobody ever claimed doing the right thing was easy," said Kapoor.

"It's a lot easier than shooting an unarmed man in the back," replied the other man. Kapoor nodded and sent him on his way.

The DCP iced his subordinates in turn. The men who'd pulled their triggers were informed their careers were over, that they'd be lucky to stay out of jail. If they thought the special powers of the man or men who'd hired them were protection enough, they were sorely mistaken, and he'd make it his mission in life to make theirs as miserable as possible. He did this with an absence of emotion that recommended itself to Kapoor, who watched the performance, waiting, hoping for one of them to come clean. Naturally, neither man did.

At least, said the older man heavily, we got the child.

That young boy had been delivered to his unbelieving parents by Smita, straight from the scene of his rescue. The mother's reaction had been predictable to Smita. The father's complete disintegration was less so. The sight of the two of them around their restored offspring would haunt her dreams for days. The strength of the bond that animated their arms around each other and their still-drugged child was an obscure source of grief to her that she would pick at in the hours and days to come.

A pediatrician had arrived to look at the child and the grandfather had come soon after. It was at that point that Smita had known her grip on the case and its dramatis personae was slipping. The old gentleman had been polite but firm, and had informed her regretfully that he'd be in touch with her and not the other way around. She'd listened in disbelief, pointed out that an investigation still continued and did he realize what that entailed? He'd smiled and offered her a cup of coffee and called the commissioner who instructed her, in so many words, to turn the cheek as the child's family exited her field of vision. Who will take responsibility if they skip town? she asked heatedly. He would, the commissioner replied coolly, telling her not to worry. They're not going anywhere, he continued. They weren't stupid and they needed to heal. As a family. Besides, he pointed out in a conciliatory tone, she'd done very well and should enjoy the moment. And the fact that a very powerful family was now and forever in her debt. At which point he hung up.

She'd watched the family disappear, with only the mobile numbers of the grandfather and parents in her purse. That, and a memory of the woman crying and embracing her child and saying, "That old bastard said he'd be safe and I didn't believe him," her husband shushing her and crying as well. She'd told the DCP what had happened, been met over the phone with a shrug that was almost audible, been instructed to join the two male officers back at HQ for the mountain of paperwork that loomed in front of them. She'd absorbed the news of the death of the child's guard, had ascertained that the woman in custody was as nonfunctional as they'd feared, turned on the TV in the recently vacated living room to find old photos of her and the DCP all over the waves, next to live images, now, of the crime scene, mercifully without the man at its center. Milk and blood still stained the road.

It was a quiet afternoon at the office. The DCP had rebuffed all attempts at interviews with a curt nod to the fact that the investigation was still alive. The three officers who'd been instructed to watch the milk-bearer had been stripped of their badges and weapons, and were already facing the first of many debriefings. The triumph of the child's return was neutralized by the knowledge that the case was now effectively at a dead end. That this would be highlighted in the press that evening and in the days to come was not lost on anyone. What heightened the surreality of the situation for Smita was the air of congratulation that hung over HQ. It was as if, she said to Kapoor, the entire police force of Delhi had chosen to close its eyes to what had happened that morning. As if the child's recovery was the endgame.

"I'm not sure," said Kapoor meditatively, "that the kid was ever in any danger."

"Because of what the builder said?" asked Smita.

"Because if they were planning to kill him, he'd already be dead."

"They're hardly professional kidnappers, sir. They didn't even ask for anything, aside from that one note."

"Exactly. It wasn't about anything at all. This whole thing's been a setup from the beginning. It's gone exactly the way it should have."

"Even the tip from the vampire?"

"No. That doesn't fit. But the tip would have come. Maybe not this soon. But it was only a matter of time."

"How can you be so sure?"

Kapoor gestured about him, his arm taking in the quiet office, the pensive silent DCP, and the hubbub of celebration outside. "We're the only idiots thinking we've failed, girl. Everyone else thinks it's time to party. Not one of our bosses has called to finger us about losing a suspect. They don't give a fuck what the media will say. Neither will the media in a week's time."

"So?"

"So this is over. We've been played. Again."

Smita nodded in sour agreement. "Funny thing. The mother. She was crying and saying the same thing over and over."

"What?"

"That some old bastard had promised her child would be safe. And she didn't believe him. Who do you think she was talking about?"

The DCP's mobile phone buzzed, its metallic hum pulling him out of his abstracted state. He sighed and reached for it, the number raising one of his eyebrows.

"Good afternoon, ma'am," he said politely. A well-bred torrent of congratulations followed over the phone, to which the DCP supplied appreciative sounds, now and again. "I didn't know that," he said at one stage, and, "Glad to have helped," at another. His shoulders sagged under the weight of the murmured approbation. He turned to his juniors when it ended.

"The minister?" inquired Kapoor. A nod.

"Happy?" asked Smita. Clearly.

"Not a word about the dead end, of course?" A shake of the head this time.

"The grandfather's an old friend?" Ancient.

The DCP sighed, got up, and took a turn about his

room. "She said something quite interesting. The old man had called her when the child was taken, had tasked her with his safe recovery. She'd told him the entire machinery of the state would work toward that end, but of course there were no guarantees. The old man had persisted, insisted, had asked her for just that, a guarantee of his only grandson's safety. Finally, she told me, she'd given in. She had furnished said verbal guarantee. She was beside herself with happiness that I had been the instrument of her keeping her promise and she didn't have the words to thank me."

Kapoor and Smita looked at each other.

"I was following your conversation, you know," said the DCP.

"The grandfather?" asked Smita in disbelief.

"The friendship of powerful people isn't always a blessing," remarked Kapoor. The DCP looked at him sharply, then nodded.

"I think she wanted me to know. To understand, almost. As if she wanted to include me."

He sat down, his hands behind his head, his feet up on his table. "Are we idiots?" he asked eventually. "The case has been brought to a successful conclusion. Nobody but a few rags no one reads will ever ask what the point of this whole operation was. The absence of a ransom, the lack of motive. Nothing. Everyone here is celebrating. There may even be a new medal on my breast at the end of this."

The other two officers waited for their senior's chain of thought to exhaust itself. He continued when he noted the resilience of their silence.

"All of Delhi is talking about this other angle. That

the whole thing was put in place to embarrass that builder and his patron. It doesn't need to be true, of course. That it's entered our conversations is enough. The damage has already been done. The builder knows and the grandfather knows and you and I all know that."

"What do we do, sir?" asked Smita desperately.

"We're the police, Smita. What do you think we should do?"

"A man's dead. Executed in cold blood."

"By our own," added Kapoor. "That doesn't sit well with me."

"What about that dead man?" the DCP asked. "Any friends and acquaintances? He must have some sort of history."

"I've asked around. He didn't get off the train yesterday." Kapoor stalked off.

Smita considered her superior officer as he mined the vein of abstraction he was currently in.

"I don't like being manipulated," she said finally, her voice loud in the almost empty office.

"Neither do I."

"Do you believe the tip would have come anyway, sir? That those nine-fingered fools just beat the men behind this whole thing to it?"

The DCP nodded.

"How do they know so much?" said Smita.

"The vampire and his crowd? Delhi's always been fertile ground for societies of all sorts. People come here from everywhere. They don't speak the language, know nobody else. They band together with men and women they think they have something in common with."

Smita waited, knowing the older man wasn't finished.

"Groups of working men play the lotteries together and split their winnings. Couples band together in committees and put in money every month so that they're guaranteed payouts sometime in the future. Student groups, political movements, neighborhood clubs. Festival committees, unions, layabouts who like Chinese movies and practice martial arts.

"Even the big colonial clubs. What are they? Vestiges of the imperial class structure. Agglomerations of men and a few women who perceive their pasts and futures in the same terms. Invitation only, closed to the rest of the world, their workings inscrutable. They're secret societies, Smita. But nobody says so, because everybody wants in.

"A society of nine-fingered men? I'm surprised it's taken this long. There's no shortage of losers and deadbeats in this city. They must be everywhere, watching everything." He tapped his mobile phone. "The only thing that's changed is this."

"That doesn't scare you?" asked Smita.

"What? That there's another layer to Delhi? Another set of men who want a slice of the pie and see that they won't get it unless they pull together?" He shrugged. "When they start breaking the law, I'll start worrying."

"They've already beaten you up," said Smita tartly.

"Maybe I deserved it," smiled the DCP. "For being so blind."

Tea arrived, the two of them sipping in companionable silence as the afternoon's shadows lengthened in the DCP's office. The day had already been a strenuous one, and they both knew their own commitment to a resolution of the case entailed more activity. Smita and the DCP fielded calls and accepted the congratulations of their peers without any apparent heat. Knowing the way forward enabled them to enjoy their respite and to treat its inevitable end with equanimity when it finally came, in the form of the builder, shadowed by Kapoor.

"He wanted to talk to us. Wouldn't take no for an answer."

The builder nodded politely to the assembly, took the offered seat, raised one leg, and put it across his knee.

"Busy day?" he offered to the officers.

They nodded their heads separately, their eyes on the visitor. He was wearing his shades inside the room and a suit that was rescued from being gaudy by its expense. His shirt, an expensive affair that looked to be a mix of cotton and silk, was open at the throat. Smita glanced at his shoes from force of habit: two-tone brogues, stylishly obnoxious in a way that grated on her.

"Congratulations," he said, taking off his glasses and placing them in his breast pocket, stem side inward so as not to disturb his silk square. His mouth smiled but his eyes remained watchful.

The DCP inclined his head slightly, acknowledging the tribute on behalf of his team.

"I spoke to the grandfather," said the builder. "He was very happy. He was particularly impressed with you, madam." He smiled at Smita; she didn't bother to reply. "He said you were smart, young. That you were principled and a credit to the force."

"Really?"

The builder nodded, the shark's smile growing. "He said you knew when to keep quiet."

"Is that an advantage?"

The builder spread his hands and shrugged. "He's an old man. His generation liked that in their women. Men my age like our women to be slightly different."

Smita felt the color rising up her neck, but she stayed focused on the builder.

"Your staying quiet is one thing, madam. But Kapoor sahib and the DCP? I would have thought men in your position would have opened your mouths by now."

"About what?" asked the DCP mildly. "The case is closed, surely."

The builder turned to Kapoor. "Uncle? Do you think the same?"

"What I think is my business," Kapoor replied heavily.

The builder laughed, switched legs, turned back to Smita. "Ten years ago, uncle wouldn't have been sitting here drinking tea with the likes of me. He'd have been out there practicing his skills on the lowlifes of this city, working out what had happened. Times change, of course. But I'm surprised Kapoor sahib has."

He leaned back, his body draped negligently in the cheap office chair.

"Ever seen uncle practice, madam? I've asked you before, of course. But it's quite a sight."

Kapoor cleared his throat, a warning sound in the still office air. The builder looked at him in mock surprise.

"Everybody needs practice, uncle. You know that. Why protect her from the inevitable?"

"Are you volunteering as a subject?" inquired Kapoor.

"Watch your tone, Kapoor," flashed the builder.

"I don't need to, son. Remember why you're here?"

"This will die down."

"Even so. One of these days you'll be coming back here. Or I'll be on the road at a checkpoint. You think those apes at your gate will be able to keep your balls out of my hand? What do you think you'll do when I start squeezing, you stupid cunt?" The older officer leaned back in his chair, one of his own legs now on a knee, the shoe pointing directly at the builder.

The builder's eyes were slits, a vein throbbing on his forehead, but his voice was still polite, the tone reasonable. "I'll find something about *you* to squeeze. You and I both know that."

"Sure," nodded Kapoor. "But you won't. You were out of line. You and I both know that. Don't we?"

The DCP laughed, his hands as ever behind his head, his feet now on his desk. After a moment, the builder laughed as well, and Smita felt herself breathe again.

"I'm sorry, madam," said the builder with irony. "Please don't misunderstand my words. We've all been under some pressure since that poor child disappeared."

Smita inclined her head in the barest of acknowledgments. Three separate eyebrows climbed up three separate foreheads, but she kept her eyes level on the builder and after a moment he lowered his own, gracefully, silently, in defeat.

"Why," asked the DCP conversationally, "are you here?"

"You don't believe that dead asshole was behind this, do you?"

"Are you asking me whether I know a setup when I see one?"

The builder laughed again, jaggedly. "If you're interested in information, sir, I may have some."

"You're assuming we don't have it already."

The builder acknowledged that as well.

"What I know is that practically nobody wants this case to go any further. The grandfather made that clear to me. Nothing I've learned since makes me want to change my mind. Am I correct?" The DCP watched the builder silently.

"Sir, we all know I'm fucked. Even with this child back home. There isn't a person in Delhi who doesn't think me responsible, or at least connected to that poor kid's disappearance. Even if they don't think so, it doesn't change the fact that the suspicion was there to begin with. Now people will think I had that guy killed this morning. To protect myself. That, or they think this whole game was set up to embarrass me. Which objective is being met just beautifully right now. I'm the only man in this city right now who wants to find the real culprit. Am I right?"

"What if you are?"

"Well," said the builder, "I was hoping I wasn't. The only one."

"What do you know?" asked the DCP softly.

"The dead man was Bengali. So is the woman, the idiot they found there. Correct?"

The DCP nodded.

"The man was a freelancer. His ustad is a Bangladeshi. He's been in and out of jail for years."

The builder threw a name out to the room. The DCP looked at Kapoor, who nodded fractionally.

"He's a hood. Burglary to begin with, some petty

extortion. Rioting on occasion. Now he's a land shark."

"Moving up in the world," said the DCP.

"I've never used him, but I know of him." He named a basti between the river and the eastern edge of the city. Smita frowned, the DCP sighed, and Kapoor looked at the ceiling.

"Tell me something I don't already know," rumbled Kapoor.

The builder leaned urgently forward, his eyes on the DCP. "Our common friend asked me to come to you, sir. She said you were the only one who could help."

Smita glanced at the DCP in surprise. Kapoor studied his hands. The DCP considered the builder quietly. That man turned to Kapoor.

"I came here for help, uncle," said the builder. "Please. You're good cops. Different from those assholes outside. Not one of them would have had the balls to talk to me the way you just did. I know that and that's why I'm here."

"Why would I help you?" asked Kapoor easily.

"Don't do it for me. Do it because it's the right thing to do."

"What do you know about right and wrong?" asked Smita scornfully.

"I may have forgotten the difference, madam. I'm hoping you haven't."

A touch of summer was in the evening air as they drove through the city toward the basti where the Bangladeshi lived. His background was as the builder had described it. He was a small-time felon who'd graduated with the real estate boom in Delhi to becoming a landlord in exactly the sort of marginal locality to which they were bound. He maintained order in his tenements and organized signatures on his papers with the help of an unending stream of men from the Bengali hinterland, men like the one who'd breathed his last in a pool of blood and milk. Alone, adrift in Delhi, brought to the slumlord by cousins who already worked for him, and now a statistic. Typical, thought Smita.

The conversation had been fairly typical as well. The builder's nod to the circumcised condition of the slumlord and his minions, Kapoor's laughing acceptance of what he said as fact, the DCP's tacit acknowledgment: it had irritated Smita to the point of almost saying something. As it was, her tight-lipped demeanor in the car was lost on no one.

"What's bothering you, girl?" asked Kapoor gently.

"Was all that talk about their being Muslim really necessary?" she replied.

Kapoor rolled his eyes and the DCP looked out his window.

"No. Seriously. We serve all the citizens of this city. Don't we?"

"Yes, we do. That's why we're hunting down a dead Muslim kidnapper's partners—so we can do something about his murder. The only people who give a shit about that man are in this car."

"I'm not sure you do care about him."

"Perhaps not," said the DCP levelly. "Can you claim you do?"

Smita looked away.

"Justice," proclaimed the DCP, "is blind to a man's religion."

"The problem is, we aren't."

The DCP thought about this for a moment, nodded his assent. "What matters, Smita, is not what we think. It's what we do."

She looked at him, at his face etched against the passing lights of traffic headed in the other direction on a long bridge over a mass of railway lines. The sun was setting in one direction, the moon already a silver presence in the other. The sky was both deep pink and dark blue and the last kites of the evening wheeled in the air.

"Do you really believe that?"

He looked into her eyes, weighed his words. "Maybe not. But it helps me get through the day and do what needs to be done. And it helps me deal with men like your uncle." He indicated the back of Kapoor's head, as that man lolled in his customary position in the front seat, next to the driver. The DCP smiled and Kapoor laughed, then turned in his seat to grin at Smita.

"Well, girl," asked that legend of the Delhi Police. "Are you going to hassle me about what I think, or help me with what we're on our way to do?"

Smita shook her head and smiled. The vehicle drove to where the one man Kapoor trusted in the local station was waiting for them. He was where he'd told them to park, at a boom barrier that guarded the privileged inhabitants of a quiet treelined colony from the hordes who lurked in the basti across the road. The muezzin's amplified call to evening prayer was electric on the air as he climbed quickly into the car, next to Smita who moved over to make room for him.

He swiftly explained the lay of the land. The basti across the road was off-limits even to the policemen, unless they went in groups. The man they were looking for was one of perhaps half a dozen enforcers whose writ was absolute in the area. The people who lived in the basti weren't all Bangladeshis. They were domestics and shop assistants and clerks and the like who worked in the houses and offices of the area, and they came from all over. But the hard men of the area were mostly Bengalis and the locals went in fear of them, especially when they'd been drinking.

"What about the local Gujjars?" asked Smita.

"They've made their peace with these bastards," said the local cop. "They had to . . . They're like rats. Small, quick, vicious. Good with knives. Don't use guns much. Don't need them around here. Razors and knives are enough: they're cutters, not killers. Keep them ten feet away from you, with your weapons on them. Get a gun on the leader as quickly as possible. Then they'll do as they're told. Don't turn your backs to them." He looked at the DCP in the rapidly fading light. "Got a warrant, sir?"

The DCP shook his head mildly. The local officer shrugged.

"Don't need one around here, really. At least half these fuckers aren't registered to vote anyway." He leaned across to Kapoor, patted his meaty shoulder. "Try not to kill any citizens, uncle."

Smita was surprised to hear her own laugh in the chorus that followed. The local cop shook his head and smiled. He gestured to the house they were parked next to, a palatial white home with a uniformed guard outside who was regarding them with lazy suspicion. A politically active lawyer, said the cop. An important person in the city, indeed all over India. If his maid or anyone in her family caught a bullet in a crossfire, there'd be hell to pay.

"We're hoping there'll be no bullets at all," said the DCP. He started to get out, then closed the door. Another car had come to a stop on the other side of the boom. A man with a lit cigarette got out, stretched indolently, smoked against the electric light of the darkening city. A passing car lit up his features and Kapoor cursed the gentleman's mother and sister.

"Fat chance of no bullets now, sir," said the local cop. "That asshole was right to be worried."

"I beg your pardon?"

"The Bangladeshi, miss. He's been reaching out to us in the station ever since the morning news. The men he knows, even those he hasn't paid off, asking for anything, any word at all. One of my informers lives close to him. He told me it looks like he's leaving town. His wife and children left for the train station just twenty minutes ago." He felt Smita's eyes on him in the dark, turned to her. "Uncle knew. I've been updating him."

"I was hoping we'd be the first ones to him," Kapoor said. "He must have known the game was up since he turned the TV on this morning."

The DCP inclined his head to the rangy form of the smoking man, which was now ambling toward their car. Kapoor thumbed a switch, the window next to him rolling down. A man with a face that would have been handsome if it wasn't so cruel leaned to Kapoor's level. He threw an unacknowledged salute to the DCP, nodded pleasantly to Smita and the local officer, turned his eyes to Kapoor.

"Welcome to the party, uncle."

"Didn't know you were invited," replied Kapoor evenly.

"You know," laughed the other man easily, "these sorts of invitations tend to get misplaced."

"You know he's ours," said Kapoor.

"That's not what I've been told."

"I'm telling you now."

"It's going to take more than that."

"What would it take?"

"A call from a number I'm assuming you don't have."

Kapoor laughed, fished out a cigarette of his own. He climbed out, leaned against the car, and lit up, taking a luxuriant puff. "It's a privilege," he said, "to be hunting the same asshole as you. Even the men you kill become celebrities."

"You've known me for longer than that, uncle."

"Even then I knew you'd go far."

"You always had an eye for talent."

"Didn't take a genius to see what your talent was, son."

The DCP joined the two of them, night settling with finality around them with a warmth that spoke of the season to come. He accepted the cigarette Kapoor offered him, declined the offer of a light from the third man, lit it himself, and leaned in turn against the car.

"Who sent you?"

"What does it matter, sir? That man's been dead since he accepted the kidnapping. Only one who didn't know it was him."

"I suppose there's no point telling you it's your duty to help in bringing this case to its conclusion?" said the DCP.

"I'm committed to just that, sir. That's why I'm here."

"Telling you your career is over would be a waste of time."

"My career's not in your hands, sir. Besides, men like me don't make it to commissioner. I'm already doing what I'm good at."

The DCP noted the dead glaze in the other man's eyes, the excitement of the chase and the sheen of whatever it was he took to ready himself for its eventual fruition. He felt another approach, smelled Smita's shampoo at his shoulder. The man across from the three of them shifted his attention to the female officer, took in the local cop who was now standing near the others, threw an absent salaam his way that wasn't returned.

"You with them?" he asked blandly of the local cop.

"I'm not with you."

The other man laughed, easily and genuinely, flicked his cigarette against the wall behind him. The guard at the gate noted his posture and bearing and turned away inside his shack, pulling the door closed.

"You picked a hell of a night to be a real cop, uncle."

"Are you threatening me, son?"

"Threaten you? Kapoor of the Delhi Police? There isn't a man alive who can do that."

"Are you still alive?" murmured the DCP.

"More so than that cunt across the road. Stay out of my way, sir. Someone's going to have to die tonight."

"Someone," said Smita recklessly.

"I'm in the mood, sweetheart. When the time comes, I won't be fussy."

"Did you kill that drug dealer?" asked the DCP quietly.

"Come on, sir. Am I the only killer in this city?" He smiled and strode off to where his team was assembling, two men of his own ilk smoking and chatting by the side of the road.

Kapoor noted Smita's involuntary shudder. "It isn't just you, girl. That cold bastard makes my skin crawl too."

"How many men has he killed?" she asked softly.

"Only he knows," said the DCP. "And for whom. Alright. This changes things." He turned to the local cop. "We've got less time than we thought. What do you think?"

The other man thought for a moment. "I spent some time in that maniac's squad. I couldn't take it, so they put me back in a uniform. But I know his methods. He'll walk in through the front door. He doesn't know any other way."

"So?"

"We go around to the back. Come on."

———————————

Nightfall by the Yamuna:

Their road lies around the periphery of the basti, the modest dwellings of the poor people to one side, the feverish fenestrations of upper-middle-class Delhi to the other. The driver speeds along the road under the instructions of the local officer, heading always toward the river. He turns off the road through a colony gate, through a boom barrier that is now raised at the policeman's instructions, picks his way across a track that is more river sand than city surface. They make their way by the light of the risen moon to the settlement whose lip sits squat on the river's edge as countless others have done in this city's water-starved history. A settlement of immigrants awaits them, lorded over by an arriviste slumlord who has made common cause with his cousins on furlough from the lands of their births. They've come here chasing a dream, but they've found this mean warren of hovels through which runs a shit-soaked drain, and the four walls of their houses enclose the sum total of their possessions. Yet these too are homes and they are, already and forever, citizens of Delhi, no matter the shit that clings to their feet as they walk to and fro.

Smita stops by the DCP's side and feels his eyes on her. She looks up at him and he asks: "You feel it too?"

She nods and he says, "No time to think anymore. Time to do."

Then they're running. Shouts go up in the air, figures materialize out of doorways, a man tries to stop them and is flattened by Kapoor's outstretched arm. Smita spies a cricket game being watched on TV through an open door, a family at play through another. A man and a woman seem to be arguing, or perhaps it's just the way they speak to each other in the loud air. A world of impressions goes whirling past, glimpsed momentarily through the corners of her eyes. She feels the cold weight of her weapon in her hand as the local officer leads them up a flight of stairs. Then they're on the roofs, vaulting from one concrete slab to another, dodging laundry, satellite dishes, and water tanks. Shouts echo up the tight lanes at their feet. They note the music of doors being slammed, they hear men in pursuit behind them, and across the brightening roofs they see other men hurtling to confront them. In the distance but closing the gap, they hear the sounds of another pursuit and she hears the officer gasp, "Not so far now." Then they hear the first shot and another and then the screaming and still they run, she feels the DCP pull away from her as he dashes shoulder-to-shoulder with the local officer. She looks over her shoulder to see Kapoor has turned and is now backing toward where they're going, his eye already sighting along the barrel of his weapon. She sees the pack chasing them with their knives raised but advancing more slowly now. She hears his bark to heed his weapon and do they, all these motherfuckers, know who he is and what he does to assholes like them when he's in the mood? She sees the local cop stop at the edge of a roof to cover a staircase up the side of the building. Then, through the door of a terrace, incongruous in that landscape of open roofs, bursts a man from whom rises like a mist the acrid stink of piss-soaked terror. Behind him comes his designated killer, his weapon held carelessly by his side. The Bangladeshi blubbers and screams. The DCP steps to one side with his weapon raised. The slumlord falls to his knees and sobs and doesn't see that the DCP's gun is trained, not at him, but at the man behind.

That man laughs and looks over to the other corner of the roof, where the local cop has his own weapon trained on two of his brother officers of the Delhi Police, rising armed and silent up the stairs. Smita monitors the situation from behind her own barrel and turns to the weeping man on the roof, taking up her position to his other side, her own field of fire at the encounter specialist unobstructed by either kneeling Bangladeshi or roof debris. The killer laughs again, takes out a pack of smokes with one hand from a pocket, shakes one out without letting go of his gun, slips it into his mouth, and puts the packet away. Out comes the lighter, a momentary flare on the moonlit terrace, then the glowing ember of his cigarette which he removes with his free hand as he blows smoke toward the heedless sky.

"Over this man, sir? Seriously?"

The DCP says nothing, his breathing even and composed behind his unwavering weapon. The other man watches him, his own gun still by his side. He smokes and measures the scene.

"You know that nobody gives a shit about this man," he says finally. "Do you really think it will make any difference what he says? If he says anything?"

"It doesn't matter what you think," says Smita. "It's what you do."

"I can still kill him, you know," he says. "Before you squeeze off a shot."

"True," admits the DCP. "But you wouldn't make it off this roof."

"My job would still be done."

"You'd still be dead. Why not leave him and yourself alive?"

"You'd kill me over that filth on the floor, sir? Are you sure you want him in your car? He's pissed himself already. The rest can't be far away."

"We'll manage."

The killer sighs. "You know that he won't make it to trial, sir. If I don't kill him, somebody else will. A cop, a criminal, a warden." He ambles over to the weeping man, fetal now on the floor. He half-kneels next to him, his weapon still at his side. "Keep your mouth shut, son. That way, only you will die."

Smita moves to his side, her weapon almost at his temple. He looks up and grins, lifts his gun and brings the other hand to it, ceremoniously throws the safety back in place. He gets up and holsters his weapon, walks over to his men who're doing the same, and, as he does so, throws a two-fingered salute to the other cops on the roof.

"I'll be seeing you," says Kapoor.

"I look forward to it, uncle," smiles the specialist. Then he's gone down the stairs with his minions, through clamorous streets filled with normal people and aspiring criminals alike, who'll always make way for men such as him.

Kapoor turns away in disgust from the throng of suddenly unsure fighters whom he was previously keeping at bay. He puts his gun away and walks to the side of the weeping slumlord and prods him with his shoe. He squats down and looks at him intently, back-hands him nonchalantly across the face, bringing the weeping to an abrupt halt.

"We just saved your life," he mutters as if to himself. "Will you be worth the effort?"

The night is warm and silver, and winter is truly at an end. Nearby is the shadowed noisome strand of the Yamuna with Ak-shardham and Noida across it. To the other side march the lit columns of Nehru Place and Ashram and Jasola, and all around a city bred on conflict calls for its prey. A pack of downcast ex–tough guys look at the bedraggled wreck of their former chief. A deputy commissioner of the Delhi Police holsters his weapon and sighs and lights a cigarette and the local cop calls now for reinforcements, and Smita, for the second time in this cool season, throws up in the night.

NECROPOLIS

Summer is only one warm night away in these latitudes. Yet Deputy Commissioner of Police Sajan Dayal didn't watch the roses of Delhi wither, nor see the dahlias fade away. He knew that the fall of the bauhinias and silk-cottons would be balanced by the flowering of the gulmohar and the amaltas, and the lagerstroemia would, in time, confirm that even the cruellest weather in Delhi has its saving graces. But what he knew at an elemental level didn't impress itself upon his consciousness, and winter's demise went unlamented in his heart.

The special task force had brought the man nominally behind the kidnapping of the preschool child into custody. But the man's incarceration had lasted barely longer than the rest of the cool weather. The music of his insight still awaited unleashing and transcription when the police van ferrying him to his first court date was intercepted and his escape facilitated. The officer and constables charged with his care were found to be woefully incompetent, but as Dayal's immediate superior pointed out with a certain relish, "What to do?" The offender had apparently wanted to relieve himself. The officer had not only stopped the van, he'd joined the offender against the nearest wall. He'd been struck on the back of his head. The driver and two constables had been similarly dealt with as they smoked by the side of the road. The Bangladeshi had disappeared, leaving not a trace behind.

It was noon.

By that evening, despite the strident protests of the local groups working in the area, police teams had fanned out through the basti. Two vanloads of Bengali speakers, their crime proximity to the missing man, were summarily deported.

Roadblocks were erected. Bulletins were issued. But the chances of actually finding the missing man, said one commissioner to his friend the journalist, "off the record, you understand, unless you withhold my name; well, it's a bit like finding a needle in a haystack, isn't it?"

That he'd been guilty of pursuing a case nobody wanted solved wasn't lost on the DCP. That his team was enjoying the infamy; that the news of their standoff against the encounter specialists had made Smita and the man from the local station celebrities worthy of free lunches and drink invitations; that Kapoor was now, if possible, even more of a legend to his nephews—these were all ironies to be savored by a man such as the DCP, who took his solace where he could.

The approbation that had greeted the apprehension of the Bangladeshi slumlord had disappeared within the space of two days, replaced by an indifference to the case that was almost eerie. The media's coverage of his disappearance had followed the same timeline, even though Dayal personally had been lionized, his apotheosis as Delhi's law enforcement savior almost complete. The DCP had been stoic about it, telling his juniors that it was only to be expected as the minders of the powerful swung into action, working the phones and other levers to make sure that what was previously unknown stayed that way. "We did," he said heavily, "what we had to do."

The DCP considered the paint on the ceiling. Kapoor and Smita sat across from him. They had just escaped the final briefing, where the DCP's fellow commissioners had ceremoniously, thankfully dropped the veil back on the case and told the special task force their energies were no longer required.

"Some things don't change," observed the DCP drily.

Smita bit her lip. "Some things do change, sir," she said finally. "They've changed right now. I know I'm the youngest person here. But don't you feel it too?"

Kapoor and the DCP glanced at each other, sighed in unison, looked away to their own individual futures.

"Well?" pressed Smita.

"Help me," said the DCP. "What exactly are you talking about?"

"All this, sir. I know that you two pride yourselves on your political tact. I know that you've built careers around both finding criminals and not pissing people off. You two know this city as it is, much more than me, who sees only what it should be. But even to you this must be different. It has to be."

The DCP considered the ceiling with even more care than before.

"I mean," continued Smita, "look at the news. People talking about money as if it's nothing. Hundreds, thousands of crores gone missing. Homes in Delhi worth a hundred million dollars each. People with mobile phones but no electricity to charge them with, mothers with babies but no water to wash them in. Men in government with the power of life and death. Death, sir. A dead drug dealer and his girlfriend. The press is compromised, the public's watching TV and thinking it's news. Our own colleagues are guns for hire. I mean," she said desperately, "come on, sir. Surely that's different? Even to the two of you?"

"The numbers might be bigger," admitted Kapoor, "but the story's still the same."

"Really?" said Smita, by now completely aflame. "And have you two always played the roles of extras?"

"Careful girl," rumbled Kapoor.

She bit her lip again and looked away. "Don't you ever get tired of burying things?" Her seniors made no reply. "This isn't why I joined the police."

"Why did you join?" asked the DCP.

"To help people. To make Delhi safer. But I don't even know who I'm keeping it safe for anymore. Or from."

"You don't want a career?"

"Of course I want a career. But not like this."

"You've only ever done the right thing. At least on this task force."

"Nobody gives a damn about what we've done."

"On the contrary. You've earned a medal and a commendation these last few months. And a notoriety for being a loose cannon that may well last forever."

She forced down her smile. "Those people are still dead."

"You did the right thing," urged the DCP gently.

"To what end?"

"You did the right thing. When the time came, we did the right thing. We could have sat on our hands like everyone else. We acted."

"When will we know if it made any difference?"

"Soon."

"You exercised your choice," said Kapoor. "Don't underestimate how hard that is." He leaned across and patted her on her shoulder. "You remember the local cop with us that night?"

Smita nodded.

"He's a good man. Let me tell you something about him." He sat back again. "His station supplies the man-power for the sweeps we do for illegal migrants. You know the score. Never the cops from the local stations, because they might tip off the ustads, who'll scatter the pack before the raid. So his boys get called in every now and then to roust out these people from under whatever godforsaken bridge they're living, provided it's not too close to their thana.

"What happens is, there's always someone who manages to hide. They'll find a hole and curl up in it and wait for the cops to leave. So you round up the kids, the younger the better, and you account for their parents. And when you find a child without its quota of adults, you take that kid and you dunk his head in the nearest barrel of water. Till he gags and screams."

Kapoor stretched and shifted. "Till he gags and screams, girl. And you keep on doing it till the parents come out. Because they always do. Unless they aren't there. In which case the kid's screaming will have been in vain.

"He's a good boy. He doesn't go looking for freebies in the shanties on the river, like the rest of the crew in that station. He knows he's pissed someone off. He's stuck on the edge of the city with third-rate business-men who wish a plague on him every time he passes.

He's got no income to speak of and no avenues for advancement and once a month, on average, he dunks a child's head in a barrel of cold water. Or he watches someone else do it."

"So?" said Smita, almost inaudibly.

"So," said Kapoor, "I gave him the chance to do the right thing. To save a man he doesn't like. For a cause he didn't know. He did it unquestioningly. That's twice now he's crossed that killer and the men who own him. He's stuck in that thana till the end of time, girl. He isn't an IPS officer like you. He doesn't have your education or your options. And he still did the right thing."

"Which means?"

Kapoor smiled and looked off into space.

The DCP laughed. "I'd disregard that speech if I were you. Your uncle's a master of the specious argument. But he did mention something of value."

Smita waited.

"Choice. We both have it, and your uncle's old enough not to care. Right?"

Kapoor's smile was unchanged.

"We're not getting played anymore," said the DCP.

"It's time to dig up some dead bodies, girl," added Kapoor.

Slowly Smita smiled as well.

"So. What are you wearing to the party tonight?"

———•—•—•———

It was cool enough for a light shawl, warm enough for bare shoulders. There were plenty of both in evidence that night. The party itself was outside, in a house that wasn't huge but had a nice lawn both out front and in the back, above which hung glass lanterns in myriad colors. Old furniture dotted the gardens. Wisps of smoke from mosquito coils worked their way up through the flower-beds, there to mingle with the smoke from the cigarettes and cigars in the hands of the revelers. There had been a sprinkling of rain that evening, enough that the women's heels sank into the soft ground, so they subsided gratefully into the couches and chairs that were ringed about with citronella candles and oil-burning lamps.

The house belonged to the braying PR man the DCP had been introduced to at the minister's party. He lived in a development that was simultaneously tony and illegal, where the plush homes within their high walls were hedged by bad roads and poorly strung electricity wires. Behind the house lurked a wasteland where herders still cropped their animals and imaginary lines in the dirt signified future wars over ownership. Beyond the walls and its guards was darkness. Within was perfumed expensive night.

The DCP and Smita had arrived early, which is to say they were actually on time. Their host, affable even in his underwear, laughed at their arrival and expended a good deal of energy making them feel at home even as he went about getting dressed. His staff scurried about with purpose, setting out ashtrays, packing ice, mopping the excess moisture off the ground. A cocktail waiter appeared with a laden tray, men with kababs made the rounds, and soon the garden was full of the conversations of reasonably well-bred Delhi.

The minister was expected, confided the PR man to the DCP. So were at least three other members of the union cabinet. One was a drug addict, he said in a loud whisper. Another, he announced, was a degenerate sex addict who hid his priapism behind his cultured drawl. "He fucked my assistant in Goa," he told the DCP and Smita. "Behind a bush!" He shook his head in disgust and delight. "She had sand in her ass afterward. What's wrong with getting a room?"

He had discovered an old connection with the DCP, he insinuated into the conversation, to the effect that their fathers had been in college together. It indicated at least one thing, the DCP pointed out to Smita: the man had done his research. That the DCP was now a hero wasn't lost on the PR man or his acolytes. Indeed, many people had already come up to him and introduced themselves, while Smita had been led away to her own admirers. The DCP studied the growing throng and listened to the shouts and trills and waited for the quiet word in his ear.

"Sajan."

He turned to her and smiled and she replied with her mouth and eyes, indeed her whole being, and it cost him a monstrous effort not to fall upon her right there.

"How distinguished you look," she said, putting a hand to his lapel. He stared at her, quietly resplendent in an almost transparent sari with a sleeveless blouse, a thin shawl across her shoulders even though her midriff was bare. He noted, as he hadn't before, the depth of her navel, the fact that it held a discreet jewel. He wondered whether it was a clip-on, or had she really bled to have it there. Her hand stayed on his breast, a gesture he wished he could reciprocate. She smiled again, withdrew her hand, accepted a cigarette, and waited for him to light it. She studied him as he lit his own, her head carefully, artlessly, to one side.

"A lovely night," he observed. She concurred, her eyes still on him.

"Know everybody?" he asked. A small shrug. Everyone that matters, it seemed to say.

"I see you brought the girl."

"She deserves to be here."

"Clearly. She seems to be enjoying the attention."

"She's young and alive. Why shouldn't she?"

Razia smiled and looked away. "How are you doing?" she asked over her shoulder.

"Fine."

"Adjusting well?"

"To what?"

"Being part of the game, Sajan. Don't be coy."

A murmur broke through the crowd. A person of consequence had arrived. The delighted bellow of their host announced the arrival of the minister. The old woman swept gracefully through the obsequious throng, a nod here, a shake of the hand there, a kiss accepted from a particular favorite. Sajan felt himself being withdrawn toward the shadows below a tree. He saw the old woman stop before Smita, saw her reach up toward his young subordinate's face, the quiet communion the old woman could summon so effortlessly even in the most crowded place. He saw the look in Smita's eyes, the happiness and joy she felt, despite herself. He felt Razia's own hand reach for his, then snake up his arm to hit him lightly on the back of his head.

"She's young," she echoed under her breath. "And alive. Why shouldn't she enjoy the attention?"

He turned to her in the shade of that giant old tree which had been left miraculously standing when this and all the other houses around had been razed. His hand felt for the warm bark, the ridges and whorls of its history. He felt as if they were there, the herders and raiders of the end of the Mughal empire, resting now for a space under its quiet shade. He smelled the winter picnics of Victorian families half a world away from home, stopping here for a bite between Mehrauli and the ruins of Tughlaqabad. He dreamed a landscape brooded over by tombs and broken by the decrepit walls of forgotten cities and he felt this land, barren sand at its heart, worthless to anyone but goatherds, abandoned once, twice, each time the city shifted somewhere else; he felt the irony truly, deeply, that this desolate land was now worth so much, and wondered what those goatherds and raiders of centuries past would have made of this. Sums beyond the dreams of any age's avarice, exchanged for land that had been used to crop goats and farm old cattle and bury the nameless unnumbered dead. To what end? he thought. This throng, these revelers, these ministers and their toadies and the men in boots and elegant women. They too will be dust. Added to this city's.

He felt Razia's hand on his chest and he blinked away the past.

"There's no difference for you, is there, between then and now?"

"Shouldn't I be the one asking you that question?"

"I think you'll find my interests are entirely contemporary."

"You were there," said Sajan. "I wasn't."

"True. I suppose that does make a difference."

The minister walked across to them. She flashed a smile at Razia, put a hand on the DCP's lapel. "What a pleasure to meet you here," she said, warmth both on her lips and in her eyes. Smita trailed in her wake. Razia and she looked at each other over the minister's shoulder. Razia dropped her eyes with a small smile, while the other woman felt the color creep up her neck.

"A chair, child," instructed the minister. Smita went and got one, which she positioned, at the older woman's instructions, with its back to the tree and facing the party. The other hangers-on were waved away, told to go enjoy themselves and not bother about this tired old lady, who was quite content to watch the fun for a bit without the need for her awful security detail. She stretched luxuriously in her solitary chair, sent Smita off to get her a drink. The DCP and Razia stayed in the shadows behind her. To anybody watching, she was alone.

"I'm so glad you're here, Sajan," she said quietly. "How did that horrible man arrange it?"

"Apparently our fathers were in college together."

"Were they?"

"It isn't worth the effort to find out, ma'am."

"Quite right. That's what I like best about you, Sajan. You're so pragmatic. You know when to dig, and when to turn away."

The DCP digested this in silence.

"Thank you for arresting that slumlord," she continued. "Much better that than the encounter those idiots had arranged. This is much neater. Fewer loose ends."

The DCP felt Razia's silent squeeze.

"Sometimes I wonder if the people on our side are worth protecting. I mean, honestly. To send that maniac after him. Luckily, we have you. I'm glad you listened to Razia. I believe you got there just in time, hmm?"

"Who arranged to have him lifted?"

"That isn't my concern," shrugged the old woman. "That he's gone is enough. You're welcome to smoke, by the way. It won't bother me."

The DCP fished out his packet, dispensed one anew to Razia, lit both.

"I miss smoking," said the minister. "I smoked all my life. Now look at me. Besieged by fools on all sides, and when I most need a cigarette, they're denied me. My doctors. My media advisor. My grandchildren. All allied against me."

She sniffed luxuriously at the smoke that wreathed the tree behind her, as the two smokers came closer, Razia's breast nestling against Sajan's side. The older woman, her back to them, laughed as she heard the rustle of Razia's sari.

"I'm glad you two are comfortable," she said. "She's lovely, isn't she?"

The DCP, knowing of whom the question was asked, nodded silently, though he knew the old woman couldn't see him.

"Yes," the old woman went on. "She's been like that my entire life, Sajan. Do you know how dispiriting it is to grow old, knowing it needn't be like that, that someone else actually had a choice in the matter?"

"Is it a choice?" asked the DCP.

The two women remained silent.

"Well?"

"I don't want to live forever. I never did. To serve was enough. I wanted, as far as possible, to live normally."

"You've lived well," said Razia gently. "You've served well."

The older woman continued as if she hadn't heard. "To love, to have a family, to grow old. I was about your age when I met her, Sajan. My children didn't need me anymore. I was perfect."

Razia laughed softly.

"Are you perfect, dear Sajan? Will you serve as I did?"

"In whose name? To what end?"

"The flame's the same. All we do is keep it."

"That wasn't my question, ma'am."

"That's why you came to our attention," said Razia.

"We liked the way you conducted yourself with those boys," said the minister. "Discreetly unbending. You always asked the right questions."

"I haven't gotten an answer yet," replied the DCP, recklessly by his standards.

Both women laughed.

"Perhaps you should meet those boys. Maybe they have a point," said the DCP.

"About what?" asked the minister without heat. "That they too want a part in the game? They'll have it, in due time. When we're ready and we think they are."

"Perhaps it's not about the action. It's about who you talk to."

"Don't speak like that, dear boy. It worries me. I can't be worried at my age."

The DCP felt Razia's hand in his.

"You must understand," the younger woman said in

his ear. "We know what we're doing. Look at this city's history. Who do you think has kept it together?"

"Look to the past," said the older woman. "Which you love so much. Men such as these have always been spoilers. Not builders."

"We'll decide when they're allowed to sit down at the feast," said the voice in his ear.

"They're already there," he replied.

The old woman waved a hand at the party. "They only think they are. Look at these people. A veneer of sophistication, but vulgar to the core. They've forced their way in, but they're still here at our sufferance. Let us deal with them first, then we'll turn to your animals."

"When will they be of this city?" asked the DCP.

"They never will. But their children may be. When they've shaken off the dirt of their fathers and mothers."

Smita was approaching them across the dew-sprinkled grass, a balloon of something warm and golden in her hands, their host gamboling at her heels.

"A long time to wait," said the DCP.

"A moment," replied Razia softly. "Eternity's a long time."

———~—+—~———

It was, he felt, a truly beautiful night. The two of them had slipped away through the heedless throng, a quick walk out the gate and up the lane and through the security fence that ringed the development, and then they were in the wasteland behind. They walked in the clear light of the moon, hand in hand, through the weeds and thickets of scrub and broken rocks and bottles. To one

side gleamed the Qutab Minar. To the other lay glowering tombs and a ruined buttress or two. Razia shivered once, delicately, drew her thin shawl more closely
around her shoulders.

"Why are we out here?" she asked.

"For the privacy."

"We can be private anywhere."

"Not like this."

"How about all these dead people?"

"Surely we're all dead to you, Razia. You'll outlive
us all."

She inclined her head a shade.

"To live as you do, as you have: at least it's good for
one thing."

A raised eyebrow.

"Perspective."

The eyebrow dropped, the head inclined again.

"The things you know," she murmured. "And yet
you don't know what I want you to do right now." She
turned her face up in the moonlight. He bent his own
to hers, kissed her with urgency, then pulled away. "Oh
why?" she said mock peevishly.

"Because, for once, I'd rather talk."

They stood face-to-face in the spectral light, on an
eroded sandy plain ringed by ancient boulders. He took
her face in his hands.

"Did you always think of this city as a prize to be
guarded?"

"Isn't it worth protecting?"

"Surely she's old enough to look after herself by
now?"

"Like me," smiled Razia. She reached up and kissed

him again, fleetingly. "We may be old enough, wise enough, strong enough. But everyone needs a champion, don't you think?"

He smiled and shrugged and pressed his question. "What is it? It might have been greed, once upon a time. Then, self-preservation. Now, what? Pride? Boredom? Ennui?"

"All those things, Sajan. Always. Never dying gets old quickly. Besides, there have always been barbarians at the walls. Who decides who gets let in and who starves outside?"

"The city itself."

"I am the city."

"Then why this charade? And why the hell do you need me?"

"You're the right age, Sajan. The right background. We'll smooth your progress."

"Commissioner?"

She made a small sound of dismissal. "Such a paltry ambition. That's your besetting failing. You won't always be a policeman."

"I suppose I should be thankful."

"No. We are. For finding you. A man of Delhi who knows where he's from."

She put her hands on his, which still cupped her face. They stood entombed in the quiet night.

"Are you actually immortal? Or is it all a game?"

"Kiss me," she said, "and see."

So he did. After a long moment in which was concentrated everything of importance to Sajan Dayal, he pulled away, his lover's eyes slowly opening to his own. He moved a hand from her warm cheek to signal them forward, so they came for her, quiet and masked and feral, their leader still wearing his kaffiyeh.

She looked at them and then at him, without heat or remorse or accusation.

"Why?"

"If you're Razia, it won't matter. There's nothing they can do to you."

She nodded and smiled.

"Did you know?" he asked her quietly.

"You think this will buy you peace with them? And those who will come?"

He made no reply, his hands back on her face.

"You're like us, Sajan."

"Not in everything."

"How are you different?"

"The future doesn't frighten me as it does you."

She looked wonderingly up at him, the men of Delhi's fringes quiet around them in the pale night. "Don't you want the city to live on?"

"The one you think you're protecting is gone."

"Sometimes I wonder if it ever existed," she said as if to herself. "Perhaps it was all a dream." Sajan made no reply so she pulled herself together. "Are these men the future?"

"Perhaps not. But they're here. Inside the gates. You can't wish them away. Or anyone else."

"You want me to talk to them?"

He nodded, his hands still on her soft face.

"That man. The slumlord. You have him," she said.

He nodded again.

"These men did it. With your help. And your men."

He nodded a third time.

"What do you hope to achieve?"

"To start with, the people who're responsible for three deaths to stand trial for them. Whoever they may be."

"How will you keep him alive?"

"I don't need to. He's told us everything he knows already. On camera. The file's already uploaded on the Internet, waiting to be made public. Killing him won't help anyone anymore."

She raised an eyebrow.

"His family's already gone," said Sajan. "He will be too. He'll know never to return once this is over. What we needed from him, we already have. Digital testimony that won't ever be tied to us." He shook his head. "God knows I don't even need a trial. As long as the truth gets out: that'll be enough for me."

She laughed then. "A new age."

"Exactly."

"You do know they'll ruin you."

"No they won't. I have you."

She peered into his eyes and felt again for his hands on her face with her own.

"What do you want from me?" she whispered.

"I want you to consider where your loyalties lie," he replied, his head bending to hers as he kissed her firmly, deeply, lovingly.

"I'm loyal to you," she said slowly.

"I know."

He watched her disappear over the crest of a low hill, a small ring of quiet men around her. He saw the bulk of Kapoor disengage itself from a tree they'd scouted that afternoon. He felt Smita's eyes on him as she walked toward them.

He was quiet and so were they, the three of them standing in the light of the indifferent moon. Kapoor lit a cigarette. They joined him and their intertwined smoke made its way toward the sky.

"What will they do to her?" ventured Smita.

"Only what she deserves," said Kapoor.

"Perhaps not even that," murmured the DCP. "She's persuasive enough."

Smita laughed first, then Kapoor, and finally the DCP. Their laughter filled that old cropping ground, echoed off the sun-blasted rocks and broken tombs, wrapped them like old memories and faded away in just the same way and then all was quiet again.

"This isn't over," the DCP said.

"So what do we do?"

"Our jobs, Smita. Keep our noses clean. Prosecute the bad guys. Protect the citizens of the city."

"From whom?" asked Smita of them both, but neither man gave a response.

"Coming, sir?" Kapoor finally asked.

The DCP shook his head. "She might still need me," he said. "If she isn't . . . you know."

"You love her, don't you?" asked Smita before she could stop herself.

"I know what I want," replied the DCP, his eyes carefully averted.

"Come on, girl," said Kapoor firmly.

The DCP listened to their heels crunching the dirt of that corner of the changing city.

EPILOGUE

The chaotic conclusion to the scandal that had grown around the kidnapping of the child coincided with the advent of the hot weather. The russet new leaves of the pilkhan trees were already turning a translucent green and the ozone smell of summer was in the noses and throats of Dilliwalas as they scanned the news for the latest developments. The explosive video with the slumlord's testimony had gone viral. Every last incensed citizen learned of the cynical attempt of a few cabinet ministers of the government of India to embarrass one of their own colleagues with a manufactured kidnapping. A child's taking, a man's death, the culpability of so many powerful men: it was a potent cocktail, and the entire political class felt the effects. All the talk around the juice stalls was of the machinations of the powerful, whose corruption, it was averred, was only matched by their brazenness. The ministers who had allegedly so conspired against their colleague were dropped from the cabinet, their protestations of innocence to no avail in the face of overwhelming public opinion. Their alleged mark was hoised as well, his own loud claims of being victim and not perpetrator lost in the noise.

Committees were formed in both houses of parliament. Junior members hoping to make their mark issued strident speeches both in the house and outside, while their senior colleagues, coerced into submission by the power of new media they didn't understand, watched in sullen silence. The fact that such an act had been committed was horrific enough, muttered the older hands. That it had been made public was beyond the pale. What was the world coming to, confided one minister to an aide, when we're actually expected to be accountable for our actions? What's the point of being in power? The sympathy of his interlocutor was no balm. Nor was comfort to be found in their own distant constituencies. The power of electronic media and the reach of the Internet meant that the wholesale shaming of the establishment continued in the inner reaches of the republic too.

The collateral damage of the video extended outward as well, with new revelations being made every day by policemen and other public servants newly eager to be found capable in the suddenly menacing citizenry's eye. A case of a dead black drug dealer and his equally dead Indian girlfriend was found to be still alive. A dossier of his clients, containing the names of some of Delhi's most influential citizens, and certainly many of their children, was discovered and published on every news site. The departure lounges of Indira Gandhi International Airport were congested with the suddenly publicity-shy. To Smita's enduring disbelief and amusement, a loud minority of Delhi's party people took to confiding to each other about how lucky they were not to have been named, since everyone knew they too used the dead dealer as a source. Still others, in a huff about not being as infamous as their best friends, proclaimed to anyone who was listening that only journeymen revelers had made their calls to that particular man, since

everybody who really partied knew his stuff was bad.
Still, went the virtuous coda to these conversations, it
was just as well it had been outed. The party scene in
Delhi was getting out of hand and who knew all these
new people anyway.

The minister had been curiously unscathed, due in
no small part to her well-publicized efforts to secure the
release of the child. It was made clear to certain depend-
able members of the press corps by the DCP that his arrest of the Bangladeshi had been at her behest, precisely
in order to stop his killing by the encounter specialist,
who was currently under suspension pending an investigation of his methods. The DCP's intercession on her
behalf wasn't lost on the old woman.

"Thank you," she said to him over coffee. They were
seated in her deep veranda, watching the sun advance
across her well-watered lawns. An ancient fan creaked
overhead.

"For what?"

"You know, Sajan. For not abandoning me to the
wolves."

"Bit of luck for the wolves, ma'am," murmured the
DCP.

She chuckled, the dogs at her ankles raising their
heads. "Clearly you're behind this," she said, a glint in
her eyes.

The DCP made no reply.

"Not that it matters. But I do wonder what you think
of me."

"I only wish you well," said the DCP.

"You don't judge me?"

"The exercise of power has its own compulsions."

"Quite right. Perhaps you see the judgments in your own future, hmm?"

"I'd like to believe my life won't come to that."

"But you know it might. Don't you, my dear Sajan?"

The DCP nodded his assent.

"You acted, in fact, much as I thought you might. Our goals may differ, but we act alike. Decisively. We chose well with you. I still believe that."

"Are you changing your mind about everything else?"

"No. I'm too old for that. But I'm not immune to self-doubt, you know. I'm not insane. I've always been open to the possibility that I, we, were wrong. Perhaps we were. Perhaps we weren't. I console myself with the fact that I'll be dead soon. I don't have to wait around to find out."

She laughed, the DCP politely joining in.

"That young man you told me to talk to. You think he'll make a good politician?"

The DCP considered the man in the kaffiyeh. He had been tapped by the ruling party to be their candidate for a parliamentary seat in Delhi, which had come vacant due to the sudden resignation of the incumbent in the wake of the kidnapping scandal. His meteoric ascendance had been questioned in the media, but his apparent and equally spectacular rise to influence in the outer areas of his presumptive seat was deemed justification enough for his nomination.

"He's clever. Venal. Ruthless."

"He'll fit right in, you mean," smiled the old woman.

"Cabinet quality," allowed the DCP.

"Our friend's spoken to me at great length about him. She was very eloquent."

"As were you, ma'am. He wouldn't have gotten past the door without your help. Or so I'm told."

The old lady looked at the DCP for a moment and then bent her head toward the coffee. He declined regretfully. "The weather," he said. "Too warm, now, for cup after cup."

"Yes," said the old lady. "The weather. This is summer as I remember it from my childhood. New leaves everywhere, and soon the trees in bloom. The prospect of a green lawn with empty beds at the edges. Fine dust in my nose, a storm in the evening. I can almost hear the bell of the ice cream man. But they don't ring bells anymore, do they?"

The DCP raised his dregs to his lips.

"I remember my brothers and I, the oldest of us must have been eight: we were put in the bathroom, the floor of which was covered in water. The water had been there all night and was cold. Then they gave us a bucket of mangoes and we spent the rest of that day eating them. I can still taste the mangoes, feel the water between my toes, smell my brothers covered in pulp. When it was all over a servant came in and threw buckets of water over us and I believe we almost swooned with joy." She looked at him with her quiet warm eyes. "Such memories, dear Sajan, this city has for me.

"People hate summer now. I don't know why. It can't be wished away. It's part of our lives and our days. To wish a season away is the preserve of the young, don't you think? Every autumn is another stitch in my shroud. It's almost ready, Sajan. But I do want to taste a mango again, smell my brothers beside me. At least I have that to look forward to."

"Your memory won't fade, ma'am. The city will remember you."

"Perhaps. But in what way? Will I even care?"

"You've served, ma'am."

"Yes. But whom? I've seen this city change. As you have, as your father did. But I'm his age and I'm still alive. I've seen this new Delhi go from a village to a metropolis in the time it's taken my summers to unwind. Sometimes I wish I'd had a space outside of myself to see everything from. Maybe then I'd have known what was right and wrong and had the guidance I craved."

"You had Razia."

"Yes. And now she has you. And she changes her mind and this city continues to perplex me." The old lady shook her head. "These past many decades. This adult life of mine. This city. Has it all been a dream?"

Then her eyes were clear and she smiled. She got up and kissed him on the cheek.

"I wish I'd met you sixty years ago. What a time we'd have had."

They burst out laughing together. Her hand was upon his arm as she walked him out.

"Be well, dear boy. Be strong. Be careful." She waved as he climbed into his car. "Take care," she said. "Take care."

———————

"And that," said Smita skeptically, "is all the evil old bitch had to say?"

The café on the terrace with the modest view rang with the laughter of the DCP and Kapoor. The traffic on the radial road that ran away from Connaught Place honked its way past their perch, but up on the roof, under the shade of the awnings, there was a semblance of calm. A warm clear day had passed, but on the horizon massed thunderheads that were moving toward the city. The kites wheeled in the blue sky above their heads, while below thirsty men jostled around the water carts in the shade of the city's fig trees.

"Seriously," said Smita, though with a smile, "after all she's done. You just let her bat her eyelashes at you?"

"What do you want me to do?" asked the DCP. "Arrest her? On what charge? Manipulating history?"

"That's what politicians are required to do, remember?" rumbled Kapoor. "Leave their imprint upon the sand. Otherwise, what good are they?"

"That's all very well," said Smita. "But aren't you forgetting she asked you to sweep the drug dealer's death under the carpet? If nothing else, she's at least responsible for that."

"True. And much worse besides. Which doesn't change the fact that we won't do anything about it. Not now, at least. We still need her."

"For what?"

"To buy us protection, if nothing else. She's still the minister. There are plenty of people on the force unhappy about the way things have turned out."

"We need her on our side, girl," said Kapoor. "On your side. If you want to stay a cop. Don't you?"

Smita looked away huffily.

"I know it isn't neat," said the DCP. "But we need our allies as well. She's a good one to have."

"Compromises," muttered Smita. "Alliances. Where does it stop?"

"It never does," answered the DCP. Kapoor nodded sagely over his cup.

"Those nine-fingered freaks too," said Smita. "What happens when they cross the line?"

"We crack the whip. Enlist someone else. Find another ally to set them off against."

"You're ready to do all that, sir?" asked Smita.

Kapoor considered the ceiling. The DCP looked away.

"Will you remember why you started doing it, sir? Or will it fade away?"

The DCP looked at her sharply.

"Ignore me," she said lightly, to nobody in particular. "I'll get over it. I'm always like this at the beginning of summer. Six months of misery to look forward to. A season's respite, then you do it all over again. That's the world, right?"

Kapoor nodded fractionally. The DCP glanced at his watch and the sky, noted the time and the lowering clouds, rose to his feet murmuring his excuses.

"See you in the morning?" he inquired gently. His juniors nodded their assent. "Good. There's work to be done."

His slim form picked its way through the packed tables of the afternoon crowd. Smita watched him leave, till she felt Kapoor's eyes on her.

"Patience," he counseled.

Smita just smiled.

"In everything," he added.

She waited.

"You can't expect him to answer questions he doesn't know the answers to."

"Really, uncle? That makes everything okay?"

"Perhaps not. Be patient for yourself, then. You still need this job. Us. Him."

She looked away.

"She's a ghost, girl. She'll fade away in time."

Smita simply shrugged.

"Maybe she'll turn on him. Or the other way around. He'll still need someone he can trust."

"So we have to wait?" she asked.

"It's what we do best."

Their laughter was light on the summer air. Then they were gone as well into the burning city.

———————————

"No more vampires."

"No more lycans."

"No more heartburn for middle-class parents."

The two of them lounged in the deep shade of a colonnade that stretched the length of a courtyard which was itself the centerpiece of a well-preserved haveli in one of Delhi's ancient villages. There was paan in front of them, a drink to each side. The first fat drops of rain were beginning to fall on the dusty ground. One, two, a few together, a dozen. An uneven pattering, a fugitive smell of wetness, a crackling in the darkening sky. A distant rumbling announced itself and she drew herself closer to her lover on their mattress.

"Happy?" she whispered against his shoulder.

"Who wouldn't be?" he replied to the listening ether.

284 ☀ N<small>ecropolis</small>

"Umm. A drink. A summer storm. A quiet night at home."

He raised his drink to his lips, leaned back against the bolsters with a tired sigh.

"What have I done to you?" Razia traced the lines around Sajan's eyes with a delicate finger, a shadow of a frown that hadn't existed the summer before. "Look at you," she said into his ear.

"Don't ask of the ruin your passage has caused me. Consider the delights you've laid before me that lead me to it instead."

Razia's laughter mingled with the sound of the increasing rain. "Again?" she said archly. "Time to add some new arrows to that quiver, DCP."

So he drew her to him. Soon they were quiet once more as the rain began to pour down in earnest, the battering of the drops against the stone courtyard a cacophony now.

"It won't always be like this, will it?" asked Sajan, his head back in Razia's lap.

She looked down into his eyes and shook her head. "But why," she said lightly, "should it remain the same? Things change, and so will we. It is the way of the world."

"You don't change."

"You aren't like me."

"So one day you'll just move on?"

She smiled and stroked his hair. "You abandoned me to the finger-stealers, remember?"

"There is nothing they could do to you. And they needed you. Revenge is a small thing beside ambition."

"True. Now they're part of the game and owe us their futures."

AVTAR SINGH ☀ 285

"And me," he pressed softly. "Am I part of your future?"

"I'll always be loyal to you."

"That isn't the answer I'm looking for."

"It's going to have to do," she whispered into his hair.

"The mask never comes off?"

"I don't know, my Sajan. I've never tried."

The courtyard was luminescent with a flash of lightning. Seconds later they heard its call.

"Does this house have a cellar?" asked Sajan.

"Of course."

So he closed his eyes and his breathing deepened and slowed and she played with his hair as he fell calmly asleep and then there was only the sound of the falling rain.

———•—•—•———

The figure sits and tells her beads in the corner. She watches the world through a stone screen that diffuses the harsh light. She hears horses approaching, the beat of their hooves amplified by the narrow lane through which they ride. A young girl runs across the courtyard, her head uncovered against the sun. Her bare feet skitter across the flagstones, skip over the steep stairs, fly across the parapet on which perches the watcher. She comes and sits by the figure's side, a conspiratorial smile on both their faces. The young girl's face joins the other at the screen as the horses thunder past. The men are in their uniforms, standards aloft. The older woman hugs the young girl to her side. Outside is the city. The fig trees are bearing fruit, the monkeys feasting among them. Summer is reaching its peak. Hot winds blow every afternoon and their household retreats to the cool cellar. But the two of them are outside in the sun watching the squadron of horsemen ride past.

"Lovely, aren't they?" says the older woman.

"Mmm," agrees the girl.

A young horseman, as if conscious of their gaze, looks up at their perch, but they're invisible behind their screen and so he passes, the clinking and creaking of his brass and leathers audible to the women.

"What's the best thing about them?" asks the older woman.

"They do as they're told," replies the girl.

The two of them smile at the familiar formula.

"When?" asks the girl.

"Soon," is the indulgent, languid reply. "Why hurry?"

The girl smiles again, leans closer to the older woman, watches the horses ride by.

Acknowledgments

Thanks are due to all those mentioned here. My naming you recognizes my debt but in no way pays it. *Necropolis* wouldn't exist without you.

Thanks, firstly, to Johnny Temple and the rest of the team at Akashic Books, for bringing this novel to the wider world.

My mother, for the reading habit. I wish she could have seen this book.

My father and sisters, for the support and not asking too many questions. And, especially, for waiting this long.

Karthika VK, editor and enabler, for pushing me to write again.

Ajitha GS, colleague, friend, and now editor. I've said it before, and it's still true: I couldn't have done it without you.

To everyone at HarperCollins who helped edit, design, and market this book in India.

Abhinandita Mathur, for Mehrauli.

All my erstwhile colleagues at the old Lajpat Nagar stand. Many of you read this book, wholly or in fragments: your advice and encouragement has been noted and appreciated.

Every single reporter at the city pages at every newspaper in India that still has them. For the entertainment, the insight, the stories.

The library at the American Embassy School, New Delhi, for the quiet and the Wi-Fi.

Pintu, Asha, Kiran, and Gulnaaz, for preserving the bubble. Figo, for puncturing it.

My friends and larger family, for helping me navigate this difficult city.

Finally, and always: Christine. For the World, and everything else.

Thank you. Thank you. Thank you.